KV-389-484

A GIFT FOR A RAKE

A GIFT FOR
A RAKE

Ann Barker

CHIVERS

British Library Cataloguing in Publication Data available

This Large Print edition published by BBC Audiobooks Ltd, Bath, 2007.
Published by arrangement with Robert Hale Ltd.

U.K. Hardcover ISBN 978 1 405 64070 1
U.K. Softcover   ISBN 978 1 405 64071 8

Copyright © Ann Barker 2006

The right of Ann Barker to be identified as author of this work has been
asserted by her in accordance with the Copyright, Designs and Patents
Act 1988

All rights reserved.

HOUNSLOW LIBRARIES	
LAH	
C0000002350809	
BBC	09-JAN-2009
L/F	£15.99

Printed and bound in Great Britain by
Antony Rowe Ltd., Chippenham, Wiltshire

For Graham, a fine colleague and a good friend

PROLOGUE

It was that strange hour which is neither daylight nor dark when Jem Cutler set off for home, his gun over his shoulder. Cully his dog was darting about in front of him, now sniffing at something just at his heels, then dashing past, in pursuit of some scent imperceptible to humans, but irresistible to one of the canine variety.

Jem had been to look over some of the undergrowth in one of the more distant woods belonging to Lord Summer, for whom he acted as gamekeeper. Now, he was making his way back to his cottage, and the thought of the rabbit-pie which Mary had been preparing for him that very morning made his mouth water. They'd not been fortunate enough to have children, but Mary was a good lass, and had never allowed their misfortune to sour her disposition. Such a good cook, she was.

His musings were interrupted by a whimpering sound from behind one of the hedges that bordered the lane along which he was walking. Jem, making his way through the gap between the bushes, saw that Cully was limping towards him with one of his forepaws held up.

'Here now, boy,' Jem said softly. 'Let's have a look at you, then.' As if understanding that

1

his master meant only his good, the dog kept still and allowed him to examine his foot. This was not very easy, given the waning light, but the man was soon able to establish that Cully had picked up a thorn in the pad of his paw. He screwed up his eyes to be able to see, for he wanted to get the thorn out first time, without causing the dog further pain.

As he studied his dog's foot, he gradually became aware of the sound of an approaching carriage, not travelling cautiously over these narrow lanes, as common sense would dictate, but moving recklessly at full tilt, with a complete disregard for other travellers. Jem thanked his stars that Cully's accident had meant that he had not still been walking down the lane.

As it careered past, probably out of control, Jem looked up. He could see that it was a curricle with two people in it. From the little he could make out in the poor light, they looked to be engaged in some kind of conflict. They'd do better to look to their driving, he thought, as he turned back to his task.

Once the thorn was safely removed, the dog leapt up, licking his master's face as if in thanks. 'Give over, you daft beggar,' said Jem, pulling Cully's ears affectionately before taking up his gun and walking back into the lane to continue his homeward journey. Moments later, he heard a shriek, to be followed by a crash combined with a horrible splintering sound, and the noise of panicking horses. Comprehending what must have happened, he ran until he reached the next corner, dreading what he might find.

A shocking sight met his eyes. The curricle had come to grief on its side, the wheel that was in the air was only just ceasing to spin, and the matched grey horses were plunging wildly. Jem did not work with horses on a daily basis but his brother was a stableman. Without fear, but cautiously, he went to their heads, taking time to calm them down, for he knew that while they were still plunging about they could make bad worse.

As soon as he was satisfied that they would remain still and quiet, he went with some trepidation to investigate what had happened to the two travellers. Both of them had been thrown clear. The gentleman lay unconscious, a large bruise forming on his head and a nasty scratch on his face. Jem placed his hand inside the man's coat and could feel that his heart was beating. What other injuries there might be, he could not tell.

The other occupant of the curricle was a lady. She lay with her dark hair streaming across her face, her cloak rumpled about her. Tentatively, fearful of overstepping the proprieties, Jem laid a hand over her heart. Then taking a deep breath, he sat back on his heels, noting for the first time the angle at which the lady's head lay. His scruples had been needless. Never again would she worry about modesty and propriety. She was dead.

CHAPTER ONE

'It's no good, ma'am, the wheel is broken.' The news could hardly have come at a worse moment. It had been some time since they had left the last sizeable place, and they still had a little way to go before reaching their destination.

Miss Eleanor Carruthers, struggling to pull herself back on to the seat from which she had just been thrown, nobly resisted berating Clay. After all, none of their present misfortunes was to be laid at his door. He had not authorized their setting off that day in threatening weather conditions. Nor was he to be blamed for the rapidly falling snow, which must have made driving very difficult. He was not even responsible for their going into the ditch, for he was the groom and not the driver.

She turned to look at Gwen, her maidservant, who was also trying to put herself to rights. Fortunately neither of them had sustained any harm beyond that which had been done to their dignity. She then turned back to Clay. 'What are we to do then?' she asked him. 'Should we wait here for help?'

The groom shook his head. 'Most unwise, ma'am,' he answered. 'Snow's coming down hard and fast, and it's very cold. We need to find shelter, before we freeze to death. But I didn't tell you the worst.'

'The worst?' she echoed, her heart sinking.

'Briggs has come off his box. He's mostly all right, but I reckon his ankle is busted or badly sprained. He can't walk, ma'am.'

Eleanor sighed. 'You'd best help us out of here, then we'll decide what ought to be done,' she said.

Once out of the carriage, she realized that the situation was every bit as hazardous as Clay had described. She stepped into snow that was already so deep that it came to the tops of her boots. It had been falling steadily for most of the day and plenty more was coming down in large flakes. The wind was so biting that for a moment it almost took her breath away.

The driver lay in the road, his normally cheerful, round face a mask of pain.

'We must get him under cover as soon as possible,' Eleanor said, looking round. 'The shelter of those trees will do.' She turned to where Clay was helping Gwen out of the carriage. 'Get the blankets from the carriage, Clay. We will be able to cover him with those whilst we go for help.'

With Clay and Eleanor helping him on either side, and Gwen following behind with the blankets, the driver managed to hop under the trees, but his face looked grey after the effort. He would certainly not be able to mount one of the horses.

'I do not think that we passed any dwellings on our way here,' Eleanor said thoughtfully. 'Unless you noticed anywhere, Briggs?'

Briggs shook his head painfully. 'No, ma'am. But I did think that I might have caught sight of a light ahead of us, and maybe a drift of smoke.'

'Then that is where we shall head for,' declared Eleanor, tying her bonnet strings more firmly beneath her chin. 'Come, Gwen.'

'Ma'am, you must allow me to go,' Clay said, looking anxious.

'You must stay with Briggs and the team,' Eleanor replied. 'Gwen and I will be far safer on the move. In any case, someone will need to walk the horses.' In other conditions she would probably have coloured. Her fear of horses was something that she was heartily ashamed of, but had never overcome.

'I could ride one to get help,' Clay pointed out. 'That would probably be quicker.'

'But that would still leave me with the other three,' Eleanor answered ruefully. 'No, better that Gwen and I should go. Meantime, while we are discussing the matter, the weather is getting worse.'

'Very well, then, ma'am,' said Clay resignedly. 'But be careful.'

'You too, Clay,' said Eleanor, as they set off.

As they left the shelter of the trees, Eleanor lifted her skirts above what was really strictly

7

speaking entirely proper, in a vain attempt to prevent them from becoming completely sodden. The need to find shelter was becoming quite urgent.

'Oh miss, I do hope we're doing the right thing in leaving Clay and the horses and all.'

'Of course we are,' replied Eleanor, wishing that she could feel as confident as she sounded. In truth, she could not see what else she might have done. To have remained sitting in the carriage whilst they waited for help to arrive would have been foolhardy in these freezing temperatures. Furthermore, the possibility of any passer-by appearing at that moment would surely have been very slim indeed.

'Do you think the driver really saw a light, miss?'

'He would hardly have said so, if he had not,' Eleanor answered.

'It could have been one of those phantoms, miss,' replied her maid, puffing along beside her. 'You know, just lit for the very purpose of luring us to our deaths.'

'If you cannot say anything sensible, hold your tongue,' snapped Eleanor. 'Phantoms indeed!' She could not help giving a little shiver, however, that was nothing to do with the weather conditions. After all, this was a very quiet part of Warwickshire and who knew what strange things might be abroad? To divert herself from these unhelpful thoughts

8

she turned her mind to the situation that had made it necessary for her to travel in the first place.

Travelling in the middle of December was not very sensible; but she had had no alternative. Her father, Sir Clifford Carruthers, was a very high-ranking diplomat, and he had been sent on an extremely delicate mission overseas. In the past Eleanor had accompanied him ever since she had been old enough to do so. This time, however, Sir Clifford had a new companion— his second wife, Monica. The first Lady Carruthers had been dead for ten years, and Eleanor's stepmother was a dainty, pretty young woman three years younger than Eleanor herself. They got on better than many do when such a relationship is imposed upon them; but this visit would be by way of a honeymoon as well as a government mission, and Eleanor had no wish to be an awkward third. She had therefore made arrangements to spend the winter in London with a school-friend. Unfortunately, however, her friend's entire household had succumbed to a most virulent attack of measles and Eleanor, who had always intended to call upon her aunt and uncle in their country house in Warwickshire, had put this visit forward.

The journey had been unpleasant from the very beginning, with overcast skies and occasional wintry showers. One of the horses they had acquired at the first change had gone lame, and when a hidden pothole had resulted in a broken wheel, Eleanor had been very much inclined to accept it philosophically as only what might have been expected from a journey which had clearly been ill-fated from the start.

Deliberately, she brought her mind back to the present. It was not yet evening, but the light had gone, and the effect of the heavy sky and constant snow was to make the hour seem later than it really was. The road was dark and unfamiliar to them, and it was impossible to see whether there were ditches on either side, or where they might begin. The light which the coachman had seen earlier must be hidden behind some trees, Eleanor decided. Had Briggs not been a reliable sort of man, she would have begun to think that it had been a figment of his imagination.

In her anxiety, she began to walk more quickly until Gwen stopped abruptly, declaring, 'Miss Nell, you'll wear me out, you will—either that or you'll have to leave me behind.'

It must have been providence that had dictated that they should stop at that moment, for as Eleanor turned to address Gwen, she saw that they were standing between two pillars which clearly marked the bottom of a drive. 'This must be the place that was showing a light,' Eleanor said, relief in her voice. 'Thank goodness. Let's hope that the drive isn't too long.'

Fortunately for them, it was not; but when they had walked its length, the house that stood in front of them did not look as welcoming as they could have hoped. It towered over them, black and forbidding, and Eleanor, who in the past had whiled away the occasional dull hour with a sensational novel or two, was suddenly reminded of some of the more unsettling portions of Mr Walpole's novel, *The Castle of Otranto*.

'It doesn't look very cheerful, does it, miss?' Gwen remarked.

'Nonsense,' Eleanor answered, trying to sound more confident than she was feeling. 'I expect that the living-area is at the back of the house, that's all.' She devoutly hoped that it was so. The fact that the steps up to the front door had not even been cleared did not bode well. Taking hold of the knocker she beat an imperious summons upon the door. The two women stood waiting, listening in vain for the sound of anyone coming to answer it. Eleanor was conscious of Gwen looking at her, and she resisted the temptation to look back. She did not want Gwen to see that she was feeling very apprehensive.

What would they do if Briggs had been mistaken about the light? We'll just have to break in, Eleanor thought to herself. We cannot possibly stay outside on such a night.

Surely no right-minded magistrate would condemn us for such an act? Then she started to wonder what would happen if in fact this was the magistrate's house, and he was simply away. Were the penalties more severe for breaking into a magistrate's house than for entering any other dwelling unlawfully?

Refusing to think any more along these lines, she lifted the knocker again, but before she could apply it to the door, she heard the faint sound of footsteps from within. This time, she could not refrain from looking at Gwen, and she knew that the relief that was evident upon the maid's face was a mirror image of her own expression.

Her relief received something of a setback at the sound of numerous bolts and locks being drawn back; and for a moment she pictured herself being taken into somewhere resembling Newgate. Then she reflected that people were entitled to be very mindful of the security of their own homes, especially in such an isolated place.

After what seemed an eternity the door slowly opened, and a man, clearly a servant, stood on the threshold, a lantern in his hand. 'Yes?' he said, in guarded tones. 'What do you want?'

For a moment, the sheer absurdity of the situation almost made Eleanor laugh out loud. Then, remembering the horrible walk that they had just had, and Clay who was tending to the horses, and poor injured Briggs, she said firmly, 'What upon earth do you imagine that we might want, standing on the doorstep in a howling blizzard? Please let us come into the dry and shelter.'

'Well, I don't know,' the man muttered, glancing over his shoulder.

Taking advantage of his momentary inattention, Eleanor said, in her best ambassador's daughter's manner, 'Come, Gwen,' and swept past him into the hall. It was such a relief to get out of the snow and the wind, that at first that was all that they could think about. Then, as Eleanor glanced around, she realized that had their situation outside not been so desperate, she would never in a hundred years have described this place as a refuge.

The house was clearly very old, possibly Elizabethan. The hall was huge and cavernous, lined with some kind of dark wood, and the staircase across the room yawned up into impenetrable darkness. The great fireplace, above which hung some tapestry the detail of which was impossible to see in this light, was empty, and the only light in the whole place that shed any illumination was that which shone from the lamp that the man held aloft. Clearly this was not a house in which there were quantities of servants available. From this evidence, Eleanor suspected that the owner must be away for the Christmas season, and must therefore have left a skeleton staff to man the place. This would explain both the lack of welcome and the indecisiveness of the man who had opened the door. It behoved some strong-minded person to take control of the situation. It was not the first time that Eleanor had done such a thing.

'What is your name, my man?' she asked him, kindly but firmly.

'Plaice,' he replied, then added 'madam,' after a brief hesitation. He looked to be about fifty years of age, and was of medium height and build. He wore his own hair which hung lankly to his collar, and while his clothing was reasonably neat, he was not in livery. Eleanor supposed him to be some kind of caretaker.

'Well, Plaice, I can see that you do not have many people to help you here, but our needs are few and simple. I am Miss Carruthers and this is my maidservant. My carriage has come to grief a short way down the road, and. . . .' she paused, as once more Plaice was glancing over his shoulder. 'Plaice, are you listening to me?'

He turned back with a start. 'I beg pardon, madam,' he said hastily.

'My carriage is damaged, my driver has been injured, and my groom is waiting with him and the horses. I would be obliged if you would send some men from the stables to give them assistance.'

'Some men, madam?'

14

The horrible suspicion came into Eleanor's mind that he might be the only person on the premises, and she said tentatively; 'Surely there must be some other men—grooms, or gardeners?'

'Yes, but. . . .' Again he glanced over his shoulder.

Eleanor sighed with relief. 'Then kindly see to it,' she said. 'As for ourselves, my maid and I are very modest in our requirements. We should be grateful for somewhere to warm ourselves, and for something to eat. Perhaps the housekeeper could have a bed made up for us? We will readily share, if it will save you trouble.'

The servant now looked more anxious then ever. 'I shall have to ask,' he said, beginning to turn away. To her horror, Eleanor realized that he was going to leave them standing in the cold dark hall. Now that the feeling of relief of getting into the dry was wearing off, both women were realizing how very cold they were.

'By all means do so.' Eleanor smiled, thinking that he meant to find the housekeeper. 'In the meantime, do you think that we might sit in the warm? It is very cold here in the hall.'

'Well, I don't know,' the man began, rubbing his chin.

At this Eleanor lost her temper. 'For goodness sake,' she snapped, 'Can you not take just a little bit of initiative? We are cold, we are tired, we are hungry, and you stand here shilly-shallying! Were your master here I dread to think what he would say to your notion of hospitality!'

At the very moment when she had finished speaking, almost as if on cue, a voice rang out from somewhere in the distance. 'Plaice! What the deuce is to do?' The voice was undoubtedly male and educated.

Eleanor looked astonished. 'Your master *is* here!' she declared. 'What of your mistress?'

'Ain't no mistress,' the other replied.

'Then take me to your master at once,' said Eleanor. 'What he must be thinking, when you leave travellers standing in the hall like this!' The lack of a mistress was not really surprising given the state of the house, but it was rather disappointing. At least with Gwen accompanying her she was not completely unchaperoned.

'I don't rightly know,' muttered the man, pausing in indecision.

'Plaice!' the voice called again.

Eleanor drew herself up to her full height, a majestic five foot and eight inches. 'Announce me, or by heaven I will announce myself,' she insisted.

Obviously Plaice did not want to do as she was asking, but equally, he could not put off answering the imperative summons from the other room. With a speed that took Eleanor by surprise, he hurried down the passage, and

16

she found herself wondering, with some amusement, if he was hoping to shake her off. She followed him determinedly, however, with Gwen scampering at her heels. Plaice paused in front of a heavy oak door, and glanced behind him. 'He won't like it,' he said, before opening the door.

The room was in marked contrast to the atmosphere that prevailed in the hall. To start with, it was well-lit with plenty of candles, some of which were placed in front of mirrors so as to make the most of the light. It was also warm, with a roaring fire in the grate. At the sight of it Eleanor almost sighed with relief.

It had only one occupant, a man who was seated by the fire, and who did not rise at her entrance. He had a rug spread over his knees. He turned his head to look as the door opened, and Eleanor found herself being observed by a pair of dark eyes, set in a handsome face, riven with lines which hinted at dissipation. For this reason his age was not easy to estimate, but she would have judged him to be in his mid to late thirties. His black hair hung loosely about his shoulders, and while it had probably seen a comb that day, it had certainly not done so since the morning. He wore no cravat, his shirt being open at the neck, and his coat was of velvet that was so dark a blue as to be almost black.

As he observed her, his eyes widened, his

17

eyebrows rose, and the corners of his mouth turned up in a rather unpleasant smile. 'Stap me, and I never believed he'd do it,' he said slowly.

'I beg your pardon,' said Eleanor faintly.

'You've come from Playell, haven't you?' said the man.

'Playell?' echoed Eleanor, not having the faintest idea what he might be talking about.

'Playell,' replied the man, obviously thinking that by her response she had confirmed what he had said. 'He told me he'd send me a wench for Christmas, and by God, he's done it.'

CHAPTER TWO

The man's words took Eleanor completely aback, and for a moment, she could not think what to say in response to his extraordinary remark. Then she straightened her spine, glared down at him and again said 'I beg your pardon?'

'*Did* Playell send you?' he asked. 'You ain't in my usual style. In fact, frankly, you're more buxom than I prefer, but I suppose beggars can't be choosers.' There was a glass of wine on the table next to him. As he finished speaking, he picked it up and took a sip, then set it down again.

'You are insulting, sir,' she said indignantly.

18

He looked her up and down and Eleanor suddenly felt as if she were clad far more scantily than she knew to be the case. Eventually, tilting his head to one side, he remarked in dispassionate tones, 'You don't look very tempting. I'd have thought you would have made more of an effort. In fact, you look as if you've been pulled through a field by your hair.'

Eleanor dragged her gaze away from her extraordinary host—for despite her indignation she was a little fascinated by him—to glance in the mirror, and only just prevented herself from giving a squeak of dismay. Her bonnet, which had been quite a stylish affair when she had set out, was now completely ruined, its original shape beyond the discernment of any but the most skilled of milliners. Her hair, its usual honey colour darkened by the damp, was escaping in untidy strands all over her head and beginning to curl in an unruly manner as it began to dry. Her cloak, like her bonnet, was sodden, and its hem, together with the hem of her gown, was filthy. In the warmth of the fire, she was beginning to steam gently.

If the man's remarks were truthful, however, they were certainly not tactful, so drawing herself up to her full height, she said, 'That sits rather oddly on the lips of a man who cannot even bestir himself to get up out of his chair! Furthermore, I wonder, sir, how *point device* you would appear, had you just had a very wet and unpleasant walk along muddy lanes from an abandoned carriage.'

His expression became alert, but still he did not rise. 'An abandoned carriage, you say. What of the horses and the driver?'

Forgetting his insults in her concern for Briggs and Clay, she said, 'My driver was injured in the accident, and his ankle may be broken. My groom remained with him and the horses while we came to seek for help, for we had no idea where we were when the wheel broke.' Remembering his insolence, she added scornfully, 'Somewhat naïvely, I suppose, I had assumed that a gentleman's residence would house a gentleman who would be prepared to offer some assistance.'

'Haughty!' he exclaimed. 'What would you like me to do?'

She stared at him. Part of her wanted to say: 'Go to the devil,' but she could not say that without sacrificing Clay and Briggs. Swallowing her resentment, therefore, she said: 'Would you be so good as to send some men to help them? It has been snowing heavily since we left them and I cannot be easy until that is done.'

'What do you mean, "we"?' he queried, a slight frown puckering his brow.

'My maid and myself,' Eleanor replied, indicating Gwen, who was standing a couple of steps behind, looking nonplussed, but also very determined to protect her mistress from one whom even her limited experience told her was a dangerous marauder.

'Your maid?'

'Yes, my maid, sir,' she responded proudly. 'Did you suppose that I would not have one? Doubtless any wench of Mr Playell's providing would have to make shift for herself.'

He stared at her in silence for a few moments before murmuring: 'It appears that there has been a misunderstanding.'

'If so, it has not been mine,' Eleanor replied, determined not to be cowed.

He grinned briefly before turning his dark gaze upon the servant who had opened the door. 'Plaice, you have neglected to announce my guest,' he said smoothly.

This remark resulted in a hiatus, for it was clear from Plaice's expression that he had completely forgotten what her name might be. Eleanor, seeing an opportunity to establish her own credentials, said: 'I am Eleanor Carruthers. I am on my way to visit my aunt and uncle, Mr and Mrs Carlisle, who live in this vicinity.'

His brows rose a little. 'Mr and Mrs Philip Carlisle of Highbridge House?' he asked her.

'Yes, that is correct,' she answered. 'They are expecting me for Christmas. Have I strayed very far from my way?'

Clearly he was startled by the fact that she was so well-connected. He made no comment upon this however, but simply answered: 'A little,' in response to her question. Then, turning to his servant again, he said: 'Go to the stables, find Brewer, and explain matters to him. He will be able to decide how many men to send. Tell him to find this lady's carriage and her servants and give whatever help may be necessary.' He turned back to Eleanor. 'Which way should they turn outside the gates?'

'To the left,' she answered positively.

'Marvellous; a woman with a sense of direction,' he murmured sardonically. Before she could rise to the bait, he said to Plaice: 'Go now. Take away Miss Carruthers's wet bonnet and cloak. And take this young woman to Cherry. He can find dry things for Miss Carruthers and her maid. Then the girl can make up the bed in the blue room.'

By now, Eleanor had had the opportunity to take the measure of her host. He was, she was reasonably sure, the kind of man whom no mother would allow within six feet of her daughter. With this in mind, she exclaimed involuntarily 'No! I cannot sleep there.'

'Indeed,' purred the gentleman. 'And where would you prefer to sleep, madam?' Eleanor flushed to the roots of her hair. 'You cannot possibly travel on tonight,' he went on. 'Even had your carriage not been damaged, the weather conditions are far too severe. The blue room, Plaice, as I said.'

'What about your dinner?' his servant asked.

'You will serve it when my guest has had a chance to change.'

'Broome won't like that,' Plaice muttered. 'He'll say it'll be ruined.'

'In fact, then, it will be much the same as usual. Go now.'

'Come on, then,' Plaice muttered to Gwen.

Eleanor made as if to go with them but her host said: 'Please remain here, madam. There will be no fire kindled upstairs as yet. Cherry, my manservant, will fetch you when he has found you some dry clothes. Now hand Plaice your cloak and bonnet like a sensible girl before you fall prey to an inflammation of the lungs.'

His suggestion was a perfectly reasonable one, so she took off her outdoor things as he had suggested; but his earlier insolence had disturbed her, and she was still unsure what to make of him. As if reading her mistress's mind, Gwen looked doubtful, and whispered: 'I don't rightly like to leave you here, miss.'

'Your mistress will be quite safe with me as long as she remains out of my reach,' said their host, smiling unpleasantly. Briefly, he lifted the blanket to reveal his motionless legs. 'I can't do her any harm. I'm a cripple, you see.'

Gwen gave one shocked gasp, then whisked herself out of the room behind Plaice. The man in the chair looked back at Eleanor. 'This is a bachelor household, and there are no women servants here. Cherry is my valet. Your maid will be quite safe with him. His morals are better than mine.' When she said nothing, he added: 'Forgive me. I have not yet introduced myself. I am Charles Christian Hurst, and this is my home.'

Belatedly, Eleanor curtsied, and Hurst inclined his head gravely in response. 'I am grateful for your help, Mr Hurst, and I, too, must ask for forgiveness.'

'Why so?' he asked her, looking surprised.

She coloured. 'I reprimanded you, quite unjustly, for remaining seated.'

'An innocent mistake,' he replied blandly.

'Nevertheless, I must apologize,' she insisted. 'I said that the misunderstanding was not mine, but I was wrong.'

'Let us say that we both made a misjudgement and forget the matter,' he replied in the same urbane manner. 'Pray, come closer to the fire, Miss Carruthers. You must be chilled.'

She looked at his face, and for a moment, she felt like a fly being invited into a web by a dangerous but nevertheless seductive spider. Then, shaking off these foolish thoughts, she did as she was bid and sat down in the chair opposite him.

'Take off your boots,' he said. She bent over to unfasten her laces, for her feet were indeed rather wet; but then glanced up and froze in her task as she saw that he was watching her. She hesitated in her task. 'Keeping them on will do you no good at all,' he went on. 'I'm afraid I cannot promise not to look at your ankles; that is, after all, a pleasure that comes my way all too rarely these days. You can rest assured that however enticing I may find them, I will not be able to act upon my inclinations.'

Seeing the sense of the first part of his speech, she quickly unfastened her right boot, but in her haste to get the other one off, she got the string into a knot, and, panicking a little, soon found that she was quite unable to undo it.

Hurst laughed softly. 'Now what are you going to do?' he asked her. 'You could, of course, come over here and rest your foot on my knee so that I could take a look at that troublesome knot; but I'm afraid I can't answer for the consequences if you do so.'

She stared up at him. 'A moment ago, you told me that you were not able to act upon your inclinations,' she said boldly, then blushed at the construction that he would place upon her remark.

He laughed again. 'Only because you are over there and I am over here. My legs do not work, Miss Carruthers. There is nothing wrong with the rest of me.'

Eleanor's bosom swelled with indignation. 'I am well aware, sir, that in some sense I have been thrust upon you, but there is no reason

25

for you to address me in this way. I do not apologize for saying that your manner towards me is not that of a gentleman.'

He grinned, showing his teeth. 'But then I'm not a gentleman,' he retorted. 'I'm a rake—or hadn't you guessed?'

At that moment, the door opened, and a man whom Eleanor had not seen before came in. He was slim and fair and looked to be about the same age as Mr Hurst. By his dress, he was undoubtedly a gentleman's personal gentleman. 'Good evening, miss,' he said, bowing politely. 'I am Mr Hurst's valet. Your maid is making the blue room ready for you, and I have found some clothes which I venture to think will be more comfortable than your own, which I can have cleaned. After you have had a chance to change, I will have dinner served.'

'Cherry,' said Hurst.

'Sir?'

'Miss Carruthers's lace has got into a knot. Pray unfasten it for her. I should hate her to feel—entangled.'

'Certainly—allow me, miss,' said Cherry, kneeling down at Eleanor's feet. She glanced across at Hurst and surprised an expression upon his face which could have been pain or regret.

*　　*　　*

Entering the room that had been prepared for occupancy by herself and Gwen, Eleanor found a good fire burning in the grate. The bed had been made up, and a truckle-bed had been placed at the other end of the room for Gwen's use, but some of the other furnishings looked as if they could do with a good dust. Gwen was there waiting for her, dressed in a dark blue gown which fitted her quite well, but which was outmoded by about twenty years.

'There are still some clothes left here from when there were maids in the house,' said Cherry by way of explanation. 'There are also some other things which have been left more recently by visitors,' he went on, indicating several gowns that had been laid on the bed. 'I trust that you will find something to fit. I will serve dinner to you and to Mr Hurst as soon as you are ready.'

Eleanor turned with some misgiving to look at the gowns which Cherry had brought. She had the gravest suspicion as to what kind of female visitors Hurst might have been entertaining, and half expected to find that they would all display nearly all of her bosom. To her relief, however, both of the evening-gowns seemed to be tasteful as well as reasonably fashionable, although as they had obviously been made for someone shorter than herself, they would probably display rather more of her ankles than was strictly seemly. She sighed, but could not think what could be done about the matter. There was nothing else for her to wear, for the gown she had arrived in was soaking wet and had been taken away for cleaning. Presumably her boots were also being attended to, for Cherry had brought her some slippers to wear before he had conducted her up the stairs.

Hair-brushes and combs were available, and it was with some relief that Eleanor looked in the mirror after Gwen's ministrations to see her hair once more in good order. She glanced up to thank Gwen, but was alarmed to see the hectic flush on the woman's face.

'Gwen, you are not well!' she exclaimed. 'How thoughtless of me not to notice! When did this start to come on?'

'Only since I got upstairs, miss,' the maidservant confessed, sounding tearful. 'But I shall be all right soon, I'm sure.'

'You must go straight to bed, Gwen, and I will ask Cherry to bring a warming-pan and a hot drink.'

'But miss, you will need me to get you ready for bed,' Gwen protested, before sneezing violently.'

'No I shall not,' Eleanor replied firmly. 'I shall manage perfectly well. And you are to sleep in the large bed. I will take the truckle-bed, and do not argue with me, if you please. When I come upstairs, I shall expect to find you sound asleep.'

'I don't suppose I shall get to sleep at all,

miss, not with worrying about Mr Clay and Mr Briggs.'

'I'm sure Clay and Briggs will be here very soon with the help of Mr Hurst's men,' Eleanor said soothingly. 'I will make sure that you are told as soon as they get back.'

'Thank you, Miss Eleanor,' said Gwen sneezing again. 'Miss. . . .' She hesitated.

'Yes, Gwen?'

'Be careful of that Mr Hurst, miss. I wouldn't trust him as far as I could throw him.'

'No, neither would I in ordinary circumstances,' agreed Eleanor frankly. 'But remember that he is unable to get out of his chair, poor man. He is not really in a position to do me any harm.'

'I wouldn't be so sure miss,' Gwen replied darkly. 'It could all be put on, just to fool you. Remember when we was in London, the other year? I heard Mr Jenkins, the footman, say he had been playing cards with a servant from the house of Hell-raiser Hurst. Do you reckon it's him, miss?'

'I don't know,' answered Eleanor more sharply than she intended. 'And I'm not going to ask him, either. Now go to bed.'

The gown that she chose in the end was sky-blue with a petticoat of a lighter shade. As she had anticipated, it was a little short, but not enough to signify. Of greater concern was the fact that although it was not cut too low across the bosom, it was a little tight, and this had the

29

effect of emphasizing the fact that she was rather well-endowed. There was not even so much as a kerchief that she could tuck in the front, which was a pity, for she had no wish for Mr Hurst to think that she was trying to entice him. Unfortunately, everything she had seen so far told her that that was precisely the kind of thing that he *would* think!

By good fortune, she bumped into Cherry as she reached the foot of the stairs and told him about Gwen. He looked very concerned.

'I'm sorry to hear that, miss, but I can't say I'm surprised,' he answered. 'You both got thoroughly wet through. You may be sure I'll see that she's well looked after. Dinner has been laid in the small dining-room, and Mr Hurst is in there already. I will conduct you there before I go to give orders for the young woman's warming-pan.'

Eleanor thanked him, hiding the misgivings that she was feeling. In ordinary circumstances it would be quite improper for her to have dinner alone with a single gentleman. Of course, these were not ordinary circumstances. He lived alone and she was the only guest, if indeed she could be referred to as such. Had Gwen been well, she could have instructed her to come downstairs and act as her chaperon; but to make Gwen do such a thing when she was on the brink of a high temperature would be most unfair. Nor could she ask for a tray in her room if Gwen was trying to settle down and rest. Like it or not, she was now obliged to sit down to dinner with Hell-raiser Hurst, if indeed it was he. To judge from his bold conversation, it seemed extremely likely.

Cherry opened the door and announced: 'Miss Carruthers, sir.' Hurst who was already seated at the table, inclined his head at her entrance, and, accepting that in place of a bow, she curtsied, then walked to where Cherry was politely holding out a chair for her, not at the far end of the table, but next to her host. She wondered where Plaice might be, and, remembering the state of his hands when he had opened the door, devoutly hoped that he was not playing any part in the cooking of their meal.

Mr Hurst was wearing the same coat that he had had on earlier, but his linen was now properly fastened, and there was a snowy cravat at his throat. His hair had been brushed away from his face, and was confined at the back of his neck with a bow.

'Welcome to my table,' he said courteously. 'You look charmingly, ma'am.' Involuntarily, she glanced down at her rather tight bodice, and looked up to see him grinning at her and showing all his teeth. 'Yes, very charming,' he added.

His openly appreciative expression gave her pause, and she hesitated, before recalling that she really had no alternative if she wanted to

31

eat dinner, and she was exceedingly hungry.

As she took her seat, she glanced down and found her attention caught by Hurst's chair. Someone had fastened a wheel to the bottom of each leg.

She hoped that he had not noticed the direction of her gaze but he said, in a tone that was no longer one of lazy amusement, but that held more than a hint of bitterness, 'You have noticed that I am quite mobile, Miss Carruthers. Oh yes, they can push me here, there and everywhere. You cannot imagine how convenient.'

'I am pleased that you have drawn it to my attention,' Eleanor replied calmly. 'If you become really tiresome, I can push you through the window and out into the garden.'

His twisted smile took on a light of real amusement. 'So you can,' he agreed. 'But don't allow the power to go to your head. I should be sure to retaliate.' A short silence fell, to be broken only when Plaice came in carrying a tureen of soup, which he set before his master.

' 'Am an' pea,' he said, before withdrawing.

'I trust you will not be disappointed with the quality of the fare,' said Hurst as he ladled out soup first for Eleanor then for himself. 'The servants only cook for me and themselves, so I tell them not to bother too much.'

'Believe me, sir, as I was trudging through the snow on my way here, I could only dream of hot soup.'

'I can imagine,' Hurst agreed. 'It is only fair to warn you, however, that the anticipation might very well be the best thing about it.' They both addressed themselves to their soup which, though thick and hot, did not really taste of very much. Hurst offered her more, which she refused. 'I don't blame you,' he said dispassionately. 'I imagine sodden paper must taste rather like this.'

'It was not . . . unpleasant,' she achieved in level tones.

'There speaks the diplomat's daughter,' he murmured. She darted a look of surprise at him. 'It's hardly a brilliant deduction,' he remarked. 'It is known locally that Mrs Carlisle's brother is a diplomat. Furthermore, I have even attended a function at which your father was a guest of honour—in Madrid, I believe.'

Before she could make any response to this, Plaice came in to clear away their dishes. While he was about his task, Cherry entered with some welcome tidings. 'The men have arrived back with your servants and the horses, miss,' he said. 'Your groom is warming up in the kitchen even now, and your driver has been taken to bed.'

'What of his injury?' Hurst asked, before Eleanor could do so.

'A bad sprain, so Brewer says, and he's good with simple injuries.' He turned to Eleanor. 'Your trunk is being taken upstairs, miss.'

'That is good news,' replied Eleanor warmly. 'Do thank the men very much on my behalf. I shall speak to them in person in the morning, of course. How kind of them, too, to bring my trunk back. I really did not expect it.'

'The men took Henry, the plough-horse, with the sledge in order to carry the groom, so they thought they might as well bring your trunk as well,' Cherry replied.

'Well, it was very thoughtful of them,' Eleanor answered. 'Pray would you be so good as to tell Gwen that Clay and Briggs have arrived safely? I did promise that she would be told.'

'Of course, miss.'

'Definitely the diplomat's daughter,' murmured Hurst, pouring some wine for both of them.

Remembering the things that he had said just before the plates had been removed, Eleanor said 'I had no idea that you had met my father.'

'Did I say that? No, that wouldn't be a strictly accurate description of events, I fear,' Hurst replied. 'I should more truthfully have said that I nearly attended the same function as your father.'

'Nearly?' Eleanor asked him.

'I got distracted on the way,' he admitted, his eyes twinkling. 'Here is the next remove, an I mistake not.'

No doubt it was a wench who had distracted

him, Eleanor reflected as Plaice and Cherry brought in the dishes. There was a fricassee of rabbit, together with fowl in plum-sauce and a joint of beef, and although the soup had taken the edge off Eleanor's appetite, the unaccustomed exercise meant that she was very ready to sample all the dishes. The beef was rather overcooked but very tasty, but the plum-sauce had a burnt quality to it and the rabbit, like the soup, lacked flavour. Nevertheless, her hunger was such that she did justice to her meal, and also to the potato-pie and the 'floating islands' that were served afterwards, and together made up the best part of the repast.

As they were finishing, Eleanor remembered something that Hurst had said earlier on and asked a question that had come into her mind. 'You said that my aunt and uncle were known locally, yet they only acquired Highbridge House this year. Has this property been in *your* family for long?'

'No. My father left me money, but no country property, just a London house. This place is called Glade Hall. My wife was a Miss Glade.'

'Your wife?' Eleanor echoed, surprised. 'I did not realize that you were married, sir. Plaice said that there was no mistress here when he admitted us.'

'I was married,' he answered. 'I am now a widower.'

'I'm very sorry, sir,' she answered.

'Are you?' he asked her quizzically. 'I expect you'll be even more sorry when you hear how she died.' Eleanor did not say anything, but simply sat watching him. 'Not curious? Well, I'll tell you anyway. I murdered her, together with my unborn child. Now how does that make you feel about staying here? Can you find a polite way of expressing *that*, Miss Diplomat's Daughter?'

CHAPTER THREE

After Eleanor had gone upstairs, Hurst sat for a brief time over his port before Cherry came to wheel him back into the salon. The floors were not carpeted in order to make the pushing of the chair easier.

'Do you want to sit here for a while, sir, or would you rather I took you straight through to bed?' After Hurst had lost the use of his legs, he had had one of the drawing-rooms converted into a bedroom, so that he would no longer be obliged to go upstairs.

'I'd rather sit in here for a while,' Hurst replied. 'Do you mind? I promise I won't keep you up too late.'

'Not at all, sir,' Cherry answered. 'I ought to go upstairs to see if Miss Carruthers needs anything for her maidservant, so I cannot retire yet.'

When he had fitted Hurst's chair with wheels, the estate carpenter had taken one arm off it at the same time, and had put it back with a hinge and catch, so that the arm could be lowered to enable its occupant to move more easily from one chair to another. Cherry unfastened the catch, then helped Hurst into his armchair by the fire. That done, he moved the other chair away, knelt down, and for a few minutes massaged the muscles in his master's legs, as he had faithfully done every day since the accident. Hurst sat with his face turned towards the fire, his eyes closed, his mouth set in a hard line. Then angrily he said through clenched teeth, and not for the first time, 'Stop your bloody ministrations for God's sake, man! You know it's doing no good.'

Cherry stood up. 'The doctor said—'

Hurst interrupted him. 'I know what the doctor said. You've repeated it to me a hundred times. There's nothing wrong with me physically. He does not know why I cannot walk. Perhaps I may walk again one day. Well, if you believe that kind of fantasy, you must have windmills in your head. Six months it's been, Cherry. Six months!'

Cherry straightened. 'I will never give up hope, sir,' he said, 'and neither must you. Now, if you will excuse me—'

'Oh go on, man, go on,' Hurst replied testily. 'Be about your good works and leave me to my brooding.'

*   *   *

After Cherry had gone, Hurst sat looking into the fire, his glass in his hand. This evening at the dinner-table had been the first time that he had spoken about his wife to anyone other than Cherry since the accident. Yes, he had thought about it often. In fact, a day never went by without his turning it over in his mind. When he had spoken to his unexpected guest in that self-accusatory style, he had only given voice to what had been festering in his head since the previous June.

He had married Priscilla Glade eighteen months before at his father's behest. He grinned wryly. No, say rather at his father's command. He had, after all, run through his own money, and had been in imminent danger of ending up in the sponging-house if someone did not rescue him. His father had consented to do so, but only if he made the marriage upon which the older man had set his heart. He had therefore, at the age of thirty-three, paid court to the very wealthy, very beautiful Miss Glade.

In worldly terms, it had been an excellent match. Hurst's family was an old one. There was no inherited property, the men of his family having perfected the ability to lose their goods over the card-table to a fine art. Hurst's own father, Robert Hurst, had never bought property for himself, being happy to rent a country house which would then revert to its owner on his death. He had escaped the gaming taint, and having acquired a modest fortune through a spell in India, he did not want to see his only son fritter it away.

From his early days on the town, it had seemed highly probable that Charles Christian Hurst—known to his friends as Chris—might do this. He neglected no opportunity for kicking up a dust, and by his early twenties, had earned the sobriquet, 'Hell-raiser'. His father had watched, hoping that in time Chris would settle down; but his hopes were vain. Eventually, a bad run of luck on Chris's part had put him into his father's power. Only his co-operation with regard to this marriage would release further funds into his grasp.

Hurst smiled wryly as he recalled how very easy he had been to persuade. He had not been at all attracted to the idea of marriage, but one look at the beautiful Miss Glade had persuaded him. In fact, as much to his own astonishment as to anyone else's, he had fallen in love with her at first sight.

Miss Glade's family had come originally from merchant stock, but they had been landowners now for three generations. Nevertheless, the taint of the shop remained, at least to some, and marriage into a family whose line did not carry such an odour had always been the aim of the Glades. Hurst's was such a family, and Miss Glade obediently did as her father bade her.

Chris had been an inveterate chaser of women since a flirtatious chambermaid had caught his eye at Eton when he was sixteen. It was, perhaps, inevitable that he should come to take his popularity with women for granted. His dark good-looks, his athletic figure, and the sparkle in his eye had guaranteed him success. For the most part he had confined his attentions to more mature ladies who knew what game he was playing, and were willing to share in it without expecting long-term fidelity. Younger ladies he indulged with the occasional flirtation, but wise chaperons kept their charges well away from him, warning them that he was a dangerous man. Needless to say, that only made him more exciting in their eyes, and he had lost count of the number of languishing glances that must have been cast his way.

By way of contrast, Miss Glade's manner towards her suitor was cool, if not cold. This did not repel him; quite the reverse. In a strange kind of way, he almost approved of his betrothed's distant manner. The fact that Miss Glade did not instantly fall at his feet gave her added allure. It made him feel like a knight in one of the stories that he had enjoyed as a boy. She would be the holy grail whose acquisition would bring him the happiness that he craved, and which he sensed, deep down, his hell-raising life could never bring. Very soon he was pursuing her not because his father had told him to do so, but in accordance with his own inclinations.

After an acceptable period of decorous courtship, he applied for permission to pay his addresses to her. This permission was duly granted, but although a formal betrothal gave him certain privileges, Miss Glade did not permit him to do more than kiss her hand or, very occasionally, her cheek. Still her coolness only fanned his passion. There had never yet been a woman with whom he could not succeed if he only put his mind to it. All he had to do was to be patient. Doubtless the formality of the marriage ceremony would give her permission to respond to him as he desired.

Hurst leaned back in his chair and almost laughed at his own *naïveté*. Their wedding night had been a complete disaster, resulting in her occupying the marriage bed alone, whilst he had sought out the housekeeper, a widow fifteen years his senior who, deprived of intimate male company for nearly ten years, had been delighted to oblige him, and whose willing response had reassured him that he had not lost his touch.

The marriage had been consummated eventually, but it had not been an act that had given either of them pleasure, and eventually

Hurst had been obliged to face the bitter truth. Priscilla had not been cold towards him out of shyness, or virtue. She had been cold because she did not like him.

To begin with, he cherished the hope that this might change. He did all that he could to please her, carefully discovering her likes and dislikes, and tailoring his life to suit hers in a way that would have seemed unimaginable to him at one time. Surely, she would eventually come to return his affections, he told himself. This did not seem to happen. She accepted any gifts graciously, like a queen receiving the bounty of a subject, and appeared at his side for formal occasions whenever required, but she did not give of herself, and made it very plain that he was barely tolerated in her bedroom. He did wonder whether there might be another man in the case, but never found any evidence of it. Man of the world though he was, the other possible explanation did not even occur to him. It was only his unexpected return home one day that had revealed to him that his wife could not, in fact, be romantically attached to any man when he had found her cosily ensconced with a female paramour.

His subsequent actions still made him wince even now. He had unceremoniously thrown his wife's lover out of the house, semi-clad as she was, and had flung her clothes after her. Thereafter, he had abandoned his attempts to make himself acceptable to his wife and resumed his hell-raising activities.

They had continued to attend various functions together, but in private they barely spoke to one another. Even the news that she was to bear his child had come to him via the doctor, and not directly from his wife. This news came as a welcome relief. He could only pray that the child would be a son and heir, so that he would not be obliged to approach his wife again. His own father had died just after his marriage and as he had no brothers, he was conscious of being the last male of his line.

His wife's pregancy, if it did not rekindle his love for her, did have the effect of making him feel tender towards her, but it seemed to have the opposite effect upon her feelings towards him. Soon they became openly hostile, and even in public she seemed barely able to be civil.

The final function that they had attended had been here, locally. He had insisted that she should spend the last months of her pregnancy in the country, but Priscilla had been against the idea. It was during the course of that evening that he had discovered the real reason for this attitude. Not only had his wife been meeting her lover in secret, but they were also planning to run away together and bring up the child between them. He could still remember the anger welling up inside him when he had made that discovery.

Unfortunately, he could not remember any

more than that. They had gone to the ball in his curricle. They had left in the same vehicle, had suffered some kind of accident and had been found by a local gamekeeper. From the moment that he had awoken to discover that his wife was dead, he had been unable to walk.

He knew what people thought about it. He had overheard more than one person saying that he had been drunk and had driven recklessly, that he deserved his fate, and that it was a judgment upon him. He had a feeling that they were right.

Here he had mouldered ever since. It had been six months since Priscilla and the baby she was carrying had died; six months since he had walked. Nothing in that time had given him the slightest pleasure or even awoken his curiosity until that handsome young woman with the honey-coloured hair had come in. She was the first visitor that he had had apart from the vicar, who had come only weeks after the accident in order to bemoan his morals. He had spoken to this clerical gentleman with such unmitigated rudeness that he had taken offence and left, never to return. Hurst's accident had made him turn in upon himself, taking no interest in the outside world, refusing to order a newspaper and hardly doing more than glance at the occasional letters that he received. Then Miss Carruthers had arrived, a lady to her fingertips, and initially he had mistaken her for the lightskirt that his friend Playell had promised him. How indignant she had been! He grinned at the memory. When Cherry came to put him to bed, he realized to his surprise that he was still grinning.

*　　　*　　　*

When Hurst had made his shocking disclosure about his wife and child, Eleanor had not known what to say. She had been glad that Cherry had come in moments later to tell her that he was a little concerned about Gwen. It had given her an excuse for leaving her host in order to go upstairs.

On her arrival in the bedchamber she had discovered that Gwen was indeed far from well. She undoubtedly had a temperature, which was climbing by the minute. Eleanor would very much have liked to send for the doctor; but she could not countenance either the thought of someone having to turn out to fetch him, or of the poor man's having to make his way to the house in such weather, even if either journey were possible. She would just have to look after Gwen herself. It was not the first time that she had attended a person with a fever, after all. Her father and Gwen had both been laid low on one occasion when they had been travelling across the Mediterranean, and because of the rough conditions, she had been the only one willing and able to nurse

45

them.

Cherry came upstairs with a jug of water to bathe Gwen's hot forehead, and asked Eleanor if she would like a cooling draught for the girl.

Eleanor shook her head. 'I do not think she will take anything at present,' she said. 'I shall see how she is in the morning. In the meantime, I have the water with which I can moisten her lips if need be.'

'Very well, miss,' said Cherry. 'I'll just get the master to bed, and lie down for a few hours myself. I'll come up part way through the night and take over so that you can get some rest.'

Eleanor smiled gratefully. 'There's no need, Cherry,' she said. 'You have your work to do in the morning and . . . and Mr Hurst may need you in the night, perhaps.'

'He is very unlikely to do so, but if by any chance he does, he can ring his bell and I will hear it.'

After Cherry had gone, Eleanor sat down beside Gwen, but although the young woman was a little fretful, and her face needed bathing regularly, her care did not absorb all of Eleanor's thoughts. She was therefore able to give her mind to the incidents that had taken place that evening.

What a strange man Mr Hurst was, insolent rake one moment, considerate host the next, then entertaining dinner companion! And what was she to make of that ultimate disclosure, that he had killed his wife and unborn child? Was it something that should be taken with a pinch of salt, or was there some truth in it? Clearly something dreadful had happened to him to make him lose the use of his legs. Had that occurrence also resulted in the death of his wife? Even whilst she shuddered at that thought, she remembered the expression of pain that she had surprised upon Hurst's face as Cherry had unfastened the knot in her lace; an expression which had not appeared to her to have a physical cause. What could have been the reason for it?

Unable to think of an answer to this question, she turned her mind to other parts of the conversation that they had had during dinner. How odd that they had almost met! She too had been in Madrid with her father, and had been present at the same function that Hurst had almost attended. Had he been married at that time? What would have happened had that meeting taken place?

She must have drifted off to sleep in her chair, for it only seemed like moments later when Cherry was gently tapping her on the shoulder and saying that it was now three o'clock, and would she like to lie down? It took a little while for her to come round, for she had been having a dream in which she had been dancing with a very tall Mr Hurst.

Quelling a sudden desire to ask Cherry how tall his master was, she turned her attention to

47

Gwen instead, and found that there was still very little change. Gratefully, she opened the door which led into the small dressing-room. Cherry had had the truckle-bed moved when it had become clear that Gwen was really ill. He had also had Eleanor's luggage placed in there, and it did not take her more than a moment or two to open her small overnight bag and take out her nightdress. She undressed quickly and climbed into bed, suddenly realizing how tired she was. Despite all the excitement of the day, she was asleep almost before her head touched the pillow.

*　　*　　*

When Eleanor awoke the following morning it was full daylight. She glanced at the clock on the mantelpiece and to her horror saw that it was just after nine. She was about to get out of bed when there was a tap on the door, and Cherry came in with a murmured apology and a cup and saucer in his hand.

'I trust you've slept well, miss?' he said 'I was wondering whether you'd like a cup of tea?'

'I would very much like one,' she replied gratefully. 'How is Gwen this morning?'

'Much the same,' he told her. 'Her temperature is high, but no worse. She's mostly quiet, although fretful from time to time.'

'I'll come and sit with her as soon as I'm

dressed,' said Eleanor.

Cherry shook his head. 'There's no need, miss,' he said. 'Plaice is sensible enough, and he's sitting with her for now. You can go to her when you've had your tea and got up and eaten your breakfast.'

After Mr Hurst's parting words to her the previous night, Eleanor was not at all sure about how she felt at having to confront him over the breakfast table. To her relief, however, the table at which they had eaten dinner the previous night was only laid for one, and she could only conclude that her host must eat breakfast in his own room. The meal, like dinner the previous night, was adequate but not very appetizing, but the coffee was barely drinkable, and after a small cup, she contented herself with water.

Before she went upstairs to see to Gwen, she wandered into one of the front rooms that overlooked the drive in order to assess the situation outside.

Had she not known that she and Gwen had trudged up to the front door the previous night, she would have had no idea that anyone had approached the house recently, for their footsteps had been completely obliterated by a later fall of snow. It was fine at present, but there was no sign of a thaw, and the sky looked leaden as if there was more to come. There would certainly be no prospect of their leaving today, even if Gwen was not ill.

Eleanor's main concern was her uncle and aunt. They would be bound to be concerned about her welfare, but that could not be helped. There was no possibility of anyone's taking a message to them. She would just have to hope that they would realize that she must have found shelter. Doubtless it would have been better had her refuge not been under the roof of a notorious rake, but beggars could not be choosers.

She looked around the room in which she was standing. It was a handsome library, panelled in dark wood, with well-stocked bookshelves from floor to ceiling, red curtains, and wide window-seats so that the avid reader could get the best light. There was no fire lit in there so it was deathly cold, and everything was covered with a film of dust. For Eleanor, books were often the only things that helped her keep her sanity on long journeys, and she sighed with regret for the neglect of what was probably quite a useful library. From what had been said so far, there was no housekeeper, and probably the only rooms that were cleaned regularly were those which Mr Hurst used regularly. If the weather continued bad and they had to stay for much longer, she might even occupy her time by cleaning and tidying in here.

Because the room was cold she did not remain there for very long, but went to the kitchens to find out how Briggs was. He was sitting comfortably by the fire with his foot up on a stool, and looking altogether much more cheerful than when she had seen him last. 'It's only a sprain, thank goodness, miss,' he said cheerfully. 'I've tried hobbling on it and it's not too bad.'

'Well, don't put your weight on it too soon and do more damage,' Eleanor told him.

'I shan't do that, miss, but I want to see to those horses myself. There's no telling whether this Brewer knows his business or not.'

After this conversation, Eleanor went upstairs to see how Gwen was faring. When she entered the blue bedchamber, she found Gwen tucked up snugly under the covers and Plaice sitting next to her, looking very much like a dog who has been told to guard something but who cannot imagine why. He gladly relinquished his post and went downstairs. After feeling Gwen's brow, bathing it, then arranging the pillows, Eleanor fetched her copy of *Clarissa* from her bag, and sat down to read.

It was not, perhaps, the most happy of choices. The tale of an unscrupulous libertine despoiling the young lady who was at his mercy struck a little too close to home, and although the tale absorbed her interest, the message which Cherry conveyed at about half past twelve, inviting her to partake of a light luncheon with Mr Hurst, brought a quite unnecessary flush to her cheek.

'Can I not have something on a tray?' she asked. 'I do not like to leave Gwen.'

'I'll be very happy to sit with her, miss,' Cherry replied. 'Some of Mr Hurst's linen needs a stitch or two and I might as well do that here as anywhere else. Besides....' He paused.

'Besides?' she prompted him.

'Begging your pardon, but Mr Hurst doesn't get very much company these days.'

'Very well, then,' she said, getting up. She paused in the doorway. 'Cherry, for how long has he ... has he...?'

'Mr Hurst has been unable to walk since June, miss.'

Eleanor walked downstairs thoughtfully. He had been crippled for six months. Had he been alone for that length of time as well? If so, to sit with him for a meal was surely little enough to ask. Her wild imaginings seemed very selfish when set alongside his misfortunes.

Hurst was at the dining-table already when she went in. As before, he inclined his head to her, and she curtsied in response. Today, he was wearing a coat of dark green, his hair was neatly tied back and his linen was clean and pressed. Obviously, Cherry took a pride in his work.

'I am glad that you have decided to join me,' he said, smiling.

She looked at him in surprise. It was almost as if he had overheard the conversation that she had had with Cherry. 'I did not want to leave Gwen, but Cherry assured me that he would be quite happy to keep an eye on her,' she responded as she took her place next to him.

'Her loss is my gain,' he said politely. 'Eating alone is a cheerless business.'

Eleanor reflected that he must have had quite a lot of experience of that, but she merely said: 'I can well believe it. At least you have this small dining-room to eat in.'

'There is another dining-room which is huge and cavernous,' he told her. 'It's really only suitable for twenty or more.'

Luncheon was a simple meal, consisting only of bread and cheese accompanied by ale or, in Eleanor's case, a pot of tea, and followed by an apple tart, and a bowl of fresh fruit.

'I apologize for the food that you have had here so far,' Hurst said, after they had begun to eat. 'Broome isn't much of a cook, I'm afraid. His wife was the cook originally, but she ran off with one of the grooms and he stayed behind to fill the post.'

'This is excellent,' Eleanor responded truthfully.

'You can't do much to a piece of cheese,' Hurst retorted.

'It cannot possibly be less palatable than a supper that we ate in London at the house of—' she paused. 'I suppose I shouldn't say really, but it was quite dreadful. Everybody remarked upon it. The champagne was flat, too.'

'Mrs Fitzroy's? Last year?' he asked her.

Her eyes widened. 'However did you know?' she asked.

'My dear girl, I was there,' he answered. 'The musicians were shocking, as well.'

'Oh, weren't they?' she exclaimed. 'I couldn't believe it when I first heard them. That was what made it so hard to bear. The rooms were so cold that one longed to dance, simply to warm up, but it was impossible to detect a beat.'

Hurst nodded in agreement. 'The last straw for me was when I discovered that they had not provided enough packs of cards for the gaming-room, and the one that I was eventually given lacked three cards. I left after that and spent the rest of the evening at my club.'

'Unfortunately, that option was not open to me,' Eleanor replied. 'There were people there whom Papa needed to see and I was obliged to remain to the bitter end.'

'Of course, there was one thing that would have tempted me to stay had I known about it.' She raised her brows in enquiry, and he smiled. 'Your presence, my dear,' he told her. 'How could you not guess it?'

She coloured, and turned her attention to the portion of apple tart on her plate. Mr Hurst, she noticed, ate very sparingly, not refilling his plate, and refusing the tart altogether. No doubt he was wise to limit what he ate when he could not take exercise, she reflected. At that thought, a huge wave of compassion swept over her, so powerful that it almost took her breath away.

'What is it?' he asked her suddenly.

'What do you mean, sir?' she replied, his question taking her by surprise.

'What made you look so tragic all of a sudden?'

'Oh.' Impossible to tell him the truth. She sought frantically for something to say, and eventually replied: 'I was thinking of the book I was reading upstairs.'

'Some improving tome, I hope.'

'It was *Clarissa*,' she answered, and blushed.

'Indeed. And you see me as Lovelace, do you?'

'Of course not,' she declared, speaking too quickly.

'No, of course you don't,' he agreed, laughing derisively. 'You would have been in some danger from Lovelace.'

'It's no bad thing, surely, to be no danger to a woman,' she said swiftly.

'You'll be saying next that this was a judgment upon me,' he retorted, indicating his chair. 'Well, you wouldn't be the first.'

By now they had finished their meal, and Eleanor laid down her napkin. 'Would you like me to push you back into the salon?' she asked him, ignoring his last remark.

'I doubt you could manage it my dear,' he replied, his tone none too pleasant. 'Rather too much dead weight for you to handle.'

At that moment, Cherry appeared, and said: 'Allow me, miss.' He took hold of the back of Hurst's chair. 'Gwen seems to me to be more settled if anything. I shouldn't be surprised if her temperature is back to normal tomorrow.'

'I do hope so,' Eleanor agreed. She watched how carefully Cherry manoeuvred Hurst's chair from under the table and round so that it was facing the doors into the salon, not noticing the brooding look upon Hurst's face as he observed her interest. Once inside the saloon, Cherry turned to close the doors and Eleanor, left alone in the dining-room, stood thinking for a moment. She tried to recall more about the party that she had attended at the Fitzroys that evening. She could not believe that Hurst could have been there without her noticing him. He was such a distinctive man, and on his feet he must have been doubly impressive. If he had spent time in the gaming-room and then left, however, she might not have had the chance to see him.

She turned to leave the dining-room by the other door in order to go upstairs to rejoin Gwen, but before she could do so, she noticed that Mr Hurst had left his snuffbox on the table. Thinking to save Cherry a journey, she opened the door into the salon, and stood on the threshold, staring. Cherry had pushed Hurst's chair as close to his armchair as possible, and was assisting his master to move from one to the other. He then moved the wheeled chair out of the way, and covered Hurst's knees with a blanket. From across the room, Eleanor could see the look of fury mingled with humiliation that was upon Hurst's face as he glowered at her.

Cherry stood upright after finishing his task and, becoming aware of another person's presence, he turned and saw her. 'I'll go back to Gwen, miss,' he said. 'You stay here for a while.' He then whisked himself out of the room before she could say anything.

'Satisfied?' Hurst asked her.

'I beg your pardon?' she said blankly.

'Is your curiosity satisfied?' he demanded bitterly.

She was utterly taken aback by his fury, and could not understand what she had done to merit it. She simply walked forward, saying 'You . . . you left your snuffbox on the table, so I thought I would bring it to you.'

'How clever of you to wait for just the right amount of time,' he sneered, his tone laden with venom. 'No doubt you were desperate to see how I manage to drag my useless limbs from one item of furniture to another. Well, now you know. Would you like to observe Cherry heaving me into bed, later?'

'That wasn't it at all,' she protested.

'So you say,' he replied disbelievingly.

'It wasn't,' she repeated, anger beginning to take the place of bewilderment. 'How can you imagine that I would be so heartless?'

'Why not?' he asked her. 'Plenty of people go to view the lunatics in Bedlam. I should imagine that this is no different.'

'Plenty of people *may* go, but I do not,' she said sharply. 'I can think of nothing more obnoxious than wanting to gloat over someone else's weakness. Now, do you want this or not?' She held out the snuffbox.

'Bring it over to me,' he said shortly.

Suddenly, the room seemed to be filled with tension, as if there were a storm on the way. Eleanor had taken a step or two towards him. Now she stopped again, aware of the heavily charged atmosphere.

'If you please,' said Hurst, with exaggerated courtesy. 'You see, we helpless invalids are entirely dependent upon the good will of such as yourself.'

Although she felt more like throwing it at him, she did take the snuffbox across the room and held it out ready to place it into the hand that he was holding out. To her great astonishment and alarm, however, instead of taking the snuffbox, he seized hold of her wrist and dragged her to him, and before she could recover from her surprise, he had pulled her on to his knee. His look of fury had now been replaced by one of triumph.

'Not so helpless, you see,' he said, pulling her against him with one arm, whilst tilting her chin with his other hand. Then he pressed his mouth to hers and kissed her ruthlessly, taking his time about it.

Eleanor was twenty-four years old and well-travelled, and this was not the first time that she had been kissed. It was the first time, however, that she had been pulled on to a man's knee and manhandled in such a way. She was a tall woman and her build was generous rather than delicate. But she found that his hands and arms were immensely strong, and although she struggled for all she was worth, she could not extricate herself from his embrace.

Eventually, he tipped her off his knee, and she staggered a little before regaining her balance. She was conscious of looking not a little dishevelled. As for Hurst, his hair, too, had become somewhat disarranged, and his face now bore an expression of unbridled glee.

She took a deep breath, drew back her hand, and slapped him hard across the face. 'How dare you, you ... you shameless rake!' she exclaimed, before stalking from the room. To her astonishment, she heard the sound of his laughter echoing after her as she ran up the stairs.

CHAPTER FOUR

Eleanor hurried straight to her room, her immediate instinct telling her to get right away from Hurst. It was not until she had opened the door, still breathless and dishevelled, that she had realized how her appearance must look to Cherry. He turned at her entrance and she could see from the expression on his face that he had formed a very accurate estimate of what had taken place downstairs. Humiliatingly, it occurred to her that this was probably not the first time that he had seen a woman dishevelled because of his master's attentions.

She blushed to the roots of her hair and said belatedly, 'Oh . . . oh dear! I . . . I have just had rather a . . . a nasty fright!'

'I'm sorry to hear that, miss,' said Cherry, looking at her steadily.

'A spider!' she exclaimed. 'Yes, it was a spider! It dropped down from the ceiling and on to my hair, and I cannot bear them, you see.'

'I see,' Cherry answered in a neutral tone. 'Would you like me to attend to your hair for you? Gwen, as you see, is nicely settled at present.'

'Oh, thank you,' Eleanor answered in some surprise. 'Can you do ladies' hair?'

'Yes indeed,' Cherry answered as she took her place in front of the dressing-table. 'I was used to do Mrs Hurst's hair at times, if her abigail was sick, or not available.'

Eleanor was silent for a time, as she watched Cherry attend to her hair with skilful fingers. When Gwen was ill, she was obliged to make shift for herself, but had never been very happy with the result. Her hair was long, thick and plentiful, and really needed expert attention. Eventually, she said, 'For how long has Mrs Hurst been dead?'

'Since June, miss,' was the reply.

Eleanor thought for a moment. 'Cherry, you told me that Mr Hurst had been unable to walk since June.'

'That's so. Mr Hurst was injured in the same accident that killed his wife. I think that will do now, miss. Is there anything more I can do for you?'

'It will—more than "do", as you put it, Cherry,' Eleanor replied. 'Thank you, there is nothing; unless. . . .'

'Yes, miss?'

'I have had enough of reading for now,' she said, eyeing *Clarissa* with a barely repressed shudder. 'Is there any household linen needing attention? The light is good today, and I would gladly sew, if there is anything that needs doing.'

'There is some sewing to be done,' Cherry admitted, 'if you are sure that you don't mind.

61

I deal with Mr Hurst's personal items myself, but everything else gets neglected, I fear.'

'I don't mind at all,' Eleanor told him. 'I should be glad of an occupation. Oh, and by the way. . . .'

'Yes miss?'

'I would like my dinner on a tray tonight, if it's not too much trouble.'

After a brief pause, Cherry said, 'Of course miss. Now I'll find that sewing for you. Then, I'll go and deal with the spider that frightened you so much.'

*   *   *

'Why did you do it, sir?' Cherry asked his master. After leaving Eleanor, he had sorted out the items of household linen that most needed a stitch or two, and had taken them to her, together with the work-basket. He knew that Hurst would probably be needing him, but judged that it would do him no harm to wait. On entering the salon, he had found his master sitting in his chair, his head leaning back, his eyes closed. Although, at first glance, his attitude suggested sleep, his expression was very far from tranquil. There was a red mark on his face that had not been there earlier.

Seeing that his master's hair had fared almost as badly as Eleanor's, Cherry went into the bedroom and came back with a hair-brush. It was as he was tying back Hurst's hair once

62

more that he put his question. 'Why?' Hurst echoed, his tone harsh. 'Well, why not? She's a wench, ain't she?'

'No sir, she is not,' Cherry replied evenly.

At once, Hurst's air of bravado disappeared and he turned his face away. 'Cherry, she came close to me; I smelled her perfume, I wanted ... wanted ... Cherry, do you know how long it is since I held a woman in my arms?'

'I've a fair idea, sir.'

'And how many women would want me like this? I'm not a proper man any more. What I can get, I must take, for I'll never get a woman's kisses any other way.' He kept his face averted. He could feel his eyes filling with tears, born of rage and frustration.

'I think you're wrong sir,' said Cherry. He paused. 'She won't come down tonight. That's your doing. You frightened her very much. Will there be anything else?'

'No, nothing.' Cherry was about to close the door on his way out when Hurst spoke again. 'What did she say to you?' he asked.

'She said a spider had got into her hair,' Cherry replied.

'A spider.' Despite his emotional turmoil, Hurst almost began to chuckle.

*　　*　　*

To decide to sew had been a mistake, Eleanor acknowledged to herself eventually. It left too

63

much of her mind free to think about what had occurred. The more she thought about the matter, the more she came to the reluctant conclusion that she was at least partly to blame for it.

In normal circumstances, of course, she would never have visited a household such as this, let alone have been staying in it. To begin with, it was a bachelor establishment, but what was worse, it was a house belonging to a notorious libertine. Circumstances had forced her to take refuge here, and she had not had any choice in the matter. Having done so, she had been obliged to stay. The accident to her carriage, the severity of the weather, and Gwen's illness had all conspired to ensure that.

But given all these unalterable facts, there were still things that she could have done to keep Hurst's advances at bay. Her very first encounter should have been enough to tell her that she would be well-advised to keep to her room. She should certainly never have agreed to dine with him. And having got his measure she should never, ever have gone close enough to him for him to be able to seize her as he had done. Even as she sat here now, she could almost feel the power of his embrace, the mastery of his lips. . . .

With real determination, she put that recollection to the back of her mind. Yes, she should have kept to her room, but how could she have done, once she had learned even a fraction of his history? It was six months since his accident, and clearly, judging by the state of the house and the lack of servants, he had not had visitors recently. How could she have refused even to dine with the man whose hospitality she was enjoying, when she might be the only guest he had entertained since the summer? She could not have done so, but for the sake of her own dignity, she must refuse to eat with him tonight. With any luck, Gwen would be much better in the morning, and if no more snow fell, they would soon be able to get away, either in her own carriage if it could be mended, or in a conveyance from her uncle's stable, as soon as she could get a message to him.

*   *   *

She was not surprised when, later in the afternoon, Cherry came to the room and said, 'Mr Hurst's compliments, miss, and would you care to join him for dinner?'

'Cherry, I told you that I would have a tray in my room,' she reminded him. 'In any case, Gwen is feeling much cooler now and I want to be here lest she should wake in a strange place and be frightened.'

'I remember what you said,' Cherry replied, 'but the master did instruct me to ask you.' He left her, but came back a short time later with a note which he gave to her. She opened it, and found a few words written in a bold, sloping hand.

Pray give me the chance to apologize. You know that I cannot come to you.
Hurst

She folded the note again, put it down, and thought for a moment. No doubt the man that he had been would have come to her room to seek her out. On the one hand she could be thankful for small mercies; but on the other, she must not trade upon his disability. Furthermore, she did not want him to think she was afraid. She turned to Cherry. 'Pray tell Mr Hurst that I will see him in the morning,' she said.

*   *   *

Gwen's sleep was deep and completely untroubled for the first time and Eleanor, sleeping in the truckle-bed which she had had brought back into the room, also enjoyed a good night's sleep. She had only just woken when she heard Gwen's voice saying, 'Miss? Miss, where are you? Where am I? What happened? Oh, I feel so weak.'

'Gwen, you are better,' Eleanor exclaimed, getting out of her bed and hurrying to Gwen's side to put a hand on her brow. 'Your

66

temperature is back to normal! Oh, how relieved I am!' She bent to kiss the abigail on the cheek. 'You have been quite ill, you know.' She gave the bell-rope a tug. 'I'm sure you'd like a cup of tea.'

'Yes I would, miss, but you oughtn't to be doing that! It's my job to ring the bell, and to be getting tea for *you.*' She looked around the room. 'I don't remember this place,' she said, wrinkling her brow.

'Don't you recall, Gwen, we struggled through the snow to get here?'

Just as Gwen was frowning to remember, Cherry came in answer to the bell, and professed himself delighted to find that Gwen was better. 'I'll fetch tea for both of you,' he said, 'and I'll let Mr Hurst know. Or do you want to give him the news yourself, miss?'

He and Eleanor exchanged a long look, before she said, 'I'll tell him.'

'Hurst!' Gwen exclaimed in horrified tones after Cherry had gone. 'Now I remember! We're in the house of the Hell-raiser! And he called you a wench, miss! Oh miss, you must take care not to dine with him, or be anywhere near him! Who can tell what he might do?'

Feeling very thankful that Gwen had not been awake on the previous day when she had hurried in, her hair all disarranged, Eleanor said, 'I have already dined with him, and have suffered no ill-effects—except that the food was awful.' She looked sideways at Gwen and

67

added craftily, 'There seems to be no one here who can tempt his appetite, poor man.'

'That's as may be, miss,' Gwen replied. 'Likely he deserves to have his stomach destroyed, the life he's lived, but I can't have *you* starving. I shall be up on my feet as soon as I can; then we'll see.'

It was only when they were sipping their tea that Eleanor had time to wonder why she had found it necessary to lie in order to protect Hurst from Gwen's disapproval.

Gwen was determined to get up that day, despite her weakness, but Eleanor did manage to persuade her to stay in bed for the rest of the morning. 'You will be no good to anyone if you collapse and have to stay in bed for the rest of the week,' she said. 'In any case, we shall want to get away from here as soon as the weather permits.'

'We certainly shall, miss.'

It would have been very easy for Eleanor to ask Cherry to dress her hair, but she sat on the edge of the bed and permitted Gwen to do so, knowing that it would please her. Then, taking her courage in both hands, she went downstairs and, after a deep breath, she went into the salon.

Hurst was sitting in his usual chair by the fire, and he looked up as she came in. Eleanor thought that he looked tired, and wondered how well he had slept. Keeping her sympathies to herself, however, she said coldly, without moving away from the door, 'I believe you have something to say to me, sir?'

'Yes I have, but I find myself unable to bawl my words across the room. I would be very grateful if you would come a little closer.' She hesitated, and he added ruefully, 'You may remain at arm's length, if you wish.'

She walked forward. She was wearing a day-dress of a warm russet shade that brought out the highlights in her honey-coloured hair. 'Well, sir?' she said.

'All right, I apologize,' he said in fretful tones, turning away from her. 'I should not have seized you in the way that I did. My roughness was unforgivable, and I trust that you do not have any bruises to show for it.'

There was a long silence, after which Eleanor said, 'Is that all?'

'All?' he demanded.

'Is that the sum total of your apology? It was hardly worth my coming down the stairs, if so.'

He stared at her for a time, after which he sighed and said, 'I should not have accused you of taking delight in viewing my . . . my misfortunes. I apologize for that as well.'

When it was clear that he was not going to say any more, she added gently, 'You should not have kissed me, either.'

For the first time since she had entered the room, he smiled. 'No, I shouldn't have,' he answered, but he still did not apologize. His gaze lowered from her eyes to her mouth, and after a brief moment, he moistened his own lips. The implication was clear, and Eleanor suddenly felt her mouth go dry.

'I have something for which I, too, need to apologize,' she said quickly before she could pursue this thought any further.

'Which is?'

'I slapped your face.'

Hurst laughed, and Eleanor remembered how he had done so the previous day as she had left the room. 'My dear girl, that has probably done me more good than anything else for a very long time,' he said.

'Why?' she asked him, puzzled.

'You forgot that I was an invalid and remembered only that I was a man,' he answered. 'I wondered whether any woman would ever do that again. Now, have we done with this mutual pardon-begging exercise; and are we both forgiven?' Eleanor nodded. 'Excellent. Tell me, Miss Carruthers, do you play chess?'

Eleanor had been well taught by her father, and the remaining time until luncheon was spent in a battle of wits over the black-and-white board.

'You play well,' said Hurst. 'I made no concessions, you know.' They had played three tightly fought games, all of which he had won, but not easily.

'Thank you for that,' said Eleanor, 'and thank you for not saying that I play well for a lady.'

'A person either plays well, or does not,' he said frankly. 'My sister plays a fair game.'

'I didn't know you had a sister,' said Eleanor in some surprise.

'I'll tell you about her after lunch,' said Hurst, 'and also about my wife.'

After they had finished their meal, Hurst instructed Cherry to wheel him, not straight into the salon, but out into the hall, and then through another set of doors which led into the library.

'Leave us for a little, will you, Cherry?' Hurst said. The man did so.

A fine picture hung over the fireplace. It was of a dark-haired, dainty young lady dressed in the fashion of about six years before. 'Mrs Hurst,' said Eleanor's host.

'She was very beautiful,' Eleanor replied, feeling like a carthorse before this slender elegance.

'She certainly was,' Hurst agreed. 'I was considered to have caught myself quite a prize.' They remained in silence for a short time. It was broken eventually by Hurst saying 'What are you thinking?'

Eleanor smiled ruefully. 'I was thinking that there are some women who have a gift for making me feel big and clumsy,' she replied.

'What nonsense!' he declared.

'Well, it was only what you yourself said when I arrived,' she answered, trying to make

71

her tone careless and only partly succeeding. "Too buxom for my taste" were, I think, your very words.'

'Oh hell,' Hurst complained. 'I should have known that would come back to haunt me. I only said it to provoke you.'

'To provoke me?'

'Why yes, of course. You'd sounded so imperious, what bit I could hear of your conversation with Plaice in the hall, that I searched in my mind to find the kind of remark that would be most guaranteed to annoy you.'

'Oh, I see,' Eleanor answered, smiling faintly.

'You're still annoyed. Aren't you?'

'No, of course not,' Eleanor replied spiritedly. 'It's just that . . . that. . . .'

He stared at her, his eyes filling with comprehension. 'You aren't annoyed; you're hurt,' he declared.

'Of course not,' she said again, turning away. But he was right. Even Monica, who had never ever said anything derogatory about her height and build, had made her feel awkward just by being the tiny person that she was. Only this erstwhile libertine had detected her true feelings. Was this perceptiveness at the heart of his success with women? Or had it been gained as a result of his accident?

He looked at her thoughtfully, gave a sigh, and said, 'Would it help if I were to tell you

72

that you were the most lusciously intoxicating armful I've held in a very long time?'

'Mr Hurst!' Eleanor exclaimed, staring at him, her cheeks turning pink.

'It's quite true,' he assured her. 'And while it's more than six months since I last held a woman in my arms, I can still remember what does and does not appeal to me—and I am a connoisseur. Does that make you feel better?'

'It ought to make me feel shocked,' Eleanor replied, 'but I fear that I have already got your measure, Mr Hurst.' He chuckled. Feeling that this conversation was becoming entirely too dangerous, she said, looking around, 'Do you never use this room now? It seems a terrible waste.'

'I haven't done so,' he admitted, accepting her change of subject with a wry grin. 'I'm afraid I've been a typical recluse.'

'I could supervise its cleaning, if you had no objection,' she said diffidently. 'Plaice could help me, and it would soon become a pleasant room in which you could sit. It would make a change for you.'

'So it would,' Hurst agreed, 'but I don't want to turn you into a maid of all work.'

'I should enjoy the occupation,' Eleanor replied cheerfully.

'Then far be it from me to refuse such an offer,' Hurst responded. 'It would, after all, enable me to peruse such volumes as *Clarissa* for useful hints. When would you like to start?'

'I'll begin as soon as I've been to see Gwen,' she answered, refusing to rise to his bait.

'Very well. I'll get Plaice to light a fire for you. Will you ask Cherry to take me back to the salon? It's deuced cold in here.'

Eleanor did as he requested, then went upstairs. She found Gwen sitting on the bed, struggling to get dressed. 'I will not be beat,' the young woman said determinedly.

'Oh Gwen, will you not stay in bed, just until tomorrow?'

'You forget, miss, I have to endure the messes that come out of that kitchen as much as anyone else,' the maid replied grimly. 'I must get down there, or do murder.'

Eleanor still thought that it would be wisest for Gwen to remain in bed, but she knew that to try to keep her there would be a losing battle, so instead she assisted her to finish doing up her buttons. 'I'll get Clay to come and help you downstairs,' she said craftily. 'You can just sit in a chair by the fire and supervise.'

Clay who, if truth be told, was as interested in Gwen as she was in him, was very happy to carry the abigail downstairs, and once Gwen had given her promise to come up to bed as soon as the evening meal had been prepared, Eleanor was ready to leave her in Clay's capable hands. She decided not to tell Gwen that she was going to clean the library. Doubtless her abigail would think it beneath

74

her dignity.

While Gwen was discovering what needed to be done in the kitchen, Eleanor found a clean apron, a mob-eap to protect her hair and some rags for dusting, slipped out with them and went to the library. To her surprise, Plaice was there, but what was more astonishing was that Hurst was there too, installed next to the fire which, although by no means burning as brightly as the one in the salon, had already begun to make a difference to the temperature of the room.

'Charming,' Hurst said as Eleanor put her cap on. 'Have you brought one for me?'

'No I have not, but I am quite sure that one can be found if you feel the need of it.'

He laughed. 'Knowing that I shall not look nearly so becoming as you do my dear, I shall beg leave to decline. But I am very willing to help in any way I can.'

'I can see that you have already made a start,' Eleanor answered, as she watched Plaice and Clay take down the last of the curtains. She was aware that Hurst had now called her 'my dear' several times. It wasn't very proper, and she knew she ought to object. This would seem a trifle absurd, however, for it was not nearly as improper as some of the other things that he had said and done.

'What do you want doing with them now?' Plaice asked.

Sternly quelling a whimsical impulse to tell

him to put them on the fire, just to see what he might do, Eleanor said 'Take them outside and give them a good shaking to get the dust out. Then come back for the carpet and do the same with that.'

'And what would you like me to do?' Hurst asked after the men had gone. In response, Eleanor handed him a duster, and pointed to a small bookcase which stood within his reach. He raised one brow as he looked at her.

'That is a duster,' she said, in the same tone that she might use with a rather backward child. 'On the bookcase and on the books is a fine, greyish-white substance, which is known as dust. You apply the duster thus'—and here she moved the cloth to and fro across the shelf—'and this will transfer the dust from the furniture to the cloth.'

'You baggage!' he exclaimed. Eleanor raised her eyebrows and looked at him with a guileless expression on her face. Before she could move away, he had caught hold of her by dint of putting his arm around her waist.

'Well, you did ask,' she replied, anxious that he should not deduce how fast her heart was beating. She did not try to struggle, but remained looking down into his face as he smiled up at her.

'So I did,' he said eventually, releasing her.

'Then let us get to work.'

For a while, there was silence in the room, whilst Eleanor bustled about, and Hurst watched her, admiring her graceful movements, whilst moving his duster back and forth over the same spot with unimaginable slowness.

Eventually, as she began to dust the mantelpiece, Hurst looked up at the picture above it and said, 'I did promise to tell you about my wife.'

'And your sister,' she prompted, lifting up a charming figurine, cleaning it, then putting it back on the surface.

'And my sister. My sister Isobel is ten years younger than I am, and like myself is widowed. Her husband was carried off some five or six months ago. Isobel writes me copious letters which I can barely read, and visits me when she can, which isn't often, because her husband's estates are in Somerset. Come to think of it, she'll have had quite a lot to deal with, sorting all that out. Our parents are both dead. My mother died giving birth to a still-born child when Isobel was three, and father died over a year ago, so we only have each other.'

He was silent for a time, during which period, Plaice, Brewer and Clay came in to move the carpet, and Cherry entered with an offer of coffee, which they both accepted. When they were left alone in the room once again, Hurst said 'I was somewhat wild in my youth.' His remark took Eleanor by surprise. She could not help it—she let out a splutter of mirth.

'What the devil do you mean by that, you baggage?' he demanded, half-angry, half-amused.

'Well. . . .' she began.

He laughed himself. 'I shall rephrase,' he said with dignity. 'I was already wild in my youth. I had run through all the money that was mine, and regularly overspent my allowance. My father decided that it was time to rein me in, and insisted that I should marry a woman of his choosing, or he would disinherit me. He chose Priscilla Glade, and I was not displeased. I knew that I must marry some day, but I always expected that I would find love outside marriage. I had not expected to fall in love with my wife.'

At this moment, Cherry returned with the coffee, and on a plate next to the coffee-pot were some biscuits. Hurst took one and bit into it. 'My God, Cherry, what's happened?' he asked. 'These are palatable. In fact, they're very good.'

'Gwen is in the kitchen, sir,' replied Cherry.

'Then make sure she stays there while they prepare dinner,' said Hurst. After Cherry had gone he said to Eleanor, 'I thought she was your abigail, not your cook.'

'Oh, Gwen can turn her hand to most things.' She put down her duster and sat down in order to drink her coffee. 'You were telling me about your wife,' she prompted.

'Where was I? Ah yes, I fell in love. I regret to say that the feeling was not mutual. In fact she cordially detested me. There was no aspect of our marriage that gave her any pleasure; *no* aspect, Miss Carruthers.'

Eleanor coloured. 'Did she love someone else, sir?'

'Yes, she loved someone else. She loved that person from before we were engaged until the day she died.'

'From before you were married? Was it not possible for her to marry him, then? Was he already married?'

'It was not possible for them to marry,' said Hurst, not correcting Eleanor's assumption. 'We were seen together as much as any other couple, but in private we barely spoke. It was not a very cheerful household as you can imagine. The fact that she was expecting my child gave her no pleasure, but reluctantly, she agreed to my request that she should pass the last few weeks of her pregnancy in the country, here at Glade Hall. While we were staying here, we attended various functions together. We were driving back after one such event when we met with an accident; at least, I assume we did. I remember nothing after bidding our hosts farewell. When I came round, I was as you see me now, plus a bump on my head and a slash across my face. My wife was dead.' He turned his face away from her, and towards the fire. 'Would to God I had never met her,' he added in tones of heartfelt sincerity. 'We neither of us ever did the other a scrap of good.'

'Who found you, sir?' Eleanor asked him eventually.

'Who found me?'

'Who found you and your wife—after the accident?'

'A man called Jem Cutler, apparently. He was a local gamekeeper. He works for your uncle now. It was he who calmed my horses down; a beautiful pair of matched greys; such sweet movers, an excellent action, never needed more than the tiniest touch of the whip, just for direction.' He sighed. 'I'll never drive those again.' Absent-mindedly he took another biscuit.

'Have you sold them, sir?'

'Sold them? No, I ought to do so, I suppose.'

'Then if you still have them, I cannot see why you cannot drive them,' said Eleanor, wondering whether she had said too much.

'You know why I cannot do so,' he said angrily. 'You see how I am.'

'Yes, I see how you are,' she retorted. 'But I do not see why you cannot sit up on the box of your carriage as well as you can sit in that chair; unless, of course, you are afraid that people will see you being helped.' When he said nothing, she added daringly, 'You told me that only your legs were affected. Presumably, then, you can still use your arms.'

He startled her by grinning wickedly. 'As you very well know,' he replied, making her blush. Then he added abruptly, 'If I drove my curricle, would you go with me?'

For a moment, her heart missed a beat. Because of her fear of horses, she had always refused to travel in any kind of open carriage that meant that she was obliged to look directly down on to the animals. Her father, knowing her weakness, had never expected her to ride in anything less sedate than a barouche. She knew, however, that to show fear now would be misinterpreted. There was only one possible answer that she could give. 'Yes, I would,' she said calmly.

'Even knowing that last time I took a woman driving I killed her?'

'I have already said that I would go,' she answered, hoping devoutly that she would have rejoined her father in some foreign clime by the time the weather had improved sufficiently for her to go with him. 'Anyway, it was an accident,' she added firmly.

'Was it?' he said provocatively.

'Of course it was,' she answered in matter-of-fact tones. 'Only a complete idiot would arrange for something like that to happen.'

'You think so?'

'Certainly. You could not possibly guarantee that such an incident would result in your wife's death, and there would always be the risk of injury to yourself, which did indeed

81

happen. Poison would have been far more reliable, I would have thought, if you had murder on your mind.'

'There speaks the diplomat's daughter,' Hurst murmured. 'Did your father have any dealings with the Borgia family?'

'No, certainly not,' she replied with mock indignation. 'Now, shall we finish cleaning this room?' She looked at the place that he had been dusting. 'That square inch is absolutely spotless,' she said admiringly. 'But what about the bits either side?' He made as if to catch her again, but she darted away and said playfully, 'Oh goodness me, look at that book up there?'

'Which book?' he asked, diverted.

'The one on the top shelf. Someone has put it away the wrong way round, with the leaves facing outward.' She pulled the library steps along, set them in place and put her foot on the bottom step.

'No!' said Hurst sharply.

'I'm right, it *is* the wrong way round,' she replied. 'I'll dust that top shelf while I'm up there.'

'No!' Hurst said again. 'You're not to go up there.'

'Oh fiddle, as if I haven't climbed a library ladder before,' she replied, beginning to climb.

'Damnation, woman!' he shouted, his tone full of anger and frustration. Then 'Cherry!' he roared, so loudly, that Eleanor was sure that she could feel the room shake. She turned her head to look at him. His face was white, a mask of fury. 'Bloody well look where you're going, woman!'

Moments later, the door opened. 'Sir?'

'Cherry, hold the bottom of the ladder whilst that damned silly female climbs down, will you?' said Hurst, striving to moderate his tone. The valet did as he was bid and Eleanor, anxious for peace to be restored, caught hold of her skirts and climbed back down.

'What now?' she asked.

Hurst ignored her, saying instead to Cherry, 'Take me back to the salon. I've had enough of this blasted tomfoolery.' Then he turned to Eleanor again. 'As for you, if you dare to set so much as one foot on that ladder, I'll tan your rump so hard you won't be able to sit down for a week.'

'Well, really!' Eleanor declared, but she did so to Hurst's retreating back, for in obedience to his master's commands, Cherry had begun to wheel the chair out of the room, just sparing her a silent apologetic grimace.

No sooner had the door closed behind Cherry, than Eleanor deliberately climbed all the way to the top of the steps, turned the book around, dusted the shelf and climbed down again. That done, she snapped her fingers and declared, '*That* for your orders, Mr Hurst!' Then she left the library, went into the hall, took a deep breath and opened the door into the salon. Hurst was alone in the room, sitting in his armchair by the fire and he was staring moodily into the flames.

'Would you be so good as to tell me the meaning of that outrageous display?' she asked him, very much on her dignity. She had quite forgotten that she was still wearing her apron and cap.

He turned his head to look at her, and for a moment, the expression that he wore was very like that which she had seen upon his face when he had watched Cherry untangling her shoe-lace. 'I should have been the one climbing that ladder,' he said.

'Perhaps,' she agreed after a moment's consideration. 'But not everyone can bear to do so, you know. My papa cannot bring himself to climb the library steps.'

Hurst made a dismissive gesture. 'That doesn't help,' he replied. 'At the very least, I should have been the one holding the bottom of them, rather than sitting helplessly in some blasted chair,' and he thumped the arm.

She raised her brows. 'You can save that display of temper for someone else,' she said calmly. 'I know you only wanted to stare up at my ankles.'

To her relief, he grinned, albeit reluctantly. 'I hadn't thought of that, but it's a deuced good notion,' he drawled.

'Anyway, Plaice can finish in there now,' said Eleanor. 'Clay can help him to hang the curtains and deal with the carpet. Shall we play chess again?'

'Certainly,' he said, trying to sound casual even though he was still deeply moved. 'And let us have some more coffee. But no more biscuits, I think. I need to be very careful how much I eat now that I cannot take exercise.'

'What about swimming?' Eleanor suggested, as she tried to locate a knight which seemed to be missing.

'What?' he asked her.

'What about swimming,' she said again. 'Can you swim?'

'I could, but. . . .'

'Well I should imagine that you still can,' she said. 'The water will still bear your weight, won't it?'

'I expect so. I trust that in your enthusiasm you will not insist that I go today? The lake might be a little difficult to find in the snow, and then I should be obliged to put Plaice to the trouble of breaking the ice.'

'Ah, there it is,' Eleanor exclaimed, as she spotted the knight. It was on the floor by his chair, just beneath his hand. She stepped forward, hesitated, and looked at him.

'By the way, did you climb that ladder after I had left the room?' he asked her.

'Surely you don't expect me to answer that question,' she replied, still hesitating. She had been thinking of how he had seized her and held her on his knee. Now, she recalled that he had threatened to spank her. He

85

smiled wryly, and spread out his hands, as if in submission. She crouched down next to his chair, picked up the knight, turned to put it on the board, hesitated, and turned back. Then, hardly knowing why she did it but responding purely to instinct, and before she could change her mind, she leaned over and kissed him gently on the mouth.

CHAPTER FIVE

She had only just placed the knight on the board when the knocker on the front door sounded with an almighty clatter.

'I am not expecting anyone,' said Hurst, staring at her as he had been doing since she had bestowed that light caress upon him. 'Perhaps someone else has got lost in the snow.' The light was just starting to go and more flakes were just beginning to come down, putting paid to the idea that there would be no more snow for the time being.

As Eleanor waited in the salon, she remembered with a start how very equivocal was her position. Of course it was perfectly reasonable that in an emergency she should take shelter in the nearest house. The trouble was that anyone visiting would not see the emergency; they would only see a single woman staying unchaperoned in the home of a notorious rake. It was too late to go and hide. In any case, given the hour and the state of the weather, this caller—whoever it might be—must have come to stay. She would be found out sooner or later. She must not look as if she were ashamed. After all, she had nothing to be ashamed of.

As she straightened her spine, she suddenly remembered that she was still wearing her apron and mob-cap, and hurriedly began to pull them off. Hurst, noticing her sudden panic, laughed softly, said; 'Here, give them to me,' and stuffed them underneath the blanket over his knees.

The sound of voices in the hall made it clear that more than one visitor had arrived. Moments later, Plaice opened the door but before he could say anything, a slim, pretty, dark-haired woman with more than a passing resemblance to Hurst, hurried in, enveloped in a black velvet cloak and carrying a sable muff. 'Chris!' she declared. 'What horrid weather you have here in Warwickshire! We have had to walk down the last two lanes!' She threw down her muff and came forward to bend down and kiss Hurst on the cheek.

'Bella, my dear, you should have told me that you were coming and I would have ordered something better,' Hurst replied. 'But you must allow me. . . .'

Clearly he was on the point of introducing Eleanor to this visitor but before he could do so two other people who had followed the first lady came in. One was another lady, fair and slender, with a heart-shaped face, light-blue eyes and bouncing ringlets. 'Oh Chris!' she whispered, her eyes filling with tears as she came forward to take Hurst's hand and raise it to her cheek. 'How it breaks my heart to see you so!'

'I was ever a heartbreaker, Patricia, or had you forgotten?' Hurst replied, a humourless grin twisting his lips.

'Oh yes, yes, but not like this!' answered the blonde, her voice breaking on a sob as she gestured towards his blanket-covered legs.

The third arrival was a gentleman of about Hurst's age, strongly built with dark-brown hair, and a crooked smile. 'Well, my friend, here we are, and rather wet from the snow,' said the newcomer in a light, pleasant voice with a slight Welsh lilt.

'Don't complain, for it means that I am obliged to give you house room,' Hurst answered. 'Egad, but it's good to see you, Playell!'

Eleanor, who had stepped back to allow Hurst to greet his friends, gave a little start, fortunately unnoticed by the company. This, then, must be the man who had offered to send Hurst a wench for Christmas!

'Likewise,' replied Playell, sketching a bow to his host. 'I must apologize for not coming to see you sooner, but in my defence, I have been much occupied with my late uncle's affairs.'

'Ah yes, he had estates in the north of England, I believe.' Hurst replied.

'Indeed, and very much neglected, with a number of land disputes with neighbours to be settled. But here I am at last, and you see I have made good my words; but too late, I fear.'

'Your words?' Queried Hurst, gently disengaging his right hand from the young woman named Patricia, who had been clasping and stroking it with both of her own.

'I promised you a wench for Christmas, and I brought you one; but I see you already have one.'

'Owen, how can you?' cried Patricia, standing up, her eyes sparkling with indignation. 'I am not a wench! I do not know what I ought to do to punish you for that.'

'Your pardon, Patricia,' replied Playell, bowing slightly in her direction. 'How, then, would you prefer that I described you?'

'That is not for me to say,' she answered, tossing her head.

'If I might be permitted, I would imagine that Patricia would see herself as an angel of mercy,' Hurst suggested, smiling.

'Indeed I would,' Patricia responded. 'Furthermore,' she went on, gesturing towards Eleanor, 'this young woman is quite clearly Chris's nurse, and cannot be described in such a manner.'

Eleanor opened her mouth to correct this mistaken impression, but before she could say anything, Hurst said 'Right, Patricia—but also wrong. Miss Carruthers is certainly not a wench, but then neither is she my nurse.' He turned to smile at Eleanor, and as he did so, adjusted the blanket across his knees, so that only Eleanor could see the fraction of white apron that he revealed for just a moment. Thank goodness I remembered to take off the apron and cap, Eleanor thought and she smiled back. Miss Reynolds's pretty pouting lips straightened into a thin line.

'And who is Miss Carruthers when she is at home?' asked Patricia in rather tart tones.

Eleanor stepped forward at this point. 'Miss Carruthers is the daughter of Sir Clifford Carruthers, His Majesty's ambassador to Peruvia, whether she is at home or away.'

Hurst gave a soft chuckle. 'Miss Carruthers is travelling to stay with her uncle and aunt, Mr and Mrs Carlisle, who are my neighbours. After an accident to her carriage, she was obliged to take refuge here, and has been prevented from leaving by the snow, together with an injury to her coachman. But I am reminded of how remiss I have been. Miss Carruthers, these visitors who have just arrived are my sister, Mrs Hulce, her friend, Miss Reynolds, and hanging on to their coat tails, insinuating himself where he is not wanted as usual, is Owen Playell.'

'Ingrate!' declared Playell, laughing. 'Were it not for the snow, I would go away and leave you to your fate—not but what it would be a delightful one, with Miss Carruthers to entertain you.' He bowed slightly in Eleanor's direction, and as he lifted his head, she saw a sparkle in his eye.

Hurst's expression lost some of its humour. 'Miss Carruthers has been the perfect guest,' he replied. 'Which reminds me, I am far from being the perfect host. Plaice,' he said to the servant who was still hovering by the door. 'Have rooms prepared for my guests.'

'What, three of them?' asked Plaice.

'Yes, of course three,' Hurst answered him impatiently. 'Did you think to house them in a dormitory like they do in the Dog and Duck? In the meantime. . . .' he turned to look at Eleanor.

'Of course,' she said, smiling. 'Ladies, would you like to come to my room and put off your cloaks and bonnets? I am afraid it will be a little while until your rooms are ready for your use.'

After the ladies had left the room, Hurst said to Playell, 'You may make use of my room if you wish. It's just through those doors.'

Playell looked at where Hurst was pointing. 'Convenient,' he remarked. Cherry came in at that moment, and stood ready to relieve Playell of his hat and greatcoat. 'Thank you, Cherry,' he said. 'It's good to see you again.'

'It's a pleasure to welcome you again, sir. I'll just take these away then I'll get you a glass of sherry.'

The two men were silent for a few moments, then Playell said 'It's devilish good to see you again, Chris. It was true what I said, you know. I have had a lot of business to see to. And besides—'

'You don't know what to say to a cripple,' Hurst finished for him.

'No,' the other man retorted quickly. 'No, I . . . well yes, partly.'

'I am the same man,' Hurst reminded him quietly. 'I ought to be grateful for your honesty, I suppose.'

'I could always slobber all over you like Patricia seems prone to do,' Playell suggested. 'My poor, dear friend.' He put his arm around Hurst's shoulders, and taking hold of his friend's right hand with his own, he gazed into his eyes with a limpid expression on his face.

For a moment or two, Hurst returned his gaze with a look of complete bafflement; then a gleam came into his eyes. He shook his hand free of Playell's, swept the two or three items from the table next to him, leaned forward, and rested his elbow on the table, his right hand opened in challenge. Playell grinned, went down on one knee, and placing his own elbow on the table, took hold of Hurst's hand. For a few moments the two men were locked in combat, their concentration fixed upon their

92

hands. Neither was aware of the door opening. At one moment, it seemed as if the contest could go either way, with first one hand then the other teetering backwards. Then at last, after a final grunt of effort, Hurst slammed his friend's hand back on to the table.

At this point, Cherry, who had been waiting by the door with wine, came forward grinning and saying: 'Well done, sir.' He set it on the table which had just been used for quite another purpose, and Hurst poured out two glasses.

'You didn't let me win, did you?' Hurst asked with a frown after Cherry had gone.

Playell threw up his hands. 'I wouldn't dare,' he said frankly. 'By the way, what's the real tale about that female who's staying here? You can tell me, now there aren't ladies present.'

'Oh, what I told you was quite true,' Hurst replied. 'She's here quite by accident, and will leave when her carriage is mended, weather permitting. Where's yours, by the way? I'll send men with the plough-horse to fetch your trunks.'

'Thank you. It's at a small-holding two lanes away. What luck for you, though,' he went on, refusing to be diverted from the previous topic. 'Shame you ain't in a position to take advantage of it.'

'Well, make sure you don't either,' said Hurst shortly. 'She's a lady and she's my guest, so treat her properly.'

93

'Of course old fellow. I'm your humble obedient servant,' Playell replied, as he darted a speculative look at his host. 'What's more, after that recent display of strength, I wouldn't dare do any other!'

*   *   *

It felt rather odd to Eleanor to be conducting two ladies upstairs in the house of a man with whom both of the ladies in question were better acquainted than she was, and she said so.

'Not at all, Miss Carruthers,' answered Mrs Hulce. 'This is my first visit to this house, so you must be better acquainted with it than I am.'

'Your first visit?' murmured Eleanor, hoping to discover more.

'I lived with my husband in Somerset, and we very seldom left home,' Mrs Hulce replied.

'And what of you, Miss Reynolds?' Eleanor asked. 'Have you been here before?'

'Certainly not,' replied Miss Reynolds rather more sharply than the question warranted. 'I cannot understand why you should think that I might have done so.'

'It is simply that you are clearly a family friend,' Eleanor explained.

'Oh,' said the other sounding a little deflated. 'No, no I have not been here. You, on the other hand, have obviously made yourself at home.' Her tone was more than a little waspish, but Eleanor did not have time to do more than glance at her in rather a startled manner before they reached the door of her bedroom. Inside, a maidservant, who was unknown to Eleanor, was waiting, and once she had delivered the two visitors into her hands, she made her excuses and left. It had occurred to her that those working in the kitchen ought to be told that there would be three extra people at table that evening. Plaice did know about them but she did not place any dependence upon his passing the message on.

As she went back downstairs, Eleanor wondered how comfortable a party they were now likely to be. Mrs Hulce seemed agreeable enough, and Miss Reynolds had been introduced as Mrs Hulce's friend, but going by the way she had thrown herself at Hurst, it seemed much more likely that her interest was in him rather than in his sister. Her manner towards her host was suspiciously like that of an old flame. This would explain why she had never visited the house before. It did not, however, explain why she had waited until now—unless, of course, she had very properly stayed out of the way during his first six months of mourning. That was a reasonable explanation of her absence. Certainly, until she knew her better, Eleanor ought to give her the benefit of the doubt on that score. Even so, she could not help reflecting that surely a woman who was sincerely attached to Hurst would have rushed to his side as quickly as possible on hearing of his accident, and to the devil with convention!

Playell's explanation of his absence was quite plausible; and by the bantering tone that the two men adopted towards one another, it seemed that they were old friends. It also occurred to her that some normal interaction with an old friend would probably do Hurst more good than anything else, and would certainly be better for him than the repulsively mawkish way in which Miss Reynolds seemed to be inclined to paw her host!

On arriving at the kitchens, Eleanor found that Gwen had matters well in hand. Someone had set a chair for her between the kitchen table and the range and she was bidding fair to queen it over all those servants who came into her orbit. She took the news of there being three more mouths to feed in her stride.

'Don't you worry, miss,' she said cheerfully. 'There's plenty of food laid in, I'll say that for Broome. It's just that he doesn't know how to prepare what's there! You won't be ashamed of my efforts, I'll promise you that.'

'Make sure you don't do too much,' Eleanor warned her. 'I don't want you back in bed again.'

'I shan't do that, miss,' Gwen replied in the same bright tones. 'I'll stay here by the fire and tell Broome what to do.' Her tone changed as she turned to Broome, who was about to put a mixing bowl on the kitchen table. 'Not there! In that dish of cold water so that it will cool down quickly!'

Eleanor smiled. She had always suspected that Gwen was happier in the kitchen than in her dressing-room. 'I'll get out of your way,' she said. 'I can see that you have plenty to do.'

'That I have, miss,' Gwen agreed, 'and right glad I am to be doing it.' She beckoned her mistress over to her and spoke quietly, so that no one else could hear. 'To tell the truth, miss, I'm glad that there are more ladies in the house. At least you'll be properly chaperoned.'

'So I will,' Eleanor agreed. 'And don't worry about helping me dress. I'm sure that Mrs Hulce's abigail will be happy to help.'

A guilty expression crossed Gwen's face, and Eleanor guessed that she had completely forgotten her lady's maid's duties in all the excitement of having a kitchen to rule over. Before anything more could be said, Eleanor whisked herself out of the kitchen and back up the stairs. It had occurred to her that Cherry would probably be preparing the guest-rooms by himself and might need some help.

She went to her own room first, and found that both Mrs Hulce and Miss Reynolds had left. The abigail jumped up quickly when Eleanor came in, and the latter strongly suspected that she had been sitting in front of the fire with her feet up.

'What is your name?' Eleanor asked her.

'Pettit, miss,' the girl replied.

'Have the ladies gone downstairs, Pettit?'

'Yes miss.'

'Do you know which rooms Cherry is preparing for them?'

'Oh no, miss,' Pettit answered, her tone suggesting that she was to be congratulated for this lack of knowledge.

Eleanor left the room and by dint of listening carefully, soon detected the sound of a broom being wielded nearby. She opened the door of the room whence the noise proceeded and, as she had expected, found Cherry busy sweeping. For the first time since she had sent eyes upon him, he looked harassed.

'You could do with some help, Cherry,' she said.

He sighed and smiled. 'I could, miss. But Plaice and Gwen are both needed in the kitchen and there is no one else to lend a hand.'

'There's Mrs Hulce's abigail,' Eleanor pointed out. 'I'll go downstairs and ask if she may be permitted to help you. She can't do anything else until she can unpack her mistress's things in any case.'

'I would be grateful, miss,' Cherry admitted, leaning on his broom.

Eleanor went downstairs. Before she entered the room, she could hear the sound of merry laughter coming from inside. As she opened the door, every face turned to look at her, and for a moment she felt like an intruder. Absurd! she told herself, then stepped forward, saying pleasantly; 'Mrs Hulce, I wonder whether your abigail, Pettit, might be pressed into service to help Cherry get the rooms ready? There are no other upstairs servants to do so and it is a lot to cast upon him, at short notice.'

'Well, I—' Mrs Hulce began, but Miss Reynolds interrupted her.

'I'm afraid that is quite out of the question,' she said smiling apologetically. 'You see, Pettit is my servant, not Isobel's, and I cannot allow her to do anything that might roughen her hands. She has my silks to deal with, you understand. I cannot risk them getting snagged.'

Eleanor took a deep breath. 'I take your point,' she said carefully. 'But the need is very great. Perhaps if she were to confine her efforts to putting the linen on the beds?'

'Possibly,' answered Miss Reynolds ungraciously. 'Anyway, what about *your* abigail? Can she not help?'

Nobly repressing the urge to say, what about *my* silks? Eleanor answered, 'She is in the kitchen, supervising the cooking of dinner.'

'Good Lord!' exclaimed Playell blankly.

'Be thankful for it,' Hurst put in. 'I assure you that her efforts are far superior to those of Broome.'

'But my dear Chris,' exclaimed Miss

Reynolds, 'this is appalling! You seem to be living in absolute squalor! For shame!'

'Nonsense!' Playell retorted. Eleanor noticed that he had coloured a little. 'No doubt Hurst needs no other servants when he is here alone. Our arrival unannounced has cast a good deal of work upon his household. I fear I've only added to it, as well, for I haven't brought my valet with me.'

Hurst laughed. 'The inconveniences suffered are little enough compared with the pleasure of seeing some new faces,' he replied. 'I hadn't realized how dull I was until you arrived.'

Eleanor took a deep breath, unsure whether she was most annoyed by Hurst's casual dismissal of all the extra work, the suggestion that she had been dull company, or by the look of triumph on Miss Reynolds's face that she could detect out of the corner of her eye. Deciding to address the first issue, she said bluntly: 'The inconveniences may be nothing to you, sir, but to Cherry I fear they are quite considerable.'

Hurst's brows snapped together, but it was Miss Reynolds who spoke. 'Oh, fudge!' she trilled merrily. 'What work is there in sweeping a room, after all? I daresay your woman could do it when she is finished in the kitchen. Do not forget that poor Pettit has the two of us to see to. Or did you intend to ask her to look after you as well?'

She then turned to Hurst to make a remark

about an unsatisfactory maid she had once employed, almost as if Eleanor had been an upper servant, just dismissed after taking instructions. Miss Reynolds would soon discover her mistake.

'By no means,' replied Eleanor pleasantly. 'Gwen will be able to find a little time for me, I am sure. But since Pcttit is so busy and Cherry already has more than enough to do, I shall see that clean linen is placed ready in your rooms, so that you can make up your own beds when you go to change.'

The effect of her remark was quite dramatic. Miss Reynolds turned to stare at her, her expression aghast. 'Upon my soul, you will next be saying that I ought to don a mob-cap and apron,' she declared. Playell stifled a laugh, whilst Hurst sat in silence, a slight smile playing about his features.

'Patricia, surely Pettit can lend a hand,' said Mrs Hulce, stepping into the breach. 'There is nothing else that she can do until our rooms are ready, in any case. She can always wear a pair of gloves, after all.'

'Oh, very well,' Miss Reynolds replied grudgingly.

Eleanor made as if to leave the room, but Mrs Hulce said; 'Pray sit down, Miss Carruthers. You are a guest here as much as anyone. I shall go and speak to Pettit.'

Eleanor did as she was bid. 'I hope that you will employ a housemaid here from now on,

Chris,' said Miss Reynolds after the door had closed behind her friend. 'It is quite absurd that you do not have one.'

'They tend not to want to be employed in houses that I occupy,' Hurst retorted, grinning wolfishly.

'Well naturally that was true before your accident,' Patricia replied, patting his hand. 'But surely, now, anyone could see that you are quite harmless, you poor man.'

Eleanor took one glance at Hurst's set face and said quickly; 'Oh would you say so, Miss Reynolds? Have you never heard about the dangers of caged tigers? Mr Hurst strikes me as being very dangerous indeed. I marvel at your temerity in sitting so close to him.'

'Just as well you are no longer unchaperoned, then, Miss Carruthers,' Hurst answered, the gleam back in his eye.

After this, Playell steered the conversation to events in town and Miss Reynolds, ready enough to talk about her many conquests, abandoned the subject of Hurst's disability for the time being. She left her host's side in order to speak to Playell, and once she had done so, Hurst made a discreet gesture, inviting Eleanor to sit next to him. After a little show of pretending to look round to see if he were referring to anyone else, she got up gracefully and took the seat that Miss Reynolds had just vacated.

'I am glad you are not too afraid to sit next

to such a dangerous man,' he murmured.

'It is the excellent chaperonage provided by Miss Reynolds that gives me courage,' she replied in the same low tone. 'I am persuaded that you would attempt nothing in her presence.'

Hurst chuckled. 'You are quite correct in that view. By the way, I am not unmindful of the burden placed upon Cherry, you know.'

Eleanor coloured. 'I did not mean to be critical of you,' she answered. 'It is simply that your household is a small one, not equipped to cope with a number of visitors.'

'My sister will make sure that Pettit helps,' Hurst replied. 'I'd have given something to see Patricia make up her own bed, though. Perhaps you could have lent her your apron and cap.'

As if attracted by the sound of her own name, Miss Reynolds turned towards them. She did not look entirely pleased to see Eleanor sitting in the place that she had vacated. 'Did I hear my name upon your lips, Chris?' she asked flirtatiously.

'You did indeed, my dear,' Hurst replied. 'I was just telling Miss Carruthers how impossible it would have been to have expected you to make your own bed.'

'I am glad that you understand me so well,' she answered, looking at Eleanor in a very self-satisfied way.

Shortly after this, Mrs Hulce came back into

the room, announcing that it was now possible for them all to go and change, since their trunks had arrived. 'You and I, Patricia, may change in your room, and when we come downstairs for dinner, Pettit will finish preparing mine.' She turned to Playell. 'Owen, your room is ready now. I will show you which one it is.'

Eleanor was surprised to experience a sensation that felt very like resentment. She was obliged to tell herself that whilst out of all the guests, she had been there for the longest, Mrs Hulce was Hurst's sister and had more right to regard herself as hostess than anyone else.

A few moments later, Cherry came in quietly to fetch his master. His entrance acted as a cue for everyone to go and change.

Life with a member of the diplomatic service had taught Eleanor to be self-reliant, and she knew that given sufficient time, she could certainly get herself ready without Gwen's assistance. The only thing that she found difficult to do was dress her own hair, so she was surprised but pleased when Mrs Hulce scratched on the door and offered her own services.

'Patricia will be primping and preening for some time yet, so I can help you before she needs me again,' she said, taking up Eleanor's brush.

Eleanor looked surprised. 'Why should she

be needing you?' she asked. 'Surely, Pettit can do all that she requires.'

'My dear Miss Carruthers, if Patricia had a whole room full of people ready to spring to her assistance, that would still not be enough. Anyway, she declares that no one can dress her hair as I can, and she will want to look her very best tonight.'

Eleanor could guess why. Miss Reynolds obviously wanted to impress her host. She glanced at Mrs Hulce's gown and secretly gave it her approval. The widow was dressed in black, as befitted her comparatively recent bereavement, and her gown was trimmed modestly as was appropriate for country wear. Eleanor herself was attired in an open robe of rich turquoise velvet, with a cream under-dress, and her only jewellery was a fine string of pearls which her father had given her on the occasion of her coming out.

After Mrs Hulce had finished dressing her hair in a fashionable but modest style, that lady said, 'I had better go back to Patricia. I shall see you downstairs.'

CHAPTER SIX

As Eleanor was making her way down to the salon, she found herself wondering about the precise nature of the relationship which existed between Mrs Hulce and her friend. When they had entered the house for the first time, she had assumed that Miss Reynolds had come at Mrs Hulce's invitation. Now, she began to wonder whether it might not be the other way round. The widow certainly seemed to feel that she must put herself at the disposal of her friend; and the abigail was in Miss Reynolds's employ. It would be interesting to learn in what circumstances Mr Hulce had left his wife. Hurst had not spoken of her being in straitened circumstances, but that was hardly surprising. She and Hurst had not been acquainted for long enough for them to be exchanging confidences. They had, in fact, known one another for less than a week.

Pondering this extraordinary fact, for she felt as if she had known her host for much longer, she entered the salon to find that Mr Playell was its sole occupant. He bowed politely and came over to greet her, saying, 'Miss Carruthers, my compliments on your ensemble this evening. You look quite delightful.' Playell himself was wearing a coat of dull gold brocade with a plain waistcoat of mustard-coloured cloth and dark-brown breeches.

'Thank you, sir,' Eleanor replied calmly. 'I am very grateful that Mr Hurst's servants were able to rescue my luggage from my coach, or I fear that the company would have become very tired of my wardrobe rather quickly.'

Playell smiled. 'I believe that you said you

are *en route* to the home of your uncle and aunt, Mr and Mrs Carlisle.'

'That is correct,' she replied.

'Will they be anxious about you? Are you expected?'

'Yes, I am expected for Christmas,' she responded. 'But as it will be Christmas in only two days' time, I doubt whether I shall get there.'

'I hope they will not be worried.'

Eleanor laughed. 'They may be a little anxious, but they are aware that I am an experienced traveller. They will trust in my good sense.'

'Pardon me for saying so, ma'am, but good sense would scarcely take you to the door of a notorious rake,' he responded frankly.

'Beggars cannot be choosers,' she answered, her colour heightened a little. 'The accident to our carriage called a halt to our journey and the weather was so appalling that I would willingly have taken shelter anywhere. Besides, I cannot really be blamed. I did not know whose house this was, you see. Mr Hurst, and others of his persuasion, should be instructed to place a warning notice for the benefit of passing females!'

'Rather in the manner of "Beware of the bull"?' Playell suggested.

'Only "Beware of the rake",' Eleanor agreed. 'In any case, sir, if I was subject to any insult from Mr Hurst, you were at least partly to blame for it.'

'I? Why so?' Playell asked incredulously.

'Because you told Mr Hurst that you would send him a wench for Christmas, and naturally—' she broke off, suddenly conscious that she was being rather indelicate.

'Oh good God,' Playell exclaimed, trying not to laugh but without much success. 'You don't mean to say that—'

'Yes I do mean to say, and it was excessively embarrassing,' Eleanor answered frankly.

'It certainly was,' contributed a third voice. 'I still blush when I recall that first encounter.' They looked round to see that Cherry was pushing Hurst into the room. Their host was dressed in a dark-red coat with matching waistcoat, and was looking exceedingly handsome.

'My dear fellow, I doubt very much whether you have blushed since the age of ten,' Playell declared.

'Not outwardly perhaps,' Hurst retorted. 'But inside, I was absolutely mortified, I can assure you.'

Cherry did not transfer his master to the armchair, for they were to go into dinner shortly, but he did pick up a rug and prepare to place it over his master's knees. Before he could do so, however, the other two members of the party came in. Miss Reynolds's appearance was in contrast to that of the other two ladies, for she had chosen to be decked out in a white gown with silver lace. She wore diamonds at her throat and wrists and in her hair, and she would not have looked out of place at one of the grand receptions that Sir Clifford Carruthers and his bride might be attending, even at that very moment. Her appearance was rather incongruous, however, at an informal dinner in a country house.

Her first action was to rush across the room and take the blanket from Cherry's hands. 'But no, no,' she declared. 'Why should a servant have the privilege of performing such intimate tasks? You must allow me! It is little enough for me to do, given all that we have meant to each other in the past.'

'You are too kind, Patricia,' Hurst murmured, his face expressionless as she tucked the rug about him.

'Not at all,' she answered, patting him on the knee. 'I must do what I can for you when you are so helpless.'

Hurst said nothing, but his face remained stony. Eleanor said quickly, 'Perhaps you could knit him different-coloured blankets to match his coats? Look at the one he is sporting now, for instance. A brown blanket with a red coat? Most unstylish, my dear sir.'

Patricia turned towards her indignantly, but before either lady could say anything, Hurst gave a crack of laughter. 'Not nearly so unstylish as something knitted by Patricia, I'm quite sure,' he said, as soon as he was able.

'Now, I think it is time we went in to dinner. Patricia, will you accompany me, a task which I am sure is much more suited to your own particular talents?'

For a moment, it seemed as if Miss Reynolds could not decide whether or not to take offence at this exchange. Soon, however, she smiled, saying; 'Indeed it is, Chris. I will leave the knitting to Miss Carruthers.'

'Shall we go, ladies?' Playell asked, offering one arm to Eleanor and the other to Mr Hulce.

Cherry wheeled Hurst to the head of the table, and Miss Reynolds, in the most subtly adept way possible, took the place on his right. 'You must take the foot, my dear sister,' Hurst said, 'and Miss Carruthers must sit to my left.' With the fifth place laid to the right of Mrs Hulce, Eleanor found herself sitting with a gentleman either side. Clearly, from her expression, Miss Reynolds was less than pleased with this state of affairs, but since she had attained her prime objective of taking the place of honour, she could hardly raise any objection about the seating of Mr Playell.

'Oh, Chris,' breathed Miss Reynolds, with tears in her eyes, 'this is quite like old times.'

'Really, my dear?' Hurst replied, his eyes twinkling. 'I have no recollection of your being permitted to attend any dinner at which I might have acted as host.'

'You know what I mean,' Miss Reynolds

answered coaxingly. 'You and I, sitting together at table, just as we used to.'

'Remind me,' said Hurst, smiling at her. At that point, Playell asked Eleanor how recently she had been in London, and so she did not hear the next part of the conversation between Miss Reynolds and her host.

From the moment when the soup appeared, it was plain that Gwen's influence had made a powerful difference. The aroma was appetizing but, unlike the first occasion when Eleanor had eaten soup at this table, the taste was every bit as good as the smell. After Hurst had taken one cautious spoonful, his face took on an arrested expression. He hesitated, then finished his bowl with every evidence of enjoyment. The removes that followed were just as palatable, and although Miss Reynolds showed a regrettable tendency to play with her food, Eleanor suspected that this was probably her normal habit.

'Did your abigail really cook this meal?' Mrs Hulce asked, half-way through her plate of stewed venison.

'I doubt whether she actually cooked it herself,' Eleanor replied. 'She has not been well, you see, so I told her that she must not stand for too long. She will just have been directing operations, I expect.'

'Not well!' exclaimed Miss Reynolds, looking down at the remains of her syllabub, to which she had not done justice in the first place. 'I trust she will not pass her illness on to us all.'

'Gwen's illness arose from prolonged exposure to the cold,' Hurst replied. 'I do not think that such things can be passed on.' He turned to Eleanor. 'I fear you may soon be looking for a new abigail,' he said with a smile. 'I do not scruple to tell you, ma'am, that I shall do all I can to tempt her away from your service.'

'Frankly, I do not think you would have to work very hard,' Eleanor replied ruefully. 'She has always preferred cooking to looking after my gowns.'

It was not long after this that Mrs Hulce gave the signal for the ladies to withdraw, and they left the gentlemen to their port, going into the salon. Eleanor and Mrs Hulce sat down straight away, but Miss Reynolds wandered over to the window. 'The moon is very bright tonight,' she remarked.

'Is it still snowing?' Mrs Hulce asked.

'No, the snow has stopped.' Miss Reynolds turned and said brightly, 'Who knows, Miss Carruthers, you might be able to get on your way tomorrow.'

'Perhaps,' Eleanor agreed.

'You must not go if there is any danger,' Mrs Hulce insisted. 'My brother can very well put you up for a little longer.'

'Perhaps there is more danger to Miss Carruthers in staying than in going,' Miss Reynolds suggested thoughtfully.

'In what way?' Eleanor enquired.

'Why, to your reputation of course. You are in the home of a notorious rake, you know, and unlike myself, you do not have a companion to give you countenance.'

It seemed to Eleanor that this was rather an insensitive way of referring to someone who was at one and the same time their host and also the brother of a lady who was present. Mrs Hulce did not seem to be at all discomposed by this comment so Eleanor simply replied: 'I must rely upon you to preserve my reputation, Miss Reynolds. After all, there is safety in numbers.'

*   *   *

Back in the dining-room, Playell was leaning back in his chair, very much at his ease. 'Damme, but that was a good meal, Chris. Good brandy, too. You always did have the best palate of anyone I know.'

Hurst inclined his head. 'I'm glad you approve,' he answered. 'Allow me to refill your glass.'

'Just a little, then,' Playell replied. 'We mustn't be too long before we rejoin the ladies. Fine-looking woman, that Carruthers female. Hope I didn't spoil sport by bringing Patricia and Isobel along.'

'I've already told you, her arrival here was pure chance,' Hurst replied, setting his glass down with a snap. 'In any case, what kind of sport do you suppose is available to me now?'

'Sorry, old fellow,' Playell declared, raising one hand in a gesture of submission whilst holding on to his brandy with the other. Then tentatively he ventured, 'Is it possible. . . ? I mean, can you. . . ?' he paused delicately.

Hurst laughed derisively. 'Oh yes, it's possible,' he replied. 'But Owen, what woman would want me, as I am now?'

'Patricia, I should imagine,' Playell replied. 'Why, when I suggested to Isobel that she might like to visit you for Christmas, Patricia could not rest until she had twisted an invitation out of me to come as well. And if you tell me that that was for the sake of my fine eyes then I should not believe you.'

'No, I have no doubt that I was the attraction,' Hurst replied. 'Whether I shall continue to be attractive to her now that she has seen how I am, I very much doubt; which all goes to prove, my dear Owen, that every cloud has a silver lining.'

'The lady is not to your taste? My dear fellow, I do apologize! I thought to entertain you! You cannot deny that she's a beauty, surely.'

'Oh, I don't,' Hurst agreed. 'She's a piece of perfection without a doubt; but she has never understood the first rule of engagement.'

'Which is. . . ?'

'A man likes to do his own chasing. Of

course, chasing has become a little difficult for me these days. Speaking of which, it's time we followed the ladies. Will you please ring for Cherry so that he can push me back into the salon?'

'I will of course,' replied Playell. Then he added diffidently, 'On the other hand, if you didn't mind, I could have a go myself.'

'Damnation!' snapped Hurst, banging his fist on the table. 'You ain't my servant, Owen.'

'No, I ain't,' the other man agreed. 'But if I took you up in my curricle, you'd trust my driving, wouldn't you?'

'I suppose so,' Hurst replied grudgingly.

'Well then, may I *drive* you, Mr Hurst?'

Hurst stared at him unsmilingly for a moment or two, then grinned suddenly. 'You may,' he said. 'But I stay in this chair. No one watches me being transferred from one to the other.'

Immediately they entered the salon, Miss Reynolds was upon them, fussing round Hurst, directing Playell into the space by the fire, and getting very much into the way thereby. 'Chris, come here and be warm,' she twittered. 'We have all missed you in here. How dull we have been!' Deliberately she bent over him with the blanket, thus giving him an excellent view of her bosom.

'Indeed!' he replied, taking in the view if only not to be ungrateful. After a moment or two, however, his attention was drawn by something happening a little further away, and turning his head, he saw Miss Carruthers incling her head to catch what his sister was saying. Suddenly, he was filled with a surge of desire, such as he had not experienced for months. To the casual glance, she seemed entirely unconscious of the intensity of his gaze, but as Hurst watched her, she gave a sideways glance, a little restless movement, and hesitantly touched her hair. She might fool others, but not him. She knew he was looking at her, and was unsettled by his regard.

For the rest of the evening, he seemed to the assembled company to be somewhat distracted. Some of those present chose to put their own construction on the matter. Miss Reynolds was inclined to attribute it to the charms of her person, whereas Playell supposed that he was brooding over his inability to pursue women as he had done in the past. Hurst could have enlightened them. The thing that preoccupied him, and continued to dominate his thoughts after he had gone to bed, was to wonder why the open display of Miss Reynolds's charms should leave him almost unmoved, whilst he should be so excited by the memory of the turn of Miss Carruthers's throat.

CHAPTER SEVEN

When Eleanor went to her room that night, she found that Gwen was there, waiting to help her undress. 'You shouldn't have come tonight,' she told her abigail as the woman unfastened her pearls and put them away. 'You know that I can manage for myself if necessary, and you have been very busy in the kitchens this evening—too busy, considering that you only rose from your sick bed today.'

'Oh, I'm well enough, miss, although I will be glad to get to my bed, I must say.'

'At least we don't keep town hours here,' Eleanor replied, looking carefully at Gwen. She did look well, although a little weary.

'That abigail of Miss Reynolds's looked black as thunder when she came down,' Gwen remarked, going behind her mistress to unfasten her gown. 'Had to do more work that she's used to, I'll be bound.'

Eleanor laughed. 'It was hardly fair that she should sit here on—'

'On her skinny backside,' Gwen put in.

'On a chair, I was about to say,' Eleanor contradicted with dignity, 'Whilst poor Cherry did everything; as if he hasn't enough to do already.'

'He's a good man, is that Cherry,' Gwen agreed, helping her mistress to step out of her gown. 'It's a wonder to me that such a worthy man should continue to be the servant of such a wicked one.'

'I don't suppose Mr Hurst is as wicked as the rumours say,' Eleanor replied, annoyed at herself for colouring. 'These things are often exaggerated, aren't they?'

Gwen looked at her with narrowed eyes. Eleanor hoped that she would put her heightened colour down to the candlelight. 'You're not getting a fondness for that rogue, are you miss?'

'Of course not,' Eleanor replied indignantly.

'Because,' Gwen went on, 'you wouldn't be the first to do so. It wouldn't do, Miss Eleanor. Not the way he is now. And besides—'

'Besides what?'

'Well, anyone can see which way the wind's blowing. That Miss Reynolds is sweet on him, and has come to make her claim. At least, that's what Pettit says. If you ask me, they deserve one another. Can you manage now, miss?'

'What? Oh, yes, yes, thank you, Gwen. You get a good night's sleep. Doubtless tomorrow you'll be needed in the kitchens again.'

'No doubt, miss. Christmas Eve tomorrow. It'd be a good thing if we could be on our way, but I doubt it.'

Eleanor laughed. 'Stop trying to sound regretful,' she said. 'You are longing to cook Christmas dinner, and you know it.'

Gwen smiled ruefully, was about to whisk herself into the dressing-room, then turned back, a horrified expression on her face.

'What is it?' Eleanor asked her.

'Plum-puddings, miss. I'll wager Broome hasn't made any, the idle good-for-nothing— not that I'd want to eat any puddings of his making. But how am I to make them and mature them in a day?'

Eleanor had to laugh at this. 'I have every confidence in your abilities, Gwen,' she answered.

It would be a strange Christmas, she reflected as she got into bed. In the past, she had certainly spent the occasional Christmas away from every member of her family. Never before, however, had she celebrated the festival with a group of people none of whom she had previously met. At least she would have Gwen, she remembered thankfully.

As a small child, Eleanor had travelled with her parents, along with her governess. Gwen, who had been nursery-maid at that time, had also accompanied them. This accounted for the closeness of the relationship between them, which was much warmer than that which normally existed between mistress and abigail. When Eleanor had been old enough to go to school, Gwen had been found other duties at Sir Clifford's country house in Bedfordshire. It was there, Eleanor suspected, that Gwen had gained her interest in cookery.

School holidays had been spent partly with friends, and partly with Mr and Mrs Carlisle, the uncle and aunt to whom she had been planning to go for Christmas this year. She had been with them for Christmas on several other occasions, but always in town. In recent years, Mrs Carlisle's state of health had meant that she was much better in the country or by the sea, so when Lord Summer had died without issue and his estate had come up for sale, they had purchased it just five months before. This Christmas was to have been the first that she would have spent with them in the country.

After she had left school, she had gone to live with her father, enjoying the varied existence provided by life experienced in a number of different foreign embassies. This year, because of her father's recent marriage, she had volunteered to spend Christmas with friends and then travel on afterwards to visit Mr and Mrs Carlisle. Then of course, her change of plan had meant that she had ended up travelling just before Christmas in the very worst of weather. Her uncle's house could only be a few miles away. How frustrating that she could not simply take wing and fly there! Instead, she was held captive by the weather and forced to associate with, among others, a spoiled beauty and a notorious rake, whose motives were as dubious as his reputation.

She remembered his kiss, ruthless and masterful, quite unlike any she had received before. Of course, he had behaved shamefully; but then, she suddenly recalled, he was not the only one, for had she not kissed him earlier on in the day?

With the arrival of the other visitors, and all the activity that that had prompted, she had forgotten that piece of audacity on her own part. It was undoubtedly a good thing that Gwen did not know about it! What a scold she would give!

Why had she done it? Had it been to reward him for his restraint, or to make up for some of the terrible things that had happened to him? Had it been because she felt sorry for him? Or, dreadful thought, had it been simply because she had wanted to? At the time it had seemed the right, the only thing to do; and even now, she had to admit to herself that given the same situation, she would probably do the same. Whatever might have been her reasons—and she was still at a loss as to disentangle them in her mind—she blushed at her own temerity.

But now Miss Reynolds had arrived, and Eleanor had seen clearly the kind of female that interested him. The young lady was made exactly on the same kind of lines as her own stepmother: small, dainty, blonde, with plenty of melting glances and a talent for flirtation. No, that was not fair; the new Lady Carruthers, despite her appearance, was intelligent, sensible and loyal. Eleanor suspected that Miss Reynolds was not any of these things, except, perhaps, for being loyal to her own self-interest, and quick enough to spot how this might best be served.

Obviously, her immediate aim was to enslave Hurst. It seemed equally obvious to Eleanor that the young lady's plans were succeeding. This had been made quite plain by the way in which the rake had leered down Miss Reynolds's front that evening. Then, immediately afterwards, he had cast a predatory look in her, Eleanor's, direction, as if to say: you see I can have any woman I want.

'Oh no you won't, Mr Hurst,' Eleanor said firmly. 'Not this one!' Upon which reflection she lay down and, by dint of trying to remember, in order, where she had spent each Christmas over the past ten years, and with whom she had spent it, she was soon fast asleep.

*   *   *

The following day dawned bright and clear, with no sign of any more snow. 'Maybe there's a chance we'll get away today, miss,' Gwen remarked as she handed Eleanor her morning chocolate.

'You don't know whether to be pleased or sorry about that, do you?' Eleanor asked her.

'I'll confess I'll be reluctant to leave that kitchen, miss,' the abigail answered virtuously, 'but I hope I know my duty. Your safety is my first consideration.'

'Gwen, I am in no danger,' Eleanor replied firmly. But even as she spoke, a picture came into her mind of Hurst's dark good looks. Danger might threaten in ways that were not entirely obvious. 'I'll get up as soon as I have had my chocolate,' she said decidedly. 'Then I'll send Clay to go and see if we can get through today.'

'I'll ask him when I get downstairs if you like, miss,' Gwen replied. 'By the way, I found out something more about the ladies.'

'You shouldn't gossip, Gwen,' said Eleanor severely.

'No, miss,' Gwen agreed in subdued tones.

There was a brief silence, then Eleanor said, 'Well, what is it, then?'

Gwen lowered her voice. 'It seems that Mrs Hulce is very short of money. Her husband left her with only a pittance. That's why they've come in Miss Reynolds's carriage.'

'I see,' Eleanor replied thoughtfully. 'Thank you, Gwen.' She felt a little guilty about gossiping about others, but did not allow the feeling to disturb her too much. She tried not to indulge in gossip merely for its own sake, but her many years of travelling with her father had taught her that all kinds of apparently trivial information could be vital in the field of international relations.

She well remembered an incident that had

taken place when her father was a high ranking diplomat in Italy. As a child of ten, she had heard two men talking on the terrace outside the salon whilst she lay in bed in the nursery immediately above. She had repeated what she had heard of the conversation to her father the following day, and he had become very thoughtful. Later on that day, he had come to find her, told her that she was a very good girl, and given her a guinea. The conversation that she had heard had given him a huge advantage in some vital negotiations.

This experience had taught her never to despise any information that might come her way. Information from Gwen would be reliable; and Gwen would never ever spread rumours about her mistress to others.

Armed with these facts, she went downstairs to partake of breakfast. She fully expected to enjoy a solitary repast as she had on every other occasion in this house, but she entered the room to find both Hurst and Playell seated at the table. There was no sign of the two ladies. This did not really surprise Eleanor. She had not expected to see either of them before noon, and she had certainly not expected to see Miss Reynolds. Owen Playell rose politely at her entrance, and Hurst inclined his head.

'You are up betimes, Miss Carruthers,' said Playell, leaving his place in order to hold out her chair. 'It is an honour to be graced with such beauty at the breakfast table, is it not, Chris?'

'An honour, and rather a shock,' Hurst replied.

'A shock, sir?' Eleanor asked, accepting with a nod Playell's unspoken offer to pour her some coffee.

'Why yes, indeed,' Hurst replied. 'I have been accustomed to coming round slowly in the morning. I am not used to being dazzled so early.'

Eleanor gave a gurgle of laughter. 'Perhaps I should take my plate into another room until you have recovered,' she suggested.

'By no means,' Hurst replied. 'I find I am already becoming accustomed.'

'You are more likely to be dazzled by the effect of the sun on the snow,' Eleanor observed.

'The sun is welcome, but the day is still very cold,' Playell observed. 'I do not think that it is thawing just yet.'

'I have sent a man out to see if the roads are negotiable,' said Hurst. 'If so, I will make arrangements for you to be taken to your uncle and aunt, Miss Carruthers.'

'Thank you,' Eleanor replied. 'Gwen was going on my behalf to ask Clay to go and have a look.'

'Brewer had already left when she came to the kitchens,' Hurst told her. 'I gave instructions that he should go first thing.

Owen, might I trouble you to pass me the toast?'

'Mr Hurst, there was no need,' Eleanor answered, feeling annoyed but not quite sure why.

'On the contrary, there was every need,' her host insisted. At that moment, the door opened and Plaice came in. 'Well?' Hurst asked.

'Drive's been shovelled clear,' he said. 'We'll do the paths round the house next.' As usual, he looked as though he would rather be almost anywhere else.

'Of course, but what of the roads, man?' Hurst asked impatiently. 'Is there any news?'

He can't wait to be rid of me, Eleanor thought to herself. Well, it was not surprising. She had been valuable as entertainment when no one else was available, but now that Miss Reynolds had arrived, she, Eleanor, was obviously expendable. She was surprised at how much this realization depressed her.

Plaice shook his head. 'It's drifted down the road,' he declared. 'No one'll get through today. Unless'n they're an angel and fly there,' he added with lugubrious humour.

'Thank you Plaice, that will do,' said Hurst. He turned to Eleanor with an apologetic smile. 'I fear you will be with us for Christmas Day.'

'I'm sorry to be a nuisance to you,' Eleanor apologized a little stiffly.

'You are not a nuisance,' Hurst assured her, with one of his most charming smiles. 'However, there is one matter in which I feel your talents might be put to use.' He glanced about him. 'If I send a man out with you to cut some greenery, would you be so good as to supervise its collection, and the decoration of the principal rooms?'

'I?' Eleanor exclaimed, amazed. 'But surely, Mrs Hulce, or perhaps Miss Reynolds. . . ?'

Playell laughed. 'Patricia will not be down until twelve. If we wait until she is ready, the men will be cutting greenery in the dark.'

'But your sister,' Eleanor protested again.

'Isobel may help later, but she has never been very artistic,' said the lady's brother.

'Then in that case, I shall be delighted,' Eleanor told him, feeling absurdly pleased to be of use. Then she added a little diffidently, 'Perhaps it might be a good idea for Plaice to clean the hall. We cannot decorate dirty rooms.'

'I'll give him the glad tidings,' Hurst replied. 'In the meantime, I'll send a message to that groom of yours, and you can give him your instructions. He hasn't got anything else to do at the moment. Take any greenery you like.' He turned to his friend. 'In the meantime, Owen, if you wish to go shooting, my guns are, of course at your disposal. You should find some sport down by the lake.' He finished this speech sounding perfectly courteous, but looking a little tight-lipped.

Eleanor opened her mouth to speak, then closed it again. She wanted to intervene but sensed that she would have to be careful. She did not wish to wound Hurst's pride. 'I'll go and put on my coat and boots,' she said. 'A breath of fresh air would do me good, I think.' Chancing to catch Mr Playell's eye, she threw him as speaking a look as she could, whereupon he said gallantly:

'I'll come and get my coat. Whether I shoot or not, some air would do me good as well. That is, if you don't mind, Chris?'

'With Miss Carruthers casting come-hither looks in your direction, who am I to spoil your fun?' Hurst answered blandly. 'Cherry shall push me over to the window, and I'll watch you from there.'

'But I can do that, old man,' said Playell, going back to Hurst.

'The devil you will,' Hurst answered tersely. 'Get along with you and enjoy the day.'

Once they were outside the room, Playell said with a twinkle as he moved a little closer, 'Well, ma'am? You wanted me for something, believe?'

'Yes, but I was not casting you come-hither looks, whatever he may say,' she insisted, taking a step back.

'I never supposed it,' he replied in a more level tone. 'How may I serve you?'

'When my belongings needed fetching from

128

my coach, the groom took one of the big horses pulling a sledge and collected them,' she said. 'I was wondering. . . .'

Playell's eyes kindled in quick understanding. 'Say no more, Miss Carruthers,' he replied. 'I'll tell them to harness the sledge, and ask Cherry to make sure Chris is wrapped up warmly whilst I fetch the guns. An hour or two's shooting will do him all the good in the world.'

Eleanor deliberately delayed her own preparations, so that she would be out of the way when the men set off. She judged it to be far more likely that Hurst would go if he did not have an audience. When she came downstairs eventually, she did put her head round the door of the salon, but finding it empty, she judged that Playell must have been successful in his persuasions.

Clay was waiting in the kitchen, and as he had already been told what was expected of him, he had taken the trouble to ascertain where the best greenery might be found. 'I'm told there's a fine holly-bush with lots of berries round the side of the house,' he informed her. 'There's other green bushes nearby, and I'll cut what you want. A lad's already been sent to find the mistletoe in the wood.'

Together they went out into the bright sunshine, and Eleanor found that she had to shade her eyes, so powerful was the reflection from the sun. When her eyes had adjusted a little, she gazed at the pristine whiteness of the surface. 'It seems a pity to tread upon it,' she remarked.

Clay merely grunted, demonstrating his opinion of this kind of sentimentality, and then said 'I believe it's this way, miss.' They walked round the side of the house, and Eleanor could not repress a cry of delight as she saw that the holly was as magnificent as any that she had ever seen at this time of year. The groom spread a piece of sacking on the ground, and on this he placed the greenery to which Eleanor directed him. They had only just begun, when a sound broke the stillness of the air, causing them both to start. Then, as the same moment as Eleanor herself had realized what it was, Clay said, 'It's just the gentlemen shooting down by the lake.'

Eleanor smiled. She liked the way in which he had simply said 'the gentlemen' without expressing any surprise that Hurst should have gone too. The more that Hurst could be encouraged to take part in normal pursuits, the better it would be for him and for all those around him, especially for those who cared about him. Of course I care about him, she told herself stoutly. He's a fellow human being, isn't he?

'Did they take the farm horse?' she asked.

'I believe so, miss,' Clay replied, as he began to cut the holly.

'They must have plenty of feed in store, with all these extra horses to look after,' Eleanor surmised, taking the holly from him as he passed it to her. 'I hope our own horses are well and comfortable.'

'They've come to no harm,' Clay answered. 'I've kept an eye on them. They're in very exalted company, I must say.'

'Exalted? Oh, Mr Hurst's matched greys.'

'Yes, miss. They're fine animals. I don't wonder at Mr Hurst's not wanting to sell them, even though he can't drive them any more.'

'But surely he could still drive, couldn't he?'

'I suppose so, miss, if he could be got up on to the driving-seat. But would he want to, knowing that his wife was killed when he was driving them?'

'I hadn't thought of that. Can you cut that big piece, just up there, Clay? It has such a lovely lot of berries on it.'

'Of course, miss.' He reached up and pulled down the branch that she was indicating. 'Apparently, the way Mr Hurst drove them that night was right out of character,' he added.

'Really?' Again, Eleanor was conscious of gossiping with the servants, but like Gwen, Clay had been with her for some time and she trusted him implicitly.

'Lashed with the crop, they were, and foaming at the mouth. Not like Mr Hurst at all, Brewer said.'

Judging that to speculate any further about

Hurst would be to go beyond the line, Eleanor changed the subject, pointing out some other trees that could also be useful to them, and after that their conversation was confined to their task.

Eventually, Eleanor was satisfied that enough greenery had been cut. Clay fetched the lad who had been cutting the mistletoe, and together they half-dragged, half-carried the sacking to the back of the house. Eleanor hoped that they would not try to carry it through the kitchen. They would certainly be in Gwen's bad books if they did so.

She paused for a moment, and looked in the direction of the lake. She hoped that Owen Playell would not keep his friend out for too long. He might not realize how very cold an immobile man could become in these temperatures.

She went inside in order to take off her outdoor things. Glancing at the clock in the hall, she was surprised to see that an hour had passed. Hurst would be chilled indeed when he returned. For the first time she began to feel uneasy about her suggestion. For a moment, she hesitated in the hall, then turned decisively and walked up the stairs. Mr Hurst was not a child for her to fuss over; and Cherry would be alive to the necessity of making sure that his master was not out for too long.

There was still no sign of the other ladies when she had put off her outdoor things.

132

Having put her hair to rights, she went downstairs and, seeking out Cherry, she suggested that the ingredients of a hot toddy should be prepared.

'That's a good thought, miss,' he answered. 'I'll give instructions for that to be done. I've just heard the gentlemen returning.'

'Then let me attend to the hot toddy,' Eleanor suggested. 'It won't be the first time I've made one.' She went to the kitchen and asked for lemons, honey, brandy and cloves, and in very little time, was preparing the steaming brew. This gave her time to look around and observe the hive of activity of which Gwen was clearly the queen bee.

'How are the plum-puddings coming along?' Eleanor asked.

Gwen threw up her hands. 'Don't ask, miss,' she said. 'There'll be something for Christmas dinner, but I can't guarantee what it'll be like. Meantime, the gentlemen have shot us some rabbits and pheasant, so however long we may be here, we shan't starve.'

Eleanor recalled that pheasants would need to hang for at least a week. 'I should hope we shall not need to eat those,' she said. With any luck, they would be leaving any day now. Strangely, the prospect did not seem to please her as much as she would have supposed.

CHAPTER EIGHT

When the hot toddy was steaming fragrantly, Eleanor instructed Plaice to carry it through to the salon. The only occupants of the room were Hurst and Cherry. Hurst was sitting near the fire, with his eyes closed, looking thoroughly chilled, whilst Cherry was massaging his legs.

'Here is something to warm you, sir,' Eleanor said.

Hurst smiled, opened his eyes, turned his head to look at her, saw Plaice with the steaming jug, and murmured, 'How disappointing.'

Flushing at his implied meaning, Eleanor turned away and busied herself with preparing a place for the jug on the hearth. When Plaice had set the jug down and left the room, she bent over, ladled out a glass of the steaming liquid and handed it to Hurst. Then, not knowing from whence came the courage, she said, 'May I help?'

Cherry looked up from his task, 'It wouldn't be fitting, miss.'

'Surely the more quickly Mr Hurst gets warm, the better,' she replied. 'Besides, I have massaged my father's feet before now.'

'Sir?' Cherry asked.

'Oh, let her,' answered Hurst resignedly.

'Unless I miss my guess, it was her idea to send me out into the cold, so she might as well do what she may to remedy the situation.'

Eleanor knelt down and proceeded to massage Hurst's right leg whilst Cherry attended to his left. It was still well-muscled, indicating that Cherry probably flexed the muscles for him from time to time. It was also very cold, and Eleanor knew that to rely simply on the heat from the fire could be injurious to him. She now began to feel guilty because it was indeed she who had suggested that Hurst should go out shooting. She had to wonder how he knew, however, for she was sure that Playell would not have disclosed this. His next comment enlightened her. 'Did you think I wouldn't guess that it was your idea, Miss Carruthers?' he asked her. 'Who else would be so determined to rehabilitate me?' She paused in her task and glanced up at him. He took a sip of the hot toddy and looked down at her, grinning. 'It was bloody marvellous to be out there. Thank you.'

'You must have a hot toddy as well, miss,' said Cherry. 'You have been outside too.'

'Of course,' said Hurst smoothly. 'You were collecting greenery. Was your task successful?'

'Very much so,' Eleanor replied. 'You have a splendid holly-tree, full of berries, around the side of the house.'

'Neither so splendid nor so full of berries as once it was, I gather,' he replied.

'Well, you did say I could take as much as I liked,' she answered defensively.

'I did indeed. How very obliging you are, Miss Carruthers,' he answered, his eyes gleaming.

In her concern for the fact that he was cold, together with her feeling of guilt because she was partly responsible for this, she had not really thought about the intimacy of the task which she was performing for him. Now, kneeling at his feet, her gaze locked with his and her hands upon his calf, she became suddenly aware of it, and found herself colouring.

'Get yourself a hot toddy, ma'am,' he said eventually. 'You may leave that now. I am warming up quite well, thanks to your offices.'

She prepared to rise, and found that he was holding out a hand to assist her. As she took it and felt the strength in his arm, she remembered how he had pulled her on to his lap and kissed her. Glad that because she was already blushing, it would not be noticeable if she did so again, she murmured a word of thanks and poured herself a glass of the warming drink.

She was about to put the jug down when the door opened and Owen Playell came in, rubbing his hands as he saw the fire and the steaming jug. 'Excellent,' he said heartily. 'Just the thing, after our morning's shooting. It was devilish cold out there, eh Chris?'

136

'It certainly was,' Hurst agreed. 'We got quite a fair bag, too.'

'You've lost none of your skill,' Playell replied, thanking Eleanor as he took his glass from her. 'Did you manage to gather your greenery, Miss Carruthers?'

'Yes indeed, I was just telling Mr Hurst that I was fortunate enough to be able to get a lot of red berries.'

'Splendid. Perhaps I could help you to put it up this afternoon?'

'Thank you, that would be very kind.'

'I do hope that you managed to find some mistletoe,' he added, his eyes twinkling. 'Christmas would not be the same without the kissing-bunch, would it Chris?'

'As you say,' Hurst answered politely.

At that moment the door opened and Miss Reynolds and Mrs Hulce came in. 'Chris, is this true?' the former exclaimed, hurrying forward so that she could take the blanket out of Cherry's hands and wrap it around Hurst's knees. 'Have you really been so imprudent as to go out in this cold weather?'

'I have indeed,' he replied. 'I don't believe I've taken any harm, thanks to, er . . . Cherry massaging my legs, and to Miss Carruthers's hot toddy.'

'You are fortunate to have such capable people around you,' Patricia answered, darting a look at Eleanor that seemed to be anything but grateful, 'but you must think of my feelings. Whatever should I do if anything happened to you?'

'Why, my dear Patricia, much the same as you have been doing for the past six months, I should imagine.'

'You are cruel,' she pouted. 'I was only trying to be kind.'

'Of course you were,' put in Mrs Hulce. 'But you were trying to manage him, you know, and gentlemen detest managing females.' She turned to Eleanor. 'Did I hear that you had been gathering greenery today? May I help decorate the rooms this afternoon?'

'Well, I shall keep Chris company,' said Patricia.

'My brother may like to come and watch the decorations being put up,' Mrs Hulce suggested.

'Thank you, Isobel, but I am not yet come to such a pass that I must simply sit and watch other people doing things,' Hurst said a little sharply.

'No, we shall be very cosy together, shall we not?' said Patricia.

Lunch was served shortly after this, and consisted of a warming bowl of soup, bread and cheese and a ginger-cake. Eleanor noticed that Hurst ate with more relish than before, and surmised that the fresh air and exercise had done him good. She hoped that he would not be tempted into forming a closer relationship with Miss Reynolds. If that lady had the power, she would wrap him in cotton for the rest of his days!

This thought was such a disturbing one that she was glad when the meal was over and Playell said, 'Now, Miss Carruthers, bring on the string! Bring on the knives! Let us transform this place!'

Some stout working-gloves were found for all of them, for handling the holly was no easy matter. Playell was entrusted with the task of trimming some of the larger pieces, whilst the lugubrious Plaice was pressed into service to help with hanging the garlands that they made, from some of the higher beams.

'I am so glad that you have taken this on,' Mrs Hulce confided to Eleanor when the two men were out of earshot. 'I am very ready to help, but I have no eye for this kind of thing; no eye at all.'

Recalling that Hurst had said as much, Eleanor ventured: 'Did you never help with decorating the house at home?'

'No, never,' Mrs Hulce replied. 'In fact, I cannot really remember very much about it. I think that the servants must have done it. I gather that things must have been different for you.'

'Yes, but not perhaps in a way that you might suppose,' Eleanor answered. 'I have celebrated Christmas in many different places, and the means to decorate a home were not always ready to hand. But I remember one year when

139

I was on holiday from school, and it was not convenient for me to go to London with my uncle and aunt or to travel to where my father was, so I spent Christmas at the home of a friend in Berkshire.' She smiled at the memory. 'It was wonderful! It snowed, although not so hard as it has this year, so we were able to go out for walks, and we collected the greenery as we have done today. All the family joined in. Mrs Wagstaff and Julia, my friend, and her younger sister and I sat round an old table that had been carried through from one of the kitchens. Then we tied the holly and the other greenery together, and arranged it in the vases. Mr Wagstaff and the two boys, Duncan and Simeon, had the ladder and hung everything up.

'Mrs Wagstaff's father, Colonel Eales, made some mulled wine, and we all stopped part way through to drink it, and eat some ginger biscuits that cook had made especially. Then, when it was all done, the children pushed their parents under the kissing-bough and would not let them go until they had made use of it. After all that, we looked outside and saw that it had begun to snow. I decided that when I had a home of my own, that would be exactly how I would celebrate Christmas.' She paused, still smiling, then turned apologetically to Mrs Hulce. 'I do beg your pardon,' she said. 'Other people's reminiscences can be rather boring.'

'Oh no,' Mrs Hulce replied wistfully. 'It

sounds wonderful; quite unlike any Christmas that I can remember. Our mother died when I was very small, and our father never wanted to celebrate Christmas very much. Sometimes, Chris would take me down to the kitchens, and we would join the servants for a while. It was much more fun than being above stairs.'

Eleanor tried to imagine the daring, dark-haired lad that Hurst surely must have been creeping down the backstairs with his sister in order to enjoy the festivities. 'But you have had your own home now for some years, have you not?' said Eleanor.

Then she inwardly cursed herself when the other lady replied, 'Being above stairs in my husband's house was not a great deal of fun either, I fear.' Then, changing the subject quickly, she went on, 'I suppose that your happy experience with your friends must have been what prompted you to suggest that the house should be decorated today.'

'Oh, it wasn't my suggestion,' Eleanor replied. 'It was your brother's idea that I should do it. I expect he simply wanted to give me an occupation.'

Playell came over to them at this moment to find out where they wanted the next garland to be hung, and so the conversation ended. But afterwards Eleanor began to think about what she had said, and to wonder whether she had perhaps hit the nail on the head. Hurst had known that Patricia would not want to take part in the decorating. Could it be that he had manipulated the situation so that he could be alone with Patricia?

At last, as the light was going, they finished their task, and stood back to admire their work.

'You have done an excellent job, Miss Carruthers,' Playell said, as he extracted a leafy sprig from his hair.

'I, and several others,' Eleanor corrected.

'Yes, but yours was the inspiration,' Mrs Hulce replied. 'I doubt if any of this would have been done without your presence.'

'No indeed,' agreed Playell. 'If you come over here, Miss Carruthers, I think you will get a better view of the whole hall.'

Eleanor crossed to where he was standing, then realized too late what she had done when he gazed impishly above his head. 'Caught fair and square, ma'am,' he said, bending to kiss her cheek. Then having done so, he remained bending over her slightly, his hands on her shoulders. 'Thank you for what you have done,' he said. She knew that he was referring to what she had done for Mr Hurst.

'I have not done so much,' she protested.

'You have brought him a breath of fresh air,' he answered, and bent and kissed her again, this time lightly on her lips.

'Charming,' said a voice from the other end of the hall. 'Absolutely charming.' Hurst was sitting in his chair watching them, Cherry behind him, and Miss Reynolds standing next to him, looking triumphant. Eleanor knew that she had done nothing wrong. She had participated in an innocent Christmas custom, well chaperoned by Mrs Hulce, who was, oddly enough, looking a little more serious than the occasion warranted. Nevertheless, Eleanor had to swallow an immediate and urgent desire to explain herself. Then, moments later, she realized that she had been leaping to conclusions, when Hurst added, 'I do not believe that this house can ever have been decorated so tastefully before.'

'Oh come, Chris,' said Miss Reynolds playfully. 'You cannot possibly know that!'

'No, but I can make an educated guess,' was the reply.

'Of course, you really need to view the hall from the other end, to see it at its best,' said Miss Reynolds, with an eye on the kissing-bunch. 'Cherry, push your master to that end of the hall.'

'Cherry, kindly do not,' Hurst said before his manservant could obey the lady's instructions. He smiled up at Patricia. 'No offence, my dear, but I have never needed the ... er ... incentive of a Christmas decoration to assist me in my courtships.'

At that moment, the clock struck, giving those who wanted it the perfect opportunity to excuse themselves in order to change for dinner. Miss Reynolds, Eleanor noticed, followed Hurst back into the salon, with a sprig of what looked like mistletoe in her hand. Clearly she was not a lady who would easily take no for an answer!

'Would you like me to come to your room and dress your hair?' Mrs Hulce asked Eleanor as they climbed the stairs. 'I am guessing that your abigail will be busy in the kitchen again, and probably worrying about tomorrow's dinner as much as tonight's.'

'Thank you,' said Eleanor gratefully. 'I must confess that I was feeling a little guilty at dragging her out of the kitchens. Foolish, isn't it?'

'Not at all,' Mrs Hulce replied. 'I think you are very tolerant, in being prepared to do without her.'

'It's all in my own interest really,' laughed Eleanor. 'You should have tasted the food when Broome was in charge!'

'I'll send Patricia's woman down to the kitchens to tell your abigail that you can manage without her,' promised Mrs Hulce.

Eleanor was on the point of saying: Dare you? but decided that she did not know Mrs Hulce well enough to risk it. Once in her room she took out her turquoise gown, and stood looking at it, hesitating. Part of her wanted to appear in front of the company in something that they had not already seen. Her other gowns could do with a press, however, and eventually she decided that she would rather not wear a creased gown in front of Miss Reynolds. She had forgotten until Mrs Hulce had mentioned the matter that Gwen was largely unavailable to her, and was consequently unable to press a gown at short notice. She would get out another gown in the morning, and ask if Cherry could press it for her in time for the evening.

She had only just made this decision when there was a knock on the door. She opened it to find Plaice with a jug of hot water in his hand. She thanked him and took it, and began making her toilet.

Mrs Hulce arrived later as promised, and was soon coaxing Eleanor's heavy, dark-golden hair into a becoming style.

'You are clever,' said Eleanor admiringly. 'Even Gwen has problems with my hair, and she knows it almost as well as I know it myself.'

'It is because there is so much of it,' Mrs Hulce replied. 'But it is beautiful hair.'

'I always hated it when I was younger,' Eleanor replied. 'I wished it could be dark, like yours.'

'And yet it is not long since golden hair was fashionable, is it?' Mrs Hulce remarked. 'I dare say it will be again soon.'

'Yes, so my aunt used to tell me. I didn't find it much of a consolation, I'm afraid. Why is it that we are never prepared to listen to our relations?'

'I don't know,' said Mrs Hulce, as she

finished the final touches to Eleanor's hair. 'Perhaps it is because sometimes they can be criminally wrong.' The statement was such a startling one, that Eleanor turned involuntarily to look at the other, an expression of surprise on her face. 'Neither my brother nor I was very happily married, I fear. In fact. . . .' She paused, then added in subdued tones; 'I have said too much and am boring you, I'm sure.'

'Not at all,' said Eleanor earnestly. 'Mrs Hulce, pray do not confide in me unless you really wish to do so. Should you choose to place your confidence in me however, I can assure you that I will not repeat anything that you may say.'

Mrs Hulce looked at Eleanor for a long moment, then sighed. 'I am sure you will not,' she answered. 'The fact is, that when Mr Hulce died this year, it was both a relief and a shock. I married him because my father insisted, but I learned, too late, that he was mean in his attitude to his dependants, whilst at the same time self-indulgent to a ruinous degree. I am left with virtually nothing, Miss Carruthers. The estate was encumbered far beyond what even I expected, and what remained of it has had to be sold in order to pay Selwyn's debts. Even my own portion is gone.'

'Did you never wish for the marriage yourself?' Eleanor asked her, getting up from her place at the dressing table, walking to a chair by the hearth and inviting the other lady to take the one opposite.

The widow shook her head. She sat down with a graceful swirl of her skirts, which reminded Eleanor unaccountably of a smooth, elegant gesture that she had seen Hurst make with his hand. 'There was another gentleman to whom I was attached,' she admitted, 'but he was only a curate who lived in one of the villages nearby, and my father refused to allow me to marry him.'

'But now—' Eleanor began.

Again Mrs Hulce shook her head. 'I think he was not as taken with me as I was with him. He married a wealthy merchant's daughter shortly after I married Hulce, and I believe that they are very happy. I do not repine about him, I assure you.'

'Did your brother know how you felt about your marriage?'

'I could not tell him,' she said. 'He was in London, and Papa had forbidden me to communicate with him because of—' She halted abruptly, coloured, then went on, 'for many reasons.'

Eleanor nodded. No doubt Mr Hurst the elder had disapproved of his son's wild way of life.

'Papa acted from the best of intentions,' Mrs Hulce insisted. 'I think he knew that he did not have much time to live, and he wanted me to be settled. Then he wanted to see Chris settle down as well.'

'I see,' Eleanor replied, thinking that however well-intentioned he may have been, the late Mr Hurst had made disastrous errors in his attempts to provide for his children's futures. 'Have you come here, then, to ask for your brother's help?'

'I was hoping to,' she admitted, 'but it's all rather difficult. You see, I was on the point of asking him for help when he had that dreadful accident, and then he had enough troubles of his own without my burdening him with mine.'

'So what have you been doing since then?' Eleanor asked her.

'It took a little while for Selwyn's affairs to be sorted out, and while that was happening, I was able to remain in the house, and keep things in order. Then I was told that there was nothing left and that all the servants would have to be dismissed, and I would have to find somewhere else to live. That was when I thought of Chris again. I wondered whether he might perhaps need me as much as I need him.'

'I'm sure he would be glad of your company,' Eleanor replied. 'I think he has been very lonely.'

'Yes, you are right, but that need not continue, need it?' She paused, looked a little anxiously at Eleanor, and went on: 'I did wonder when I first saw you standing beside my brother's chair, whether you were ...

148

well—'

'Oh no, no!' Eleanor exclaimed colouring. 'My arrival here was quite by chance.'

'Yes, I know that now; he responds to you in the way that he does to every beautiful woman. But now that Patricia is here. . . .' her voice tailed away.

'You think that they might make a match of it?' Eleanor asked in a carefully neutral tone.

'Patricia has always been interested in Chris, even though when she first met him he was already married to Priscilla,' she replied. 'She is an orphan with a sizeable inheritance. Her trustees are two indolent old men who allow her to do exactly as she pleases. One of them is her uncle, who brought her up and spoiled her dreadfully because she was so pretty. Since coming out, she has made her home with a number of different society matrons, all of whom she has chosen because they permit her to have her own way. Now that she is over twenty-one, she may please herself, of course.'

'So—forgive me for asking this, Mrs Hulce—'

'Isobel; you must call me Isobel,' put in Mrs Hulce.

'Thank you, Isobel; and of course you must call me Eleanor. Did you come with Miss Reynolds, or did she come with you?'

A flush crossed Mrs Hulce's rather pale cheek. 'I have to admit that I rather took advantage of her,' she confessed. 'After I had been obliged to leave my husband's old house,

149

I went to stay for a while with friends, while I decided what to do next. I wanted to come here but was at a loss as to how to find even the fare on the public stage. Then Patricia appeared in the neighbourhood and I told her—very casually, you understand—that I was hoping to come and see Chris, but that I had had to dispose of my carriage, and was temporarily at a loss.'

'So Miss Reynolds offered you a seat in her carriage,' Eleanor surmised. 'Did Mr Playell appear at the same time?'

'Yes, he did,' answered Mrs Hulce, colouring a little, darting a glance at Eleanor, then looking away.

Suddenly, Eleanor remembered how Mrs Hulce had looked serious when Playell had kissed her under the mistletoe. Did the widow perhaps have an interest in Mr Hurst's friend? Did she suspect that Eleanor herself might have designs upon him? If so, she must disabuse her of that idea.

'Mr Playell seems a very agreeable gentlemen,' she said casually. 'Have he and Mr Hurst been friends for long?'

'Since they were at school,' Isobel replied. 'It sometimes seems as if I have known Owen all my life.'

'I take it that Mr Playell is not already married.'

'No, he is not married,' Mrs Hulce confirmed. 'Or . . . or even attached, as far as I know. The field is clear for you, Eleanor,' she added with another little sideways glance.

This was just the chance that Eleanor had been hoping for. 'For me?' Eleanor exclaimed with a little laugh. 'Oh no, no. I already have an attachment, you see.'

'Oh, I see,' Isobel answered.

'You do not think that Miss Reynolds has any interest in Mr Playell?' asked Eleanor, not because she suspected such a thing, but because she wanted to get away from the previous subject before Isobel began to make enquiries about the identity of her mythical admirer.

'No indeed,' Isobel responded firmly. 'All her interest is in my brother. But if he and Patricia do make a match of it, there will be no place for me.'

Eleanor did not feel that she knew Hurst well enough to hazard an opinion on the matter. Furthermore, she, too, could not imagine Miss Reynolds wanting to share an establishment with another woman. Instead, she simply said: 'You must tell your brother how you are placed, you know. I am sure that he will want to help you in some way.'

'Yes, but I don't want to impose,' Isobel replied. 'He has enough problems of his own, hasn't he? I do want to make my own way in the world, but with Chris's help this would be so much easier.'

After this, they went downstairs to join the

others. But as they went, Eleanor thought back to the lie that she had told about having another attachment, and wondered why it did not seem like a lie at all.

CHAPTER NINE

It had been quite a pleasant evening, Eleanor reflected later, as she was preparing for bed. Miss Reynolds had been permitted to take her preferred place, the one next to Hurst on his right, and as he had been quite happy to indulge her with a flirtation, she had been well content.

Once again Eleanor had found that, whilst she was on Mr Hurst's left, she had had Mr Playell as a neighbour on her other side. He had been an entertaining dinner companion, as ready to talk about her concerns as his own, and after his quick-wittedness that morning over the shooting expedition, she had felt very much in charity with him. He had also talked to Isobel with all the ease of long acquaintance; but from the warmth of his glances, it occurred to Eleanor that Playell's interest in Mrs Hulce might go beyond the kindness naturally extended to his friend's younger sister. This would indeed be good news, if the interest was mutual, as her earlier conversation with the widow certainly led her to suppose. She was glad that she had played her part in clearing the field by assuring Isobel that she was not interested in Playell.

Eleanor had also been careful not to look too much at her host, and had allowed Miss Reynolds to take most of his attention. If questioned afterwards, she would have found it difficult to say why she had done this. Possibly, she had not wanted anyone to suspect that she was setting her cap at him, least of all the flirtatious Patricia or even the man himself!

When Cherry had come to push his master back through into the salon, Eleanor had thought that the valet was looking pale, and she had not been surprised when Hurst had called an end to the evening quite early. 'Cherry's got one of his heads coming on, and ought to be in bed himself,' he had said.

'Surely he can put it off until you are in bed yourself, Chris,' Patricia had complained. 'It is too bad that our pleasures should be curtailed just for the whims of one servant.'

'Cherry has a great deal to do,' Eleanor had put in. 'I fear the household would struggle without him.'

Miss Reynolds had simply shrugged, but had not said any more.

It was only as Cherry had been about to take his master through to bed that Eleanor had thought to say, 'Mr Hurst, tomorrow is Christmas Day.'

153

'It is indeed, Miss Carruthers,' Hurst had replied, with a quirk of his eyebrow.

She had coloured. 'I was just wondering whether we are to mark the day in some way?' she had asked him. 'We cannot get to church, so. . . .'

'So you are proposing a service of some kind here?'

Miss Reynolds had sniggered. 'Imagine, Chris! A church service in the house of the Hell-raiser!'

'At what hour would you like your service?' Hurst had asked Eleanor, ignoring Patricia's derision.

'Perhaps at ten o'clock?' she had suggested diffidently. 'Then the servants would be able to attend.'

'And a female parson to lead it!' Miss Reynolds had laughed scornfully. 'Well do not expect me to be there. It seems to me that one of the few things to be thankful for in being marooned is that we do not have to drag ourselves to some icy church to hear a wretched cleric drone on and on.'

'No one will expect you to attend, my dear,' Hurst had answered with his most charming smile. Then he had turned to Cherry. 'Ask Plaice to have a fire lit in the library tomorrow morning, will you?'

Once Hurst had retired, no one had seemed very inclined to stay up. After Patricia had made a few spiteful remarks about some of her acquaintance, she had declared herself to be ready to retire, and the ladies had gone upstairs whilst Playell had wandered into Hurst's bedroom for a chat.

Eleanor had already prepared for bed and was about to climb in when she suddenly thought about her prayer-book. She usually carried it with her, but she had very foolishly left it behind in church on the last occasion when she had attended. She had no doubt that she would eventually get it back, for her name was in it and she was known to the vicar in whose church she had left it, but it did mean that she would have to find another one to use on the morrow. She did not really want to put off looking for one until the next day, for she wanted to read through the appointed passages before she went to sleep.

Half-remembering seeing a prayer-book on the Hell-raiser's bookshelves, she put on her dressing-gown and slippers, took up her candle, and made her way downstairs.

It was certainly cold in the library. Plaice would need to light a fire in good time for the room to be warm the next morning.

She went to the shelf where she thought she might find what she was looking for, and soon spotted three prayer-books next to two large Bibles and a book of sermons. She opened one and saw that it had once been the possession of Priscilla Glade, given to her by her mother in 1775. It must have belonged to Hurst's wife, she decided, putting it back with an unaccountable feeling that she was trespassing. The second volume she took out was rather more worn, and contained no inscription, so after a brief perusal of the shelves nearby—but very brief, because it was cold—she left the library, closing the door behind her.

She was about to go upstairs when she heard an unmistakable cry of pain proceeding from the room which she knew to be Hurst's bedchamber.

She looked around. Cherry would attend him, she thought; then she remembered that Cherry had not been well that evening. Again she hesitated, but before she could decide to return to her room, she heard a groan, and before she could have second thoughts, she tapped on the door and entered, saying diffidently; 'Sir? Are you unwell? Can I help you in any way?'

Hurst lay in bed, his dark hair tousled, his face contorted with agony. His bedclothes were rumpled, as if he had been pulling at them. 'God yes,' he exclaimed. 'I've got cramp in my left foot and my calf. Find someone—anyone—to massage it, will you? Oh God!'

Eleanor put the candle down, and came over to the bed. 'The left, you said,' she remarked, unfastening the covers on the left hand side of the bed.

'I didn't mean you,' he bit out.

'Then whom do you suggest? Plaice? Or

156

shall I wake Mr Playell, or even Miss Reynolds? She would be charmed to help you, I'm sure.'

'Go on, then,' Hurst replied, wincing. 'My case is too desperate for me to argue with you.'

She uncovered his foot and calf and saw that the muscles were indeed bunched and very tense.

'You will know my legs by now,' he drawled in a calmer tone.

She coloured a little, but without hesitation, she took hold of his limb and began massaging and flexing, until the knots of tension began to disappear and the muscles relaxed. He had well-shaped legs and feet, she noticed. How odd that she should be performing this task for him for the second time today!

'Is that better, sir?' she asked him at last.

'I'm afraid not, ma'am, he answered blandly. 'In fact, there is barely any improvement. Pray continue.' His lips twitched slightly.

'Mr Hurst, you are a liar,' Eleanor said, without heat.

'I simply like what you are doing,' he answered shamelessly. 'I didn't want you to stop. But regretfully, I have to confirm that you are correct. The problem is now rectified. Thank you. Cherry is upstairs in bed having taken laudanum at my instruction, and would not have heard me.'

'Then I will tuck in the bedclothes, and leave you to your rest, sir,' Eleanor replied, getting up and covering his legs.

'One moment,' he said. 'Playell and I enjoyed a glass of brandy before we retired. The decanter is still over there, I believe. Would you be so good as to pour me a small measure? I feel as if I need it.'

'Of course,' Eleanor replied. As she stood up, she suddenly became aware that she was in her night-attire in the bedchamber of a notorious rake. The fact that her nightgown was certainly cut higher at the neck than the gown that she had been wearing earlier that evening, did not seem to make any difference to her feelings of embarrassment. She was glad that she could busy herself for a few moments with her back to him so that he would not see the heat in her cheeks.

'What were you doing downstairs anyway?' he asked her.

She told him the nature of her errand. 'I did not want to leave it until the last minute,' she said to him, as she handed him the glass.

He took it, and held it up to her in salute. 'To you, Miss Carruthers—or does such service as you have performed for me this evening give me the right to call you by your given name?'

'I think it must do,' she answered, smiling. 'You may call me Eleanor, sir, if you wish. Now, if you are comfortable again, I must leave you.'

'Stay for a few moments,' he urged her,

patting the bed next to him.

'I should not.'

'Stay until I have drunk my brandy. I don't want to run the risk of knocking the glass off this little table in the night.'

'Very well,' she agreed, picking up an upright chair and bringing it to the bedside, then sitting down.

Hurst grinned wryly, regretfully smoothing down the coverlet. 'All right, Eleanor, you win that one. And since I am now calling you Eleanor, you must call me Chris. I am glad you have decided to stay. There is something about which I need to ask your opinion.'

'Of course, sir—I mean, Chris.' There was a brief silence, then she asked him curiously, 'Have you always been called Chris?'

'My father is the only person who has ever called me Charles,' he answered her. His tone did not invite further enquiry. There was another silence. 'What do you think of Isobel?' he asked her eventually.

'What do I think?'

'Is all well with her? We don't know each other as well as we might. I was off to Eton when she was three, and after that, much of our lives has been spent apart. I was never very sure how she felt about her marriage. Our father decided that I was a contaminating influence, you see, so the letters that I wrote to her were returned to me unopened.' He was silent for a moment. 'I didn't much like the things that I heard about Hulce, but there was nothing specific that I could really object to.'

'I see,' Eleanor replied, thinking it was strange that both Hurst and his sister should choose to confide in her in this way.

'So what do you think? Is she all right?'

'I think she would be glad of a chance to discuss her future with you,' Eleanor answered, not wanting to break faith with Isobel.

'She's talked to you, has she?' Hurst said astutely. 'Well, I shan't ask you to betray her confidence. But if you can find a way of taking Patricia away tomorrow, I should be grateful.'

'I ought to go now,' said Eleanor, eying his almost empty glass. 'Is there anything else that I can do for you before I go?'

He grinned, showing all his teeth. 'Oh, there's a great deal that I would like you to do for me, Eleanor, but for now, perhaps you would just stoke up the fire.'

She did as he asked, bending over the grate with her back to him. Her hair, released from the elaborate style of that evening, hung down her back in a long plait.

'So all that lustrous golden beauty is your own,' he remarked. 'I did wonder.'

'All my own,' she agreed, straightening from her task and turning to face him.

'I don't suppose you would consider loosening it for me?' he asked, smiling impishly.

160

'You would not make such a request, sir, if you had any idea how long it takes to achieve this,' she answered in matter-of-fact tones. Her reply was not entirely truthful—she could, in fact, plait her hair quite quickly—but she needed to say something to diffuse the feeling of crackling tension that had begun to fill the room.

He smiled ruefully. When she came back to his bedside, he was holding out the glass. 'I've finished my brandy now,' he said. She had to move closer in order to take it, and as she did so, he reached out with his other hand, hooked it in the neckline of her night gown, and pulled her towards him. Two buttons of his own night shirt were unfastened at the neck, revealing a few strands of dark chest hair, and the sight made her strangely breathless. When she was close enough, he let go her night gown, put his hand around the nape of her neck and pulled her closer still until their lips met. His kiss was warm and searching, but when she pulled away, he released her immediately.

'Thank you for staying,' he said, smiling. 'That was particularly pleasant.' He stretched out a hand towards her neck line once more. 'If I might but unfasten a button or two,' he murmured.

'Certainly not, you shameful rake!' Eleanor declared, springing back in alarm. Her face was aflame, but she could not completely prevent herself from smiling back at him.

He sighed ruefully. 'And there was I, thinking that I'd really got a wench for Christmas,' he murmured.

She went to the door, opened it, then turned back to look at him. 'Happy Christmas,' she said.

'Happy Christmas, Eleanor,' he answered.

It was only when she got back to her bedroom that she realized that she had left the prayer-book behind. Oh well, she decided, she would just have to read the service without seeing it first. At least she knew where the books were to be found. Then, feeling that she probably needed prayers after her shameless dalliance with a man of doubtful reputation, she settled down for what proved to be a very restless night's sleep.

CHAPTER TEN

She was woken the following morning by Gwen's voice saying, 'Good morning, Miss Eleanor,' as she drew the curtains.

'Good morning, Gwen,' answered Eleanor. 'Happy Christmas.'

'And the same to you, miss. You've a good colour this morning.'

Eleanor laughed self-consciously. 'I ... I must have been sleeping with my head under the covers,' she said. At the very moment when she had woken, a dream that she had been having had come into her head. In the dream, she had not drawn back when Hurst had reached out for the fastening of her nightgown. In fact, she had leaned forward and permitted. . . .

'Gwen, I have a gift for you,' she said quickly. Before she could remember any more of that shocking dream, she swung her legs out of the bed, went to the chest of drawers under the window and took out a package. 'Here you are.'

'And I for you, Miss Eleanor,' Gwen replied.

Eleanor had purchased a new shawl for her abigail, and this was much appreciated. 'It's beautiful, miss,' said Gwen, fingering the soft material.

'I know how much you like blue,' Eleanor replied, unwrapping her own package to reveal a set of handkerchiefs embroidered with her initials. 'These are lovely, Gwen,' she said admiringly. 'I had no idea you were making them.'

'You don't know about everything I do, miss.' Gwen replied demurely. 'Would you like me to fetch your water, now?'

'Yes, please,' Eleanor replied. After Gwen had gone, she got back into bed and sat sipping her chocolate. She picked up her handkerchiefs to admire them, then dropped them as a thought suddenly occurred to her. Oh my life, she thought. I've nothing for

Hurst, or Playell and the ladies!

When Gwen came back with the water, it was to find her mistress frantically rummaging through the contents of the chest of drawers. She frowned when Eleanor explained her problem. 'You didn't know you were going to be stranded here, miss,' said Gwen. 'Nobody could hardly expect you to have anything for them.'

'No, but it doesn't seem right,' Eleanor replied.

'Well, let me have a look, whilst you have your wash,' said Gwen.

'At the very least, I must find something for Mr Hurst,' said Eleanor. 'After all, he is my host.'

'Yes miss,' said Gwen. 'Are you going to wear your russet dress today?'

'Yes please. Aren't you needed in the kitchen?'

'Presently, miss. We made an early start, so that we can all be in the library for morning prayers.'

'Oh, my stars, I forgot that I had that to do, as well,' Eleanor exclaimed.

'Let's get you dressed first, miss.'

By the time Eleanor was dressed, Gwen had had time to sort through her mistress's things, and had found a few items for her inspection. 'There's this fine lace that that Spanish diplomat's wife gave you,' she said.

'Oh yes; beautiful stuff, but all black,'

Eleanor answered. 'That would do very nicely for Mrs Hulce, wouldn't it?'

'Just what I was thinking miss, her being in mourning. Then there's those handkerchiefs you saw and bought for yourself only a couple of weeks ago. You've not used them yet.'

'No, and I shan't need to, now that I've got those lovely ones that you've embroidered for me. Those will do for Miss Reynolds. What about the gentlemen?'

'Do you remember that you bought Sir Clifford that snuff, and by chance overheard him saying that he no longer cared for the mixture? I have it here. Perhaps that could be for Mr Hurst. And you have several gifts for your uncle. Could you spare one of those for Mr Playell?'

Eleanor pondered for a moment. 'There is a pair of driving-gloves, which I bought for Uncle Philip before I discovered that his cousin had already sent him some,' she said thoughtfully. Then: 'Hand me that paper that we wrapped each other's presents in. That will do to wrap the ones that we have just chosen.'

There was not quite enough paper to wrap everything, so Eleanor simply tied a length of ribbon around the jar of snuff and used the paper for the rest. That done, she went downstairs in order to partake of breakfast.

Hurst and Playell were both at the table, and cordially wished her a happy Christmas, which greeting she returned.

'Sad for you not to be with your family at Christmas, Miss Carruthers,' Playell remarked as he served her with some bacon from one of the covered dishes on the table.

'It would not be for the first time, Mr Playell,' she replied calmly.

'In fact you are to be envied, Eleanor, for no doubt you will have another Christmas to enjoy when you arrive at your uncle's house,' Hurst put in.

'Yes, you are right,' Eleanor agreed. She was aware of a startled expression on Playell's face, then she remembered that of course he would not have heard Hurst call her by her Christian name before. In for a penny, in for a pound, she thought to herself before saying, 'Chris, might I trouble you to pour me some coffee?'

'Of course.' Hurst smiled. He turned to Playell. 'Formality seems a little unnecessary in such a small gathering, does it not? Eleanor might even allow *you* to call her by her first name if you ask her very nicely.'

'I would be honoured if you would permit me to do so,' said Playell. 'Pray call me Owen.'

After they had finished their repast, Hurst said to Playell, 'Are you to join us for prayers this morning?'

Playell looked first at the young lady whose idea the morning service had been, then at his host, who clearly meant to attend, and tugged at his cravat. 'Well, ah, that is to say, not very religious myself, but, ah, as it's Christmas, well,

166

why not?'

'Splendid,' Hurst answered. Then he turned to Eleanor. 'You will be joining us, I take it?'

'Joining you. . . ?' she murmured. She had been under the impression that the onus was upon her to read the service for the benefit of the others.

'Why yes,' he answered. He picked up a little book that had been at his elbow throughout the meal, but which she had overlooked. She recognized it immediately. It was the one that she had taken from the library the previous night. 'I have read the service to myself, and having thought the matter through, I have decided that I shall lead the household in prayers as its master should.'

Those attending the service gathered in the library just before ten o'clock. All the servants were present, including Eleanor's own staff who had found a refuge at Glade Hall, and she wished them all a happy Christmas. The gift of money which she usually presented to her own servants for the season, she would give the following day as was traditional. Briggs was walking unaided, and with only a hint of stiffness, so his ankle was obviously recovering well.

Cherry had wheeled his master to the end of the library before everyone assembled. Eleanor was pleased to see that the valet looked much better, and told him so.

'Thank you, miss,' he said in his usual polite

tone. 'A good night's sleep always puts me to rights. I hate to leave Mr Hurst on his own, though.'

'I contrive to manage,' Hurst murmured, glancing up at Eleanor with a wicked grin which made her blush.

At first it seemed as though neither Mrs Hulce nor Miss Reynolds would make an appearance, but the widow arrived just before the service began, and made her way quietly to the front, where she took her place next to Eleanor. In the end, the only two people who did not make any appearance were Miss Reynolds and her abigail.

Hurst might have been known as the Hell-raiser, but he read the service well and with dignity, and by the time it had finished, Eleanor felt that she had begun Christmas Day in a proper fashion.

The servants trooped out to be about their various tasks and Eleanor, getting up to leave the room, encountered a speaking look from Hurst, which reminded her of their conversation the previous night. She turned to Playell and took his arm, saying 'Tell me about your family, sir. Do you not have brothers and sisters who will be missing you at this season?'

As she did so, she was aware of Mrs Hulce getting up, and Hurst saying to her 'Don't run away, little sister. I'd like a word with you.'

'I have a sister, who is married with four unruly children who are all under ten,' Playell said ruefully as they strolled into the salon. 'I make a point of avoiding their household during major festivals; or, indeed, at any other time,' he added reflectively.

Eleanor laughed. 'I am sure you are too harsh, sir,' she said. 'What are their names?'

'Oh, good Lord,' he exclaimed. 'Now you have me! Is one of them called Norman? No, that was what the first one would have been called, had it been a boy, but it wasn't. They called her something else instead, I think.'

'Mercifully,' Eleanor murmured.

'What? Oh yes, of course!' laughed Playell. 'There is no excuse for me, Miss Carruthers. You have now revealed what a hopeless uncle I am, but I swear I shall improve—just as soon as they do. I'll put a guinea under the seal of my letters to the boys when they go to Eton, and when the girls come out, I'll drive them around Hyde Park and introduce them to all the notables.'

'That's very good of you,' laughed Eleanor. 'The problem is, will they want to be driven around by a middle-aged man?'

Playell laughed in his turn. 'You have a point, there. But what of yourself? Are you an aunt?'

'No; I am an only child; but you have reminded me that I might, perhaps, have a brother or sister one of these days.'

'Indeed?'

'Yes, my father has just married again, and

my stepmama is a delightful young woman.'

Playell made some response to this comment, but Eleanor did not hear it. All at once, she had found herself wondering whether she would ever have the pleasure of holding a child of her own.

*   *   *

Having asked Isobel to stay behind, Hurst could not now think of a way to begin. He watched her as she paced up and down restlessly in front of him, and noted, with some surprise, that she cut a very elegant figure. He had always been fond of his little sister, but the difference in their ages had meant that although there had always been affection between them, there had never been intimacy. Once he had made his home in London and begun his wild style of living, the attitude of their father had meant that the separation between them had been more than merely physical. Now he was convinced that his sister stood in need of help. He wanted to give her all the assistance that he could—after all, she was all the family that he had—and the most obvious way to do this would be to offer her a home. On the one hand, however, he could not risk hurting her pride, but on the other, he did not want to make her feel obliged to come to his aid. The problem was that he did not feel that he knew her well enough to be sure of the best way to proceed, and he found himself regretting that distance between them which had been largely of his making.

Before he could say anything, however, she ceased her pacing and turned to look at him, twisting her black-edged handkerchief between her fingers. 'Chris, I . . . I expect you are wondering why I have come?'

'Not at all, my dear,' he replied, smiling at her. 'I'm charmed that you have come to see me, and I hope this will be the first of many visits.'

She darted a sideways glance at him. 'That is exactly what I was going to speak to you about,' she said quickly. 'You see I . . . I—' She halted abruptly.

Hurst waited for a few moments, then when time went on and her sentence remained unfinished, he said gently, 'Bella, what's wrong?'

She looked up from the handkerchief that she was clutching so tightly, and he saw that there were tears in her eyes. 'Oh Chris, I don't know what to do. Selwyn spent everything and there is nothing left. The house . . . even my portion—' She gulped, blinked away her tears, and straightened her back. 'I was wondering whether . . . whether—'

'My dear Bella,' Hurst interrupted, 'you may come and live with me for as long as you wish.'

Isobel hurried to his side and knelt down next to his chair. 'Chris, I don't want to impose upon you,' she said. 'I must confess that I was hoping that you would invite me to stay, but only until I could make some other arrangements.'

'Other arrangements?' queried Hurst.

'I thought that perhaps I might become a . . . a companion, or a governess eventually,' Isobel replied.

Hurst took hold of both her hands firmly. 'My dear Isobel, no sister of mine is going to become a companion or a governess as long as I have breath in my body,' he told her. 'I believe the Spanish have a saying which, directly translated, means "my house is your house". I've always been a great admirer of the Spanish.'

She reached up from her kneeling position and kissed his cheek. 'Chris, I accept your offer, and oh so very thankfully,' she told him. 'Indeed, I do not think that I shall ever be able to stop thanking you.'

'My dear sister, I pray that you will at least try,' he drawled. 'That, I fear might become a trifle tedious.'

She gurgled with laughter. 'Very well, then. But we must promise to be honest with each other. If I start to do something that irritates you, pray tell me.' She looked at him, then looked swiftly away. 'And of course, should you find someone to . . . to share your life, I should absolutely expect to move out immediately.'

'I do not think it likely,' he said in an even

tone. 'But did such a situation occur, my dear, you would of course continue to make your home here for as long as you wished.' Then he went on, with a lightening of tone, 'However, it seems to me to be far more likely that *you* will receive an offer of some kind. I shall probably find suitors beating a path to my door in search of you. I wouldn't be at all surprised if Owen Playell is one of them.'

'Oh do you think so indeed?' Isobel asked eagerly. Then she coloured, looked down and said in more subdued tones, 'Of course, I am not out of mourning yet.'

'That's true. But you must not take anything for granted, little sister. You may have some competition there. Eleanor Carruthers seems quite taken with him, for instance.'

'No, you are mistaken there,' his sister informed him. 'Eleanor told me, only yesterday I think it was, that she had another attachment.'

Hurst's immediate instinct was to demand to whom she might be attached, but he held his peace on that subject. 'Shall we join the others?' he suggested. 'Patricia might have come downstairs, perhaps. I would not want to be remiss.'

'I think I'll go up to my room for a few minutes,' his sister replied. 'I'll ask Cherry to take you to the salon.'

While Hurst waited for Cherry, he thought about what his sister had just told him.

Eleanor Carruthers already had an attachment. Why should the news have come as a shock to him? She was a very desirable woman. He himself desired her; it followed therefore that other men would do so as well, and one of them obviously enjoyed her favour. He would be well advised to put her out of his mind, and settle for what he could get.

Eleanor and Playell were still conversing easily when the doors opened and Cherry pushed his master into the room. There was no sign of Mrs Hulce. 'My sister has gone upstairs for a few minutes,' Hurst said, by way of explanation. 'She will be down directly.'

Looking at his face, Eleanor could detect no sign to show her how the conversation had gone. Knowing how much he disliked being observed whilst Cherry moved him about, she wandered over to the window to look outside while the manservant helped his master into his armchair.

Playell followed her, observing, 'The snow seems to be melting a little, ma'am. I think you may be able to reach your destination before many days have passed.'

To her surprise, when she heard his words her first sensation was one of consternation. This feeling she ruthlessly suppressed, saying in cheerful tones, 'I do believe you are right. I shall soon be gone. You will be glad to be rid of me, no doubt.' Unthinkingly, she turned back to look at her host, and found his gaze locked unsmilingly with hers, as he allowed Cherry to straighten his legs before spreading the rug over his knees. Oh no, she thought, I have turned round too soon.

'You are mistaken,' Hurst said politely. 'Naturally those to whom you are . . . attached, will be glad to see you, but the loss of your company will create an unwelcome gap in our fellowship.'

'Not to mention the yawning gap in our stomachs as they refuse to return to Broome's appalling cooking,' Playell put in.

Everyone laughed. 'You are very right,' Hurst agreed, smiling. 'I shall have to find some means to tempt Gwen to stay with us.'

'That is easily done,' Playell replied, walking to the sideboard in order to pour sherry for them all. 'All you have to do, my dear fellow, is tempt Eleanor to stay, and Gwen will do so as well.'

'You are mistaken, Owen,' Hurst said, his smile gone. 'There is nothing here to tempt her to stay, and there are other attractions elsewhere.' Eleanor could feel her face flaming. She was glad that Playell immediately engaged his friend in conversation on another matter. She had just realized how easily she could be tempted and was very afraid that her expression might give her away.

A short time later Miss Reynolds appeared. She was clearly in buoyant mood. 'Happy Christmas to you all,' she exclaimed, 'and especially to you, my dear Chris.' She swayed over to Hurst's side, her hands behind her back, and as she reached him, she brought out the piece of mistletoe that she had been hiding from view. 'May this coming year bring all that you most desire.' Bending, she kissed him lingeringly on the mouth.

'Thank you, my dear,' Hurst replied courteously. 'I applaud the sentiment; but my nanny always used to say that to have all that I desired was not very good for me.'

'And mine said the same,' Playell agreed. 'What of yours, Eleanor?'

'Oh, indeed,' Eleanor responded, feeling rather annoyed with Miss Reynolds for making such a spectacle of herself. 'I am sure that most of us would have ended up completely spoiled, had it not been for our nannies.'

'Mine was not like that at all,' Miss Reynolds remarked; then she looked around in surprise when they all laughed.

Luncheon was a simple meal, consisting of cold meat, bread and butter, and a lemon-cake, but no one complained, for all were aware of the sterling efforts that were being expended in the kitchens on their behalf. Miss Reynolds, seated again at Hurst's right, made great play with her eyelashes, and she often seemed to find it necessary to lean forward and lay her hand on her host's arm for emphasis.

Mrs Hulce, sitting at the head of the table,

looked as relaxed as Eleanor had ever seen her. She could only conclude that the conversation between her and her brother must have gone well.

The meal was almost over when Miss Reynolds said, 'When shall we exchange gifts?'

'Might I suggest that a formal gathering would be inappropriate when some of us are here by accident, and others had no knowledge of this visit?' said Playell.

'Oh, pooh,' Miss Reynolds replied scornfully. 'We are not children to be upset because we do not have gifts to open, are we, Miss Carruthers?'

Eleanor smiled. She knew perfectly well that Miss Reynolds would be counting on the fact that she, Eleanor, would be the only one with nothing to open. 'Certainly not,' she agreed. 'Half the fun of presents is seeing how others react to the gifts that one has wrapped for them. I am looking forward to seeing you open my gift, Miss Reynolds.'

A look of chagrin crossed the beauty's face, and Eleanor wondered with some glee how soon Miss Reynolds would make an excuse to go upstairs, so that she could find something to give in return.

'I have gifts for all those present,' said Hurst, 'so no one will have the mortification of having nothing to open. Shall we exchange gifts after dinner, when the tea-tray comes in?'

'What a good idea,' smiled Miss Reynolds. 'I

shall be sure to have mine ready.' She strolled over to Hurst, stroked his cheek, murmuring 'Pray excuse me. I have letters to write,' and left the room, turning to blow him a kiss from the doorway.

'A game of piquet, Owen?' Hurst asked his friend, as Cherry pushed him through into the salon.

'Splendid,' Playell replied. 'Where do you keep the cards?'

Mrs Hulce turned to Eleanor, who was still smiling at seeing her suspicion about Miss Reynolds confirmed so quickly. 'What about a stroll along the terrace?' she suggested. 'The sun is warm and a little fresh air will do us good.'

'Take care, it may be slippery,' Playell warned.

The ladies promised to do so, and in a very short time were walking along the terrace enjoying the winter sunshine. Eleanor noted that whoever had remarked upon the snow melting earlier on had been quite correct. Here and there the sounds of dripping water could be heard, and she herself only narrowly escaped some large droplets falling down her neck.

As soon as they were out of the house, Mrs Hulce said, 'I thought you might like to hear about my conversation with my brother.'

'Naturally I would,' Eleanor agreed, 'but pray do not break any confidences. I am only pleased that you managed to talk to him as you wished.'

'Well, I will tell you,' the other lady replied. 'After all, you know about my circumstances anyway.' She paused briefly. 'I told Chris everything—the debts, the sale of the house, everything. It turns out that he did have concerns about Selwyn even before the marriage, and wrote to me and to our father, but Papa did not say anything, and never gave me any letters.'

'Good heavens!' exclaimed Eleanor. 'How . . . how unprincipled!' She recalled that Hurst had also said much the same thing.

'I think he must have known that Chris would support me, and that was why,' Mrs Hulce went on. 'Anyway, Chris says that there is no question but that I must come and live with him here.'

'Isobel, that is wonderful news,' said Eleanor warmly.

'Yes, I was so pleased, because it means that perhaps I may be of service to him,' Isobel replied. 'I did venture to say to him that I did not want to intrude if he should perhaps marry. He told me that he did not expect to do so, but that if he did, any wife of his must be prepared to welcome me as well. Was that not kind of him?'

'Very kind,' Eleanor agreed, wondering what Miss Reynolds would think of this.

'This is certainly a very beautiful house,' Mrs

Hulce said after a few moments. 'What age do you suppose it is?'

Eleanor readily accepted this change of subject, and they chatted about the house and other houses that they had known until they both felt that they had braved the cold for quite long enough.

The two men had not played piquet together for some time, so the first hand was spent rediscovering one another's game. Soon, however, they were well into their stride and everything else was forgotten in their absorption with a pastime at which they both excelled.

After Playell had beaten Hurst, albeit by a very small margin, they paused for a glass of Madeira, which Playell poured for them. 'Perhaps I should tell you that when you leave, you will only be escorting one lady,' said Hurst as he took his glass.

'Good God!' exclaimed Playell, almost dropping his own wine. 'You must have taken leave of your senses!'

'To invite my sister to reside with me?' Hurst queried, grinning impishly. 'I thought it was rather a good idea.'

'To invite. . . ? Damnation, Chris, you know very well what I thought.'

'In short, you supposed that I must have succumbed to the fair Patricia.'

'Well, yes,' Playell agreed. 'And I still say, you would have taken leave of your senses even to consider such a thing.'

'Actually. . . .' Hurst murmured.

'Never say you have considered it!'

'You have to admit that the notion of marrying Patricia does have quite a lot to commend it.'

Playell pursed his lips. 'She's not a hardship to look at,' he agreed. 'But when you've said that, you've said it all.'

'She's been prepared to travel quite a distance to see me,' Hurst put in.

'Yes, well, thereby hangs a tale,' Playell told him. 'I'm not one to bandy a lady's name about, which is why I didn't say anything before, but it was all round the clubs, so if you'd been in London, you would have heard anyway. I picked up the latest gossip when I dropped into White's the other week. She made a play for young Drysdale, the match seemed certain, and all of London was waiting for the announcement. She called round to see her fiancé-to-be one fine afternoon; she was left there, with the understanding that Lady Harne, her future mama-in-law, would be chaperoning her. However, neither Drysdale nor his mama was in, but Harne was.'

'The deuce! Not Harne the hunter?'

'Precisely,' Playell agreed. 'Lady Harne came home with Drysdale and her bosom friend, Ruth Presse—'

'The tongue of the *ton*,' Hurst interrupted.

'As you say,' Playell agreed. 'Anyway, they all

181

arrived to find Harne and Patricia enthusiastically enjoying one another's company, shall we say?'

'So her departure from London was politic.'

'Very politic. Drysdale cried off, of course, and Patricia fled to Somerset, to put as much distance as possible between herself and London.'

'Her estate is in Somerset,' Hurst observed, 'but rather too close to Bath for discretion, I would have thought.'

Playell nodded. 'That may have been why she sought out Isobel, only to find her on the point of visiting you.'

'So she decided to come as well.' Hurst thought for a moment. 'Don't think me ungrateful for your company my dear fellow, but where exactly do you fit into this party?'

Playell coloured a little and pulled at his cravat. 'Well, I'd already decided to pay you a visit—don't look at me with your brows raised, I *had* decided to do so—but knowing that she was now alone, I wondered whether Isobel might want to come, so I popped in—'

'You popped in to see my sister in Somerset on your way to my house in Warwickshire from your own estates in Derbyshire, via your London club?' Hurst exclaimed, his brows raised. 'My dear chap, you really weren't attending when they instructed us in the use of the globes, were you?'

'All right, I admit it,' Playell growled. 'I've

182

always admired Isobel. She's never thought of me as anything other than your friend of course, but I still have to be of what service I can. Perhaps when her mourning is over, you'll allow me to call upon her.'

'Come whenever you like,' Hurst answered, 'but I don't know whether she'll want to marry again. I think she had a pretty rotten time of it with Hulce, although she's never said much about it.'

'I guessed as much. So there you have it. I went to visit Isobel, intending to come on and see you—and to prove it, I have got a gift for you which I did procure in London before I left—and found myself escorting not only Isobel but also Patricia.'

'Who is clearly after me because she's desperate, having managed to burn all her boats,' Hurst remarked, with bitter humour. 'I'd say we'd make a pretty good pair, all told—both of us at our last prayers.'

'Poppycock,' Playell answered brutally. 'I arrive here, with the charitable intention of providing you with a woman, and find you already have one—and a very attractive one, too. You always were a lucky dog.'

'Lucky?' demanded Hurst. 'Hell, Owen, would you really say so? You can have my place and welcome.'

'I didn't mean that,' his friend replied in subdued tones.

'No, I know you didn't.' He paused. 'She is

lovely, isn't she?' he went on in quite a different tone.

'Luscious, I think would be the word,' Playell agreed.

'But not for me, I'm afraid.'

'Shouldn't she be the best judge of that?'

'I have it on good authority that she has another attachment,' Hurst replied, 'and perhaps it's just as well under the circumstances.'

'What circumstances?' Playell asked him, genuinely puzzled.

'These circumstances,' Hurst retorted, pointing to his legs. 'Do you think I want her pity? A woman like that deserves a man whose arm she can take, not one who needs blankets wrapped round his knees. Let Patricia do that! She's good at fussing and petting me and treating me as if I were a pet poodle.'

'Could you endure it?' Playell asked curiously.

'I'd rather endure that than see the woman I—' he broke off abruptly. Then he resumed in a different tone, 'To be honest with you, I've rather a fancy for having a woman in my bed again, and you must admit Patricia would do very nicely.'

Eleanor, who had been on the point of entering to see if the gentlemen would like tea, turned and followed Mrs Hulce slowly up the stairs. So, Mr Hurst had decided that he wanted Miss Reynolds, had he? Well, it was not surprising. Once a rake, always a rake—that was what people said. The fact that he was unable to walk did not alter the kind of man that he was. She supposed that she must be thankful that she had not succumbed to him the previous night. The truth was, that she had been sorely tempted to allow him to unfasten those two buttons, and he would almost certainly not have stopped at two!

She exchanged a few words with Isobel about meeting later, but could not have told anyone either what she herself had said or what the other woman had replied. It would be a very good thing if she could go on to her uncle's on the morrow. What a blessing it would be to get away from the fascinating Mr Hurst while she was still heart-whole. That, at least, was what she told herself.

CHAPTER ELEVEN

Christmas dinner was every bit as good as the company had come to expect from Gwen. The goose was cooked to perfection, and set off admirably by the side-dishes that had been prepared to go with it. Somehow—no one ever managed to find out how she had managed it—Gwen had been able to conjure up a plum-pudding, and everyone declared it to be excellent—apart from Miss Reynolds, who declined it because of its richness and played with a bowl of jelly instead.

On this occasion, Eleanor found herself seated at Mr Hurst's right for a change; and although Miss Reynolds sought to dominate the proceedings with gossip from London, Hurst seemed more disposed to talk about some of the foreign places which he and Eleanor had both visited, at different times.

'St Petersburg can be beautiful in the spring,' Eleanor said, smiling reminiscently.

'Indeed,' he responded, 'but deucedly cold in winter. I remember—' He broke off suddenly, and turned those dark eyes upon her. Suddenly, she felt her heart start to race. Her hands were in her lap, and to her astonishment, she felt him catch hold of her left hand with his right and squeeze it tightly, so that she almost cried out. 'I wish I could walk beside the Neva with you,' he said in a low tone, then swallowed convulsively.

She sat transfixed by his gaze, and for a few moments, everyone and everything else in the room seemed to disappear. So powerful was the sensation that she almost reached out to take him in her arms and pillow his head on her breast, so that she might give him the comfort which he so desperately needed. Then someone moved a chair, making a scraping sound on the floor and she was jolted back to the present. Glancing round quickly, she saw to her relief that at that moment, Playell was keeping the other two ladies very well entertained with an amusing story.

She smiled back at him, squeezed his hand in return, then said in a louder, brighter tone than she normally used, 'By all means if you say so, but for my part, I find nothing very much to admire in Russian ladies!'

At once, his expression changed, the flirtatious grin returned and he replied, 'But then, Eleanor, your point of view is not the same as mine.' His gaze flickered down to the low-cut bodice of the handsome, dull-gold gown that she had chosen to wear that evening.

'Undoubtedly,' she answered a little tartly. 'Would you like your eyes back now, sir?'

He laughed, Playell made a comment, Patricia claimed her host's attention again, after a little glare at Eleanor, and the conversation became general. A little later, however, when the attention was turned away from Hurst again, he looked at Eleanor, smiled, and raised his glass in a silent toast.

After the meal was over and the gentlemen had spent a brief time over their wine, the party reassembled in the salon in order to exchange gifts. To her surprise, Eleanor had three parcels to open; one from Hurst, one from Miss Reynolds and one from Isobel. She had suspected that when Miss Reynolds had gone upstairs, it had been to turn over her belongings very hastily in order to find something that she might give to her. She was not entirely surprised, therefore, when her gift turned out to be a small bottle of perfume that was not quite full. She thanked the donor very sincerely, but could not help reflecting that she must be inherently more deceitful than Miss Reynolds. Like her, she had searched among her belongings for items that would serve as gifts. In Miss Reynolds's place, however, she was convinced that she would have topped the bottle up with water, and pretended that it was unused!

Miss Reynolds professed herself delighted with the handkerchiefs that she received, and Mrs Hulce, looking at the lace admiringly, declared that she had never seen anything so fine. 'I shall trim my black satin with this tomorrow,' she promised. Isobel's gift to Eleanor was a tiny silver brooch in the shape of a snowflake. 'I thought it might make a pleasant memento of your stay here,' she remarked.

'Indeed it will,' Eleanor agreed, hoping that the other woman had not given her something precious that could ill be spared.

She saved Hurst's gift until last, and when she opened it, she found that it was a framed drawing of the Grand Canal in Venice. 'Why, this is lovely,' she exclaimed. Peering at the bottom of it, she saw the initials C.C.H. She looked up at him in sudden comprehension. 'Did you do this yourself?' she asked him.

He inclined his head. 'My only talent,' he murmured.

'It is a very impressive one,' Eleanor replied.

'Chris has always been able to draw,' Mrs Hulce remarked. 'I wish that I could.'

Miss Reynolds, who until then had been looking very well pleased with the pearl necklet that he had given her, eyed the picture with unmistakable chagrin. 'I don't think you have got the distance quite right, Chris,' she said.

'Nonsense,' Eleanor replied, her eyes still on the picture. 'It is just as I remember.'

'Oh well, if *you* are satisfied,' said Miss Reynolds scornfully; then she flushed as she realized that in her haste to belittle the woman whom she perceived to be a rival, she had seemed to criticize the very man whom she wanted to impress. 'Of course it is a very good drawing.'

'Thank you, my dear,' Hurst replied, amused. He opened the parcel that she had given him, and admired the snuffbox that it contained. 'This is charming,' he declared. 'Quite charming. Thank you.' Miss Reynolds preened herself, darting a sly glance at Eleanor as if to say that she knew the other woman would not have given anything half as suitable.

Eleanor thought of the presents that she had wrapped for the two gentlemen. She had not done as Gwen had expected when she had attached the labels, and was now worrying that perhaps she had made a dreadful blunder. Oh that she had bestowed them as Gwen had suggested! Hurst would then have had something to put in his new snuff-box, and she would have been spared the inevitable forthcoming embarrassment.

Playell did not have a parcel from Eleanor to open, but he professed himself delighted with the jar of snuff. 'This is just my sort,' he declared, his tone unmistakably sincere, so that she knew he was not just being polite. 'Thank you, Eleanor. Now I am put to shame, because I have nothing to give you in return; but I do have an excuse. Like Isobel and Patricia I had no notion you would be here, but unlike them, I have no ingenuity.'

'It really doesn't matter,' Eleanor replied.

'Besides,' Hurst put in, 'you went up to the loft on my behalf and found a suitable frame.'

'So I did,' declared Playell, brightening.

'Then you must share in part in Mr Hurst's gift,' Eleanor responded.

'Chris,' Hurst corrected her. He began to open the parcel that she had given him and she could feel her heart begin to race. What if he thought she had been cruel and insensitive? Suddenly, she realized that she would not hurt him for all the world.

At one point during the proceedings, everyone had been opening gifts and chatting amongst themselves. Now, as luck would have

190

it, everyone seemed to be quietly watching Hurst open this last gift. He took off the wrappings and stared down at the driving-gloves in silence.

Miss Reynolds was the first to speak. 'Good heavens! How insensitive!' she snapped at Eleanor. 'He will never drive again! As well give him a pair of spurs!'

After what seemed like an eternity, Hurst looked up from his contemplation of his gift. 'That is not what Eleanor thinks,' he said, looking at her. 'I shall endeavour not to disappoint her.'

The conversation soon became general, but under cover of some talk between Playell and Hurst, Miss Reynolds turned to Eleanor and said: 'Why he should be concerned about not disappointing you I cannot imagine. He barely knows you. Anyway, you will soon be gone, and I will still be here.'

Eleanor could not think of a polite way to respond to this kind of rudeness, so instead she turned to speak to Isobel. The next time she looked around, Miss Reynolds was fussing over Hurst again.

On the whole, the rest of the evening was very enjoyable. There could be no music performed—evidently the late Mrs Hurst had not been musical for there was not a spinet or pianoforte to be seen—but Hurst directed Playell to a cupboard in the library where he thought some games might be found. Most of these were of the nursery level, but the company passed an entertaining hour or two, and even Miss Reynolds seemed to be in a mood to be pleased.

'What an agreeable Christmas Day this has been,' Playell remarked as they prepared to part for the night.

'Much more agreeable than I expected to have, certainly,' Hurst responded.

'If we had not descended upon you, you would have been dull indeed,' Miss Reynolds put in. Then, as if she had spoken thoughtlessly, she added a little artificially: 'Apart from Miss Carruthers, of course.'

Eleanor smiled politely. Alone of everyone in the party, she and Miss Reynolds had continued to address one another in formal terms. Glancing at Hurst, she saw that he was smiling too.

'Ah yes, who could be dull with her about?' he replied.

'Indeed,' Miss Reynolds agreed. 'Her conversation is so instructive.'

'I think I must retire before all these plaudits make me conceited,' Eleanor remarked.

With that, the gathering broke up. Patricia swayed over to Hurst and pressed an affectionate kiss upon his cheek. 'What a happy Christmas it has been,' she breathed. 'The first of many, I hope.'

Mrs Hulce, too, crossed to her brother, and also bent to kiss him. 'Thank you, dear brother,' she said. Eleanor knew that she was speaking of more than just the Christmas festivities.

Eleanor curtsied politely to her host, and left the room with the ladies, closely followed by Playell, who said; 'Good night, old chap. Perhaps if the snow clears, we'll take a drive down to the lake in a day or two.'

'Perhaps.' Hurst smiled. As she reached the foot of the stairs, Eleanor heard Hurst call out her name, and she went back into the room, passing Playell on her way.

'I have instructed one of the grooms to look at the road first thing tomorrow,' Hurst said. 'With any luck, you may be able to join your uncle and aunt for the rest of their festivities.'

'Thank you,' Eleanor replied. 'You are very kind.'

'Not at all,' he answered. 'I feel that I am the one who should be thanking *you*.'

'Why?' she asked him.

'You've encouraged me to think that my life can still have meaning,' he told her frankly. 'You've helped me to see that I can still be a man—even like this.'

'Even like this, you are more of a man than many I have met,' Eleanor replied, colouring at her own temerity.

'Come over here.'

'Why?' she asked again; but she went all the same.

'Patricia and Isobel kissed me before they

left. I would be glad if you would do the same.' She bent to salute him upon his cheek as the two other ladies had done a short time before. 'No,' he said, before she could do so. 'Not like that. Give me your lips, Eleanor.' She hardly hesitated. She turned her head, and pressed her lips to his, thinking to herself, this may be for the last time. Their mouths touched, clung, then with a groan, Hurst put his arm around her, caught the back of her head with his other hand, and deepened the kiss, coaxing her lips to part, and savouring the inside of her mouth with his tongue.

When at last they parted, they were both breathless. After gazing at her for a long moment, Hurst said, in a voice that was not quite steady, 'Thank you, my dear. You add to your kindness. Leave me now.'

Shaken and unable to think of anything to say, Eleanor dropped a rather disorganized curtsy and withdrew. Her legs were shaking so much that she could barely climb the stairs. She was a little afraid that Miss Reynolds might have lingered to discover why Hurst had called her back, but fortunately there was no one in sight to witness her flustered ascent.

She hurried into her room, closed the door and leaned back against it, as if pursued. She stood there for a long time, reliving the kiss that they had shared and that had had such a shattering effect upon her. Had he been similarly affected, she wondered? Of course not, she told herself impatiently, as she made herself prepare for bed. He was a rake, wasn't he? The conquest was everything to him. Now she had revealed herself so thoroughly in her response to his kiss, he would want no more to do with her. Had she not heard that very afternoon that he meant to bed Patricia? Then why was she brooding over him, for goodness sake?

Thanking her lucky stars that Gwen had not appeared to get her ready for bed, she finished her preparations, and was just doing up the buttons of her nightgown when she paused, remembering what he had said. *Thank you, my dear. You add to your kindness*. That was what he had told her. Her kindness? What had he meant by that? Did he think that by kissing him, she was being kind? Did he, heaven forbid, think that she had embraced him because she pitied him? The truth of the matter was that she was deeply attracted to him. Could he really be unaware of the effect that he had upon her?

Suddenly, it seemed very important that she should tell him that she had not kissed him out of kindness. Quite what else she would say, she did not know, but she must at least tell him that, especially as there might well be no further chance of private speech with him. She pulled on her dressing-gown, slid her feet into her slippers, and picked up her candle. Then after a moment's thought, she put it down again, unfastened the top two buttons of her nightgown with trembling fingers, and opened her door.

She encountered no one on her way down the stairs, but as she turned towards the door to Hurst's bedchamber, she saw that it was slightly ajar. Then, from inside she heard Miss Reynolds's voice. 'I'll close the door, shall I, Chris? We don't want a draught, do we?'

Suddenly, Eleanor felt rather sick. As she returned to her room, she told herself determinedly that she was thankful that although she was a fool, at least she had not made herself look foolish in front of others, especially Hurst and his fancy piece.

But that night she dreamed that she and Hurst were walking together by the Neva, her hand tucked in his arm. When she awoke, there were tears on her cheeks.

Long after the house had gone quiet, Hurst lay wide awake, staring up into the darkness of the canopy above his bed. 'Hell and the devil confound it,' he muttered to himself, 'I must be demented. A beautiful woman comes to my room and offers herself to me; and I turn her down! Idiot!' He thumped the bedclothes with his fist.

Patricia had appeared shortly after Cherry had bade him goodnight. He had still been sitting up in bed, with pillows piled up behind him which he would discard when he wanted to settle down. Resting on the covers in front

196

of him was the sketch-book which he had asked Cherry to bring to him before he retired. It was the one that he had brought back with him from Russia, and he had been leafing through the pages, remembering his visit there some three years before.

It had been a very happy time, during which he had stayed with Count Alexei Yefimovitch Volkhov. Together, he and the handsome Russian nobleman had disported themselves in many and various ways. But the moment that remained with him the most clearly had been the morning when he had got up early—or rather, gone to bed late—and seen the early morning sunlight gleaming on the River Neva in St Petersburg. He had hurried to his room in the Volkhov palace and collected his sketching things. Then he had almost run back to the river in order to capture the beauty of the moment.

It had been that incident that had darted into his mind at dinner. Suddenly, the glowing health of the woman beside him had brought back to him the beauty of the scene on that crisp April morning in St Petersburg. He had almost been overcome by the moment, and had been unable to dismiss it from his mind. It was this dinner-time conversation that had prompted him to send for his sketch-book.

The draught from the opening door had interrupted his reverie. At once, he had slipped his hand under the pillow next to him in order to find his pistol. He did not expect intruders, but he was quite isolated downstairs in this part of the house, and he had no wish for any house-breaker to catch him unawares. Almost at once, however, he had heard Patricia's voice. He was surprised at the depth of his disappointment. He would almost have preferred an encounter with a burglar.

'Patricia, my dear, this is a surprise,' he had said, feeling his way.

'Surely not,' Miss Reynolds had murmured seductively as she crossed to the bed, and sat down next to him. Her matching pink nightgown and wrapper billowed about her. The neckline was very low, and as she sat, she had deliberately leaned forward, giving Hurst a better view. He had found himself thinking that she looked far better in stays. 'Chris, you must know that I am very fond of you,' she had said.

'It is kind of you to say so,' he had answered her blandly.

'Chris, you are not making this easy for me,' she had complained, glancing up at him through her lashes. 'I was wondering whether I could . . . do anything for you.' She had placed her hand on his, stroking it gently. He had been surprised at how little it had affected him.

'Again, I am very appreciative of your kindness, Patricia, but Cherry has done all that I require,' he had responded.

'Chris—' she had begun, but he had interrupted her.

'Patricia, I am grateful that you have come to enquire about my welfare, but I must insist that you go back to your own room,' he had said gently but firmly. 'You are not dressed for sitting about in this draughty house. I should hate you to catch cold.'

She had stood up, a faint flush touching her cheeks. 'I wonder what your response would have been, had it been Miss Carruthers who had come to your room,' she had said.

'That, my dear, is something that we shall never know,' he replied.

She had paused briefly, then, as if the words had been wrenched from her, she had exclaimed 'I cannot understand you! It is not as if you are going to be flooded with offers.'

'Perhaps it is for the best, then,' he had answered. 'You would surely not wish to be saddled with a man whom you cannot understand.'

She had left without saying anything more.

Laying aside his sketch-book, Hurst had discarded the extra pillows and had blown out his candle before lying down to think. What a fool he was! He had determined to accept Patricia and all that she was so willing to give him. He had told Playell as much. Why, then, had he refused what had been so blatantly offered? Patricia had said that she did not understand him; but he understood himself

199

only too well.

The answer lay in the person of Miss Eleanor Carruthers. How ironic it was that he had chased after women for most of his adult life, and only fallen in love twice. The first time, the object of his affections had been Priscilla Glade, and she had proved to be beyond his reach, because her inclinations lay elsewhere. Now, he had fallen in love again, but because of his physical disability he could not bring himself to ask the woman of his choice to share his life. Call it pride, but he did not want her to accept him out of pity; and how could he ever be sure that pity did not play some part in her feelings for him? Furthermore, even if he could dare to address her, she would probably refuse him because of the attachment of which Isobel had spoken. Even bearing all of that in mind, the plain fact was that because he was in love with Eleanor Carruthers, he could not make do with Patricia Reynolds, or with any other woman.

So where did that leave him? Sitting by the fire with a rug over his knees whilst this unknown suitor and his like courted the woman of his choice? 'Damn damn damn damn damn!' he said out loud. He lay back, staring up above him, and thought that he would never get to sleep. But when he did, like Eleanor, he dreamed of walking by the Neva.

CHAPTER TWELVE

When Eleanor came downstairs the following morning, it was to discover that a servant had been able to ride through to inform Mr and Mrs Carlisle of their niece's whereabouts.

'The message I have received is that Mr Carlisle will come over this morning and fetch you,' Hurst said as they sat at breakfast. At first, it had seemed as if Playell would be the only other person to make an appearance. As Eleanor took her place, however, the door opened to admit Mrs Hulce. 'My dear Isobel, this is quite unexpected,' said Hurst, his tone ironic. 'Are you sure you are quite well?'

'Perfectly well, thank you dear brother,' answered Mrs Hulce, sketching an impertinent curtsy. 'I could not risk Eleanor's leaving without my being able to say goodbye to her.'

'I will hardly be a thousand miles away,' Eleanor told her. 'You must come and visit me whilst I am there.'

'With pleasure,' Isobel replied, 'and you must come back and see us here.'

'Of course,' Hurst said politely. He doesn't really mean it, Eleanor thought to herself, remembering how she had heard Miss Reynolds's voice coming from inside his bedchamber. He has his wench now.

They chatted desultorily of this and that, but

now that Eleanor was going, she could play no part in any plans being made for the day. In the minds of the others seated at breakfast, she had as good as gone already.

After the meal was over, Eleanor excused herself and got up from the table. 'I must prepare to leave. Do you know whether Gwen, Briggs and Clay have been told that we shall be going today?'

Three horror-stricken faces were turned towards her. 'Not Gwen,' Playell faltered. 'What will we eat?'

Eleanor took one look at them and burst out laughing. 'She is my abigail, you know,' she reminded them.

'Of course,' Hurst agreed. 'You must naturally take her with you. But if you would be so good as to enquire of Mrs Carlisle as to whether she knows of anyone who can cook and is prepared to come here, I would be eternally grateful.'

'By all means,' Eleanor replied. 'I don't think any of you deserves to be left to Broome's tender mercies.'

'Tender?' Hurst exclaimed. 'Pray choose your words with more care, Eleanor. The last piece of meat he cooked was like shoe-leather!'

Still smiling, Eleanor went back upstairs to her room. She was on the point of going in when to her surprise, Miss Reynolds emerged from her room and walked towards her. 'You are up betimes,' Eleanor remarked, then blushed as she thought again of what she had heard the previous night.

'I wanted to see you off,' Miss Reynolds explained. Her tone seemed to imply rather that she would like to see the back of her.

'That was kind of you,' Eleanor replied, taking the words at their face value.

'You have done so much to make us all comfortable—you and Gwen, of course,' said Miss Reynolds, smiling. 'We are very grateful to you.'

Torn between annoyance at being lumped together with the kitchen staff and amusement at the way in which Miss Reynolds sounded as if she were using the royal 'we', Eleanor simply answered, 'I was glad to have been able to help.'

'You must call and see us again,' the other said politely. 'Perhaps in the spring, when the weather is better.'

'I doubt if I shall still be here then,' Eleanor responded. 'I expect to be joining my father and his wife in a few weeks.'

'I should not really be issuing invitations yet, of course,' the other woman went on, with pretty bashfulness. 'I am hoping that I shall be able to persuade Chris to see a doctor I know. He has had much success with people who have sustained such injuries.'

'Do you think that Chris will go?' Eleanor asked her.

Miss Reynolds smiled smugly. 'If *I* ask him, I am sure that he will,' she replied. 'The treatment that the doctor recommends involves living in a warmer climate, so perhaps this time next year, we shall be spending Christmas in Italy.'

'That should certainly be warmer,' Eleanor agreed. 'Well, if you will excuse me, I must finish getting my things together.' Miss Reynolds gave a nod, which looked very much a signal of dismissal, and glided on along the corridor and down the stairs. Eleanor watched her departure, thinking to herself, she'll ruin him, and there isn't a thing I can do about it.

She entered her room to find Gwen doing the packing. 'Breakfast's all done, miss, and I've put everything out ready for Broome to do for the rest of the day. He could hardly make a mistake, given the instructions he's got, so they should eat properly for today, at least.'

Eleanor sternly repressed a feeling of guilt at taking Gwen away. 'I don't suppose they'll starve,' she replied.

'Of course not, miss,' Gwen agreed. 'But I'll be sorry to think of Mr Cherry eating poor food. And Mr Hurst,' she added, almost as an afterthought.

'I thought you likened Mr Hurst to the devil incarnate,' said Eleanor.

'Maybe he's not so bad, miss, if Mr Cherry stays with him. I've just finished this, so may I go down to the kitchen to say goodbye to Mr

Cherry and the others?'

'Certainly,' Eleanor replied, wondering whether Clay ought to look to his laurels if he was not to find himself usurped in Gwen's affections by Hurst's capable valet.

Gwen had done an efficient job as usual, and packed everything, even down to the drawing which Hurst had done for Christmas and which was now safely in the trunk. Feeling an unaccountable urge to look at it again, Eleanor went to the trunk to open it, but before she could do so there was a knock at the door and Mrs Hulce came in.

'I just thought I would come and see if you needed any help, but you seem to have done everything.'

'I will have to correct you there,' Eleanor replied ruefully. 'Gwen has done everything. I do apologize for taking her away, but I really could not do without her.'

'Of course not,' Isobel acknowledged. 'Are you to make a long stay with Mr and Mrs Carlisle?'

'I'm not sure,' Eleanor admitted. 'That depends partly on the weather and partly on what guests have been gathered together for my amusement.'

'Will the gentleman with whom you have an understanding be there?' Isobel asked diffidently.

'What gentleman?' Eleanor asked, honestly puzzled.

'You said that you had an attachment,' Isobel replied.

'Did I?' queried Eleanor. Then she blushed as she remembered the conversation. 'Oh, that. It's nothing really. He doesn't actually . . . that is, he never thought of me in that way, and I . . . that is . . . look, can we just forget the whole matter?'

'Why yes, yes of course,' answered Isobel looking a little puzzled herself.

A short time after this, Isobel went back downstairs, and Eleanor followed her not long afterwards. She had only just reached the bottom of the stairs when there was a knock at the door, and Cherry, who happened to be crossing the hall at the time, opened it to reveal Mr Carlisle standing on the doorstep. He came in, and at the sight of his niece, his rather pale, thin face flushed with pleasure. 'Eleanor, my dear! How lovely to see you! We have delayed Christmas on your behalf!'

Eleanor hurried forward to kiss him on the cheek. 'I hope you weren't too worried about me,' she said.

'No, not at all,' he replied. 'We were concerned naturally, but had every confidence in your good sense and that of your groom and driver.'

'We were fortunate,' Eleanor told him. 'Although the coach came to grief, we managed to walk here and get help. But come, I must take you to Mr Hurst, who has been my kind host over the past few days.'

'I have heard of Mr Hurst but have not met him,' Mr Carlisle informed her. 'I shall be glad to make his acquaintance.'

Eleanor led the way into the salon, where the rest of the little party had gathered. Playell and Hurst were playing chess, Mrs Hulce was trimming a collar with some of the new lace that Eleanor had given her for Christmas, and Miss Reynolds was hanging over the back of Hurst's chair to observe his next move. They all turned to look at the newcomers and, as on a previous occasion, Eleanor felt like an outsider. Then the feeling passed as Playell rose to make his bow, and Hurst made the familiar gracious inclination of his head, as Eleanor introduced her uncle to those present.

'I am indebted to you, sir,' Mr Carlisle said to Hurst as he took the chair that his host indicated. 'Mrs Carlisle and I have no children of our own, and this young lady is very dear to us.'

'I am sure she is,' Hurst replied politely. 'You will forgive me for not rising, sir, but as no doubt you have heard, I am sadly incapacitated.'

'I have heard it, and regret that I have not called upon you sooner,' answered Mr Carlisle. 'But as you know, we are comparative newcomers to the district.'

'Do you have time to join us in a glass of wine before you leave?' Mrs Hulce asked. Out of the corner of her eye, Eleanor noted that Miss Reynolds was looking decidedly put out. She wondered whether anyone had told her that Hurst's sister was to remain in residence. Nothing that Miss Reynolds had said had suggested that she was privy to this information. If she were really as intimate with Hurst as she pretended, would he have failed to inform her about his plans for his sister? For the first time since she had heard Miss Reynolds speaking to Hurst the previous night, she felt her spirits lift, but could not entirely understand why.

So absorbed was she in these thoughts that Playell had to ask her twice if he might pour wine for her. Her uncle, she discovered, had accepted, saying that it would take a little while for her belongings to be collected from her room. Her room! It would not be hers now for very much longer.

In a very short time, it seemed, her luggage had been brought down, the wine was finished, and it was time to leave.

'There is no need for you to go to the door, Chris,' Miss Reynolds said protectively. 'You must not sit in a draught. Mr Carlisle and Miss Carruthers will not mind if you say goodbye to them here.'

'But I shall mind very much,' Hurst replied pleasantly. 'Owen, will you drive?'

'With pleasure,' Playell answered. He manoeuvred the chair into the hall, and the whole company followed, Miss Reynolds and Mrs Hulce bringing up the rear.

Eleanor turned to them first saying, 'It has been a pleasure to meet you. I hope that the remainder of your stay is enjoyable.'

'Thank you, I am sure it will be,' Miss Reynolds replied smugly. Eleanor felt sure that she would have liked to add the words: *now that you've gone.*

'I, too, have enjoyed your company, Eleanor,' Mrs Hulce said warmly. 'I hope that you will permit me to call on you as soon as the weather improves.'

'Please do,' Eleanor replied. She turned to Owen. 'Kindly beat Chris at chess, for my sake,' she said. 'He always wins when he plays against me.'

'As indeed he should,' Miss Reynolds put in. 'Chess is hardly a lady's game, after all.'

Eleanor laughed merrily. 'You would agree very well with my father,' she answered. 'He has often said the same.'

'Only when you beat him,' her uncle pointed out.

'The beauty of the whole situation, Miss Reynolds, lies in the fact that it was my father who taught me, so he does not really have a leg to stand on,' Eleanor explained.

Miss Reynolds did not say anything, but merely smiled politely. Playell laughed, however, as he raised her hand to his lips.

'I'll do my best to thrash him very thoroughly

on your behalf,' he laughed. 'We shall miss you, Eleanor. Your company has been enlivening.'

She then turned to her host. He smiled at her, his eyes twinkling, then glanced upward. He was sitting immediately beneath the kissing bough. 'You must pay the penalty before you leave, Eleanor.'

She smiled, then bent over and kissed him on the cheek. The memory of the very different kiss that they had shared the previous evening was in both their minds. 'Goodbye, Chris,' she said.

'Goodbye, Nell,' he replied in a lower tone, his smile suddenly vanishing. 'God keep you.'

As they hurried out into the fresh air, Eleanor hoped that her uncle would believe that it was the cold that was making her eyes sting. It was a far more likely explanation than the real one, namely, that his niece was crying because she had just said goodbye to a dyed-in-the-wool rake, with whom, as she had only just realized, she had very foolishly fallen head over heels in love.

CHAPTER THIRTEEN

Eleanor's welcome at Highbridge House was everything that she could have hoped. As soon as the carriage drew up outside the front door,

Mrs Carlisle came hurrying out on to the step, her face wreathed in smiles. She was very like her brother, Eleanor's father, and consequently very like Eleanor herself in feature, although whereas brother and sister shared the same dark hair colour, Eleanor had inherited her thick, wheat-coloured hair from her mother.

'Eleanor dearest!' the older lady exclaimed. 'At last! We have been so worried about you!'

'Really, Aunt June?' she replied in an amused tone, stealing a glance at her uncle before walking up the steps to embrace her aunt. 'And here was my uncle telling me how much you were both comforted by thinking about how sensible I was!'

Mrs Carlisle enveloped her niece in a loving embrace. 'Of course we knew that you would be sensible,' her aunt assured her, as she led her into the house. 'But however sensible one is, there are always accidents that occur. Think of your carriage's broken wheel, for example! If I have said it once, I have said it fifty times; what a pity you were not just a little nearer when it occurred, then you would have walked to this house rather than to Mr Hurst's residence.'

'There is no guarantee that I would have done so,' Eleanor replied, flushing, no doubt, from the effects of coming from the cold atmosphere into the warm house. 'Remember that Gwen and I do not know this countryside well. We could easily have wandered the wrong way in the dark.'

'Very true,' her aunt responded. 'In fact, when one thinks about it, you were exceedingly fortunate to have found any kind of shelter.'

'And are you pleased with your new home?' Eleanor asked as she stood in the hall admiring the classical beauty of the light-coloured marble and black-and-white checked floor.

'It hardly seems new to us now,' her aunt replied. 'Of course, I had forgotten that this is your first visit here. You must tell us what you think when you have seen the whole of it. But for now, come upstairs and let me show you to your room, so that you can put off your outdoor things.' She led her niece up the wide, white-stone stairs and into a corridor lined with pictures all of which were landscapes from foreign climes. 'You will remember your papa's gifts over the years,' Mrs Carlisle said smiling. 'I have had them all hung here together and I think that they look well in this setting.'

'I hope you won't guess what your Christmas present from Papa is from the shape of the parcel,' Eleanor remarked with a rueful grin.

'If it is another picture, then I could not be more delighted,' replied her aunt positively. She opened a door which led into one of the rooms off the corridor. 'We have put you in the green bedchamber this time,' she said by way of explanation. 'There is another room that is prettier, but it has two outside walls, so we think you will be warmer in here.'

'It's lovely,' Eleanor responded, looking round. 'Before we could occupy the rooms at Mr Hurst's house, we had to clean them first.'

'How extraordinary,' her aunt responded. 'Does Mr Hurst not keep any servants, then?'

'Very few,' Eleanor replied as she took off her cloak, bonnet and gloves. 'He has lived a solitary life since his accident.'

'Oh yes, I recall. It was a shocking affair. Not that I was surprised when something dreadful happened. They were both in a towering rage when they left the ball.'

Eleanor turned to stare at her aunt. 'You were there that evening? I did not think that you were. Uncle said that he had never met Mr Hurst.'

'No, we did not meet him, or his wife,' Mrs Carlisle confirmed. 'It was quite a big occasion; they had not been in the country for very long, and we were only visiting in the area at that time. I quite thought that he would murder her, the way that he was looking at her. Then of course she did die as a result of the accident. There were some who were very ready to say that it was a judgment upon him, for he had committed murder in everything but name.'

'What nonsense!' Eleanor exclaimed in a heated tone. 'No one could possibly have arranged such an accident as that.'

'Exactly so, my dear,' Mrs Carlisle responded, looking at her niece curiously.

Not wanting to make her aunt suspicious by championing her former host any further, Eleanor said, 'Enough of Mr Hurst. Have you been very dull over Christmas, or have I missed a lot of parties?'

'Neither really,' Mrs Carlisle replied. 'We have a few guests staying, but we have been quite quiet. As you know, because of the weather there has been no chance for anyone to come or go.'

'Do I know them?' Eleanor asked, as she got up from the dressing-table having tidied her hair.

'I believe so,' her aunt replied. 'Mr and Mrs Court are here, with their son and daughter. You will remember Mrs Court, I'm sure.'

'Oh yes. Didn't the two of you come out together?'

'That's right. Then we also have Captain and Mrs Richards, and they have brought Captain Richards's brother Henry with them. So we shall be a comfortable number around the table.'

'I hope they won't all expect Christmas presents,' Eleanor said devoutly. 'I have already given away any extra items that I had with me to Mr Hurst and his guests.'

'Oh no, you do not need to concern yourself,' Mrs Carlisle assured her. 'When we gave out our gifts on Christmas Day, I explained that they were from you as well as from ourselves. How many guests were staying with Mr Hurst apart from yourself, my dear?'

'There were three others,' Eleanor responded. 'A friend of Mr Hurst's named Playell, Mrs Hulce, who is a widow and Mr Hurst's sister, and a friend of hers named Miss Reynolds.'

'What a blessing that they were there,' her aunt said as they went back downstairs. 'I dread to think what damage might have been done to your reputation had you been obliged to stay there unchaperoned.'

Eleanor wisely decided not to say anything about the time that she had spent at Glade Hall before the others arrived, and also determined to have a word with Gwen about being similarly discreet on the subject. Instead, she simply observed, 'Surely there would have been no harm done. After all, the poor man cannot get up out of his chair.'

'I daresay,' her aunt replied rather tartly. 'But a rake is always a rake, you know.'

Remembering how Hurst had seized her and pulled her on to his lap, Eleanor silently concurred with this view.

They descended the stairs and Eleanor found herself reflecting how much this house differed from Glade Hall. It was a comparatively new property, having been built approximately thirty years before, and the paintwork and furnishings were all clean, bright and in good condition. She could be certain of every modern comfort, she decided.

'Did you sigh, my dear?' her aunt asked her.

Eleanor blushed. 'I'm afraid I did not sleep well last night,' she said truthfully. 'I was worrying whether I would be able to get to you today or not.'

'Well, now you are here and all worries and discomforts are at an end.' Mrs Carlisle beamed.

Would that that were really so, Eleanor thought to herself ruefully.

When they arrived back downstairs, all the party were assembled ready for luncheon. Eleanor recognized Mrs Court straight away, but she had not seen Miss Catherine Court for some years, and discovered that the rather plump, awkward child of five years before had developed into a lively, buxom eighteen-year-old, who was clearly setting her cap at Henry Richards. Mr Richards, who was a clergyman, seemed gratified by this interest, and Eleanor wondered whether they would make a match of it. Certainly, Mrs Court did not appear to be disapproving.

She recognized Captain Richards, for he had at one time been stationed as military attaché at one of the embassies in which her father had served. His wife was small and dainty, with hair as sandy as that of her husband. After lunch, she and Eleanor sat together for a

216

while, and the captain's lady divulged the interesting news that she was expecting their first child.

'Are you hoping for a boy or a girl?' Eleanor asked her.

'I don't really mind,' Mrs Richards confessed. 'Andrew says that he is hoping for a girl, but I don't believe him.'

'It's true,' the captain protested as he joined them. 'I would like to have a girl as pretty and dainty as her mama.'

Mrs Richards blushed. 'But to whom would you leave your presentation sword in that case?'

'We would just have to hope for a boy next time,' he answered blandly. Then, leaning closer to his wife with the intention that nobody else should hear, he added, 'The fun's in the trying!'

Eleanor did overhear and tried not to blush. For some reason, his whispered words brought to her mind the time when she had sat with Hurst in his bedchamber, and he had kissed her.

Luckily for her, diversion soon arrived in the form of Mr Felix Court, Catherine's older brother, who wandered over, saying: 'I have been trying to recall how long it is since we last met, Miss Carruthers. Can it really be five years?'

'Why yes, I believe so, Mr Court,' Eleanor replied. 'I hope that you are not going to say that the years have not been kind to me.'

'By no means!' he replied, laughing. 'To me, you look exactly the same, which is why I find it impossible to believe that it has been so long.'

'In that case, I forgive you,' she answered, smiling up at him. He was a fresh-faced young man of about her own age, slender, with wavy light-brown hair and warm brown eyes.

'Mrs Carlisle tells me that you have been travelling around with your father, but that he has now married again.'

'Yes, that is so,' Eleanor agreed. 'I have a charming stepmama, who has made my father very happy.'

Mrs Richards got up to go to speak to her hostess, Mr Court took her place next to Eleanor on the sofa, and for a few minutes, the two of them chatted about some of the places that they had both visited.

'I hope to go to St Petersburg before long,' Felix said eventually. 'I am told that it is very beautiful.'

'It certainly is,' Eleanor agreed. 'I was talking with Mr Hurst about St Petersburg only a short time ago.' She was pleased with herself for not blushing at the mention of his name.

'Oh yes, your aunt mentioned that you had been obliged to accept his hospitality,' the young man answered. 'That was an awkward business.'

'Awkward? Why so?' Eleanor asked

defensively.

'Why, because you were not expected,' Felix replied in reasonable tones.

'Oh ... oh yes, of course,' Eleanor responded, colouring as she had not done at Hurst's name. 'It was a little difficult at first, perhaps, but my servants were able to help, and so we all managed. And that reminds me of something. Aunt June?'

Mrs Carlisle, who had just been ringing the bell for more tea, turned around at the mention of her name. 'My dear?'

'Mr Hurst has no one to cook for him, and he asked me to make enquiries in the district. Do you know of anyone who might be available to go to work for him?'

'I don't know of anyone myself, but Lamb might know,' she replied, referring to her butler.

'No one to cook at Christmas!' exclaimed Mrs Court. 'Why, whatever did you do?'

'It was quite simple,' Eleanor answered. 'Gwen, my abigail, is an excellent cook, so she prepared the meals whilst I was there. But naturally I could not leave her behind.'

'I don't suppose you would have dared to do so, in such a household as that,' Mrs Court replied, pursing her lips.

'Oh Miss Carruthers, was it very exciting?' Miss Court asked. 'Was he terribly wicked? It must have been thrilling to stay in the house of a—'

'Catherine!' exclaimed Mrs Court before her daughter could finish her sentence. 'Kindly hold your tongue!'

Eleanor was grateful for the interruption which gave her time to take a deep breath and avoid leaping too obviously to Hurst's defence. 'It was not particularly exciting,' she replied in matter of fact tones. 'Mr Hurst is an invalid now, and does not keep late hours; and the party was quite small.'

'Rather a change for him, then,' remarked Mr Court, a tall man with his son's wavy hair and brown eyes. 'Time was when the place would have been full of—'

'Paul!' said Mrs Court in reproving tones.

'I was only going to say "guests",' Mr Court replied indignantly. 'How long is it since he had his accident, Miss Carruthers?'

'About six months, I believe,' Eleanor replied.

'Didn't he kill his wife?' uttered Catherine in hushed tones.

'She was killed in the accident which injured him as well,' Eleanor corrected firmly.

Moments later, the tea-tray was brought in, and it seemed as if the subject had been dropped, as the party split up and people started chatting amongst themselves. Eleanor took her place in a chair by the window, where she was approached by Captain Richards.

'Forgive me, Miss Carruthers, but there is something I would like to ask you; it's a matter on which you may be able to enlighten me.' She indicated the window-seat which was just beside her, and he took his place there. 'I wonder, ma'am, whether you had the chance of inspecting Mr Hurst's stables?' Her expression must have been very surprised for he laughed, and went on: 'Yes, it is an absurd question. Of course you did not go inspecting the stables in the depth of winter. But did you hear, perhaps, whether Mr Hurst has disposed of his greys?'

'You are right, Captain Richards, I certainly did not go anywhere near the stables,' Eleanor told him, smiling. 'But I can tell you that Mr Hurst's greys are still in his possession. He mentioned them in my hearing.'

'Surely he can't drive them now.'

'I see no reason why he should not,' Eleanor replied, trying not to feel irritated. 'His hands were not affected by his accident.'

'No, but—' Richards began, then he stopped, perhaps sensing some of her disapproval. 'Oh well,' he went on, 'they do say that a pair or a team of horses is only as good as the man who drives them, and Hurst was one of the best.'

'Really?' uttered Eleanor curiously.

'Oh, undoubtedly,' the captain replied. 'I saw him take part in a race once. He was competing against Colonel Warrener, driving his greys against the colonel's chestnuts. I've never seen anyone so cool. He hardly used the whip, and such light hands!'

'How extraordinary,' she mused.

'Why so?'

She considered for a moment before speaking, then, concluding that it could not possibly be a confidential matter, answered: 'After the accident, his horses showed every sign of having been treated to a dose of the lash.'

'You do surprise me,' answered the captain. 'Perhaps he was in a foul mood.'

'Yes, perhaps,' agreed Eleanor. But it did not seem to be a very satisfactory explanation.

*   *   *

Once the thaw had begun, it continued steadily, and soon it became possible for members of the house party to explore the grounds, as long as they kept to the paths. The gardens became more picturesque than ever as tiny streams were transformed into torrents.

The party that Mrs Carlisle had assembled was a congenial one. None of the gentlemen was a rake, and all of the ladies were too good-natured to be competitive. There was only one reason why Eleanor should find herself thinking back nostalgically to the time that she had spent at Glade Hall. When she found her thoughts straying too much to its master, she tried to divert them into other channels. To think sentimentally about him could not possibly do her any good. He had the wench that Playell had brought him for Christmas, and was probably as happy with the situation as was Miss Reynolds herself. She ought to be glad for them both. She ought to be, but she wasn't. She'll ruin him, she told herself exasperatedly, and not for the first time. He needs to be encouraged to do the things that are within his power, not wrapped up in a blanket and slobbered over!

Very often, she found her mind going back to the time that she had spent with him before the others had arrived. How companionable they had been! It had been over that time that they had spent together that her love for him had grown, and there had been times when she had been sure that her feelings were in a fair way to being returned. Then Miss Reynolds had arrived, and soon afterwards, the weather had changed, giving Eleanor no reason to stay. Miss Reynolds had remained, however, and was probably even now worming her way into Hurst's affections, establishing her place with him. The problem was that Eleanor could not see what she could do about it.

CHAPTER FOURTEEN

After Eleanor had left Glade Hall, Miss Reynolds sighed and said, 'Well, thank goodness for that.'

'Thank goodness for what, my dear?' Hurst asked. His tone was bland, but there was something in his eye that made Patricia weigh her words.

'To be among old friends, of course,' she replied innocently, her eyes wide open. 'They say there is no friend like an old friend, don't they? However agreeable Miss Carruthers might have been—'

'And she was very agreeable,' put in Mrs Hulce.

'—we do not know her very well,' Miss Reynolds concluded.

'Well, for my part, I would be very glad to know her better,' said Playell. Then he looked at Isobel, coloured, tugged at his cravat, cleared his throat and added, 'As a friend, of course, that goes without saying.'

Miss Reynolds watched this little bit of byplay and gave a brittle laugh. 'You see what I mean,' she said lightly. 'Miss Carruthers clearly sows dissent wherever she goes. What do you think, Chris?'

Hurst stared at her for a moment, then said, 'I do trust that Gwen organized the kitchen before she left. The thought of returning to Broome's cooking is too horrible to be borne.'

This was only the first of a number of barbed comments concerning Eleanor Carruthers that proceeded from Miss Reynolds's lips over the next few days. As if by arrangement, Isobel and Owen seemed to take it in turns to say something in Eleanor's defence. Hurst's response was to say nothing about her at all in Patricia's hearing. He and Playell did go shooting again on two occasions. Whilst down by the lake, their talk was all of the activity upon which they were engaged. As they were coming back on the second occasion, however, Playell ventured to say, 'I'm glad you've begun to take part in normal activities again. It was Eleanor Carruthers who suggested it, you know.'

'I had guessed,' Hurst replied. 'She has always had an interest in rehabilitating me.' Playell almost said that he thought that perhaps there was a personal reason for Eleanor's interest, but something told him to keep his counsel, and he contented himself with a grunt. In a moment or two, he was rewarded when Hurst said, 'Do you think I could drive again?'

'I don't see why not,' Playell answered, barely repressing a whoop of delight. 'It would be a pity not to make use of those new gloves.'

Their expedition had been a morning one, and consequently, when they returned to the house, Patricia had not yet left her chamber. Isobel was downstairs, however, and she had prepared a hot toddy for the men to enjoy after their chilly outing.

The sight of her pouring out the steaming liquid reminded Hurst of how Eleanor had performed the same task on a previous occasion. He remembered how she had massaged the warmth back into his legs and he smiled reminiscently.

'What are you smiling at?' Isobel asked him. Playell was still in his room and Cherry had left them, so Hurst told her exactly what Eleanor had done.

'It was purely out of kindness, of course,' he concluded, taking a sip of his hot toddy.

'Fiddlesticks!' Isobel replied. He stared at her. 'Well, of course she was being kind,' Isobel qualified, 'but I am sure that there was more to it than that.'

'There wasn't,' Hurst answered. 'Remember that she already has an attachment. You yourself told me so.'

'Yes, that was what she said earlier. But on the day when she left here, I taxed her with it, and I could swear that she had made the whole thing up.'

'Made it up? But why the deuce should she do that?'

His sister coloured. 'I had said something to the effect that Owen might be interested in her, and I think that she guessed that ... well. . . .'

'I see,' Hurst responded thoughtfully. 'So you think that she is unattached after all.'

She looked directly at him. 'I think that she is probably as unattached as you are.'

'Bella,' he said, so gravely that she hurried to kneel by his chair, and took his hand. 'Bella, if

226

a man . . . if Owen was . . . would you? Could you?' He fixed her gaze with a look of painful intensity.

She squeezed his hand. 'Yes, of course I could; if I loved him.'

There was a long silence, then he said; 'Bella, can you find out where Cherry put my driving-gloves?'

*   *   *

About a week after Eleanor's arrival at Highbridge House, on the finest day that they had yet had, all the gentlemen went out shooting. Miss Court and Mrs Richards both went into the library to write letters, whilst Mrs Carlisle, who had a headache, went back to bed, leaving Eleanor and Mrs Court to entertain one another. Eleanor was just describing the gown that her stepmother had worn for her wedding when the butler came in with a note addressed to Miss Carruthers. After a brief 'excuse me' Eleanor opened the note and read it.

My dear Eleanor,
You see, I have taken your advice and have driven myself here. Pray let me show you my skill. I promise I shan't overturn you.
                        Hurst

'Oh, good heavens!' Eleanor exclaimed,

227

suddenly feeling sick. 'Mr Hurst is here to take me for a drive!'

'There is no need to go if you do not wish to do so,' Mrs Court replied soothingly. 'In any case, you are not dressed for driving.'

Eleanor stared at her. Of course, Mrs Court was not aware of how acute was her fear of horses. She probably thought that she, Eleanor, was simply wary of going on an outing with a notorious rake. 'That does not matter,' she replied. 'Of course I must go.'

She hurried upstairs to get ready, deliberately forcing her mind to focus on the clothes that she was to wear, the coldness of the day, the pictures on the wall, Mr Hurst himself, anything to stop herself from thinking of having to climb up into the carriage and sit looking down at the animals that she had feared for more years now than she cared to remember. She would have given anything not to have to go; but she had encouraged Hurst to drive again—she had given him gloves for Christmas, for goodness sake!—and she had said that if he went driving, she would go with him. Now she was going to have to make good her words, and any hesitation on her part would be put down by him to reluctance to be driven by a man who could not walk. She had been longing to see him again ever since she had walked out of the front door of Glade Hall. Now she had her chance. She could only wish with all her heart that it had come in another way.

As soon as she was warmly dressed she hurried downstairs as fast as she could. The sooner she got up into that curricle, the sooner she would be able to get down again, then the ordeal would be over.

When she got outside, she found that the curricle was waiting at the door, with the groom standing at the horses' heads. Even Eleanor could see that they were beautiful creatures; but she looked away from them as quickly as possible, and up at Mr Hurst who was sitting in the driver's seat. He was wearing a tricorne hat and a warm, caped greatcoat, and he had a rug over his knees. Anyone who was unaware of his disability would not have been able to detect that there was anything the matter with him.

He grinned down at her. 'Good morning, Eleanor,' he said cheerfully. 'You see, I am putting my new gloves to good use.'

'Yes. Good morning,' she replied, her voice sounding a little shaky despite her best efforts.

'I'm afraid I can't help you up,' he said, looking at her a little curiously. 'However, if Brewer will leave their heads, I'll undertake to hold them steady whilst he gives you a hand. I've taken the edge off them, so they're not too fresh.'

'Very well,' she replied. She had fully intended to move. She told herself firmly that all she had to do was to put one foot in front of the other in order to walk forward; but somehow, although she knew in her mind that that was what she needed to do, she suddenly seemed to have become rooted to the spot.

'Well, are you coming or not?' Hurst asked her, with a slight edge to his tone.

'Yes, of course,' she said. In her determination not to remain where she was, she moved a little too hastily. Brewer left the horses' heads at that moment and came towards her; and the horse nearest to her, catching sight of her quick movement out of the corner of its eye, tossed its head. Eleanor gasped, her face turned white, and she stepped back shaking her head. 'No; no, I can't; I'm sorry.'

Hurst's face took on a stony look. 'You didn't mean it,' he said slowly. 'You were lying to me, weren't you? You don't trust me. You're like all the rest. Your pretty lips are full of promises, but when it comes down to it, you simply have nothing to give. Your word means nothing.'

'No,' she said. 'No, it's not like that.' She might have stepped forward again, despite her fears, but the tension in Hurst's voice and his hands had communicated itself to his high-bred pair. They began to move restlessly and she shrank back.

'Damn you, Eleanor,' he said, his voice not quite steady. 'Damn you for making me hope that . . . oh, damn it all to hell!'

He touched his horses, Brewer, seeing which way the wind was blowing, scrambled up behind, and they set off down the drive at the gallop. Eleanor began to run after them, not knowing what she could do, but desperate that Hurst should not leave thinking that she did not trust his skills. The curricle reached the bottom of the drive and, with scarcely a check, passed through the gateway which Mr Carlisle had said was too narrow as they had arrived a few days ago and which he was intending to widen at a later date. As the curricle disappeared from view, Eleanor saw something being flung out of it. She paused, then walked to the gateway, and without surprise, she found the gloves that she had given Hurst for Christmas lying on the ground.

She picked them up, and as she held them, she found that her eyes were filling with tears that would not be held back. What had she done? She had been entirely at fault in the whole business. If only she had been honest with Hurst from the very beginning and told him that she was afraid of horses, this situation would never have arisen. What could she do? How could she put this right?

So absorbed was she in her own thoughts that it was a moment or two before she realized that she was being addressed. 'I beg your pardon?' she said, turning to the woman who had come out of the cottage by the gate.

'I said, are you all right, miss? Would you

231

like to come in for a cup of tea and p'raps a sit down?' The woman was about twice Eleanor's own age, neatly and simply dressed, and her comely face wore an expression of anxious concern.

Eleanor thought for a moment. The last thing that she wanted to do at the moment was go back to the house and face Mrs Court. It would be far better to pretend that she had simply been for the drive and returned; but to do that, she would have to wait for a little while. Her aunt and uncle would never believe that she had gone driving, but she could tell them the truth privately; or at any rate, a version of the truth. Meanwhile, to spend half an hour in the gatekeeper's cottage would suit her very well.

'Thank you, I would like that very much,' Eleanor replied. 'I am just a little—overset at the moment.'

'Come this way, miss,' said the other. 'I've a good warm fire going and I've just made some scones. My Jem is mortal fond of scones.'

The smell of cooking was very inviting when Eleanor entered the little cottage and she was pleased to accept her hostess's invitation to take a seat by the fire, and wait while a fresh scone was buttered for her. 'You must forgive my manners, miss,' said the woman as she took the kettle from the hob and began to make the tea. 'I am Mary Cutler, and my husband works for your uncle.'

'You know who I am, then,' said Eleanor in some surprise.

'Oh yes, miss,' answered Mary cheerfully. 'I look after the gate, so I know everyone as comes and goes. Very anxious, they were, Mr and Mrs Carlisle, when you didn't turn up for Christmas. If he was down here with a lantern once, he was here a dozen times was the master, looking out for you. And my Jem set off down the road to look, but you couldn't be seen anywhere.'

'I'm sorry to have been so much bother to everyone,' Eleanor remarked.

'Oh, 'twasn't no bother, miss, and very glad we all were to hear that you were safe at Glade Hall.'

Eleanor sat in silence for a moment. It occurred to her that Mary Cutler must have been drawn outside by the sound of Hurst's curricle leaving. 'Mr Hurst came to take me driving just now,' she said.

'Yes, I did see him, miss. Is he able to walk now?'

'No, I fear he is not,' Eleanor answered.

'Well I'm glad he is driving again,' said Mary comfortably as she brought Eleanor's tea. 'A gentleman needs to occupy himself. Did you know as it was my Jem that found him and poor Mrs Hurst after the accident?'

'Of course,' Eleanor exclaimed, glad not to have to explain to Mary why she had clearly not been for a drive with Hurst. 'Mr Hurst told

233

me that himself, but I had forgotten.'

'That was when the estate belonged to Lord Summer,' Mary went on. 'We were living in another cottage then, but it wasn't in a good state, so Mr Carlisle moved us in here, and right glad I am that he did.'

Eleanor nodded, then paused for a short time before saying, 'You were telling me about the accident.' She did not want to seem impatient when the woman had been so kind.

'Oh yes. Fair shook my Jim up, it did, to find them lying there. Well, at first he thought that they were both stone dead; her lying so still, and him with that slash across his face. But it hasn't scarred him, has it, miss?'

'No, it hasn't,' Eleanor agreed, thinking of Hurst's handsome countenance. 'I wonder what made that mark?'

'My Jem thought it looked like the mark of a whip or a crop or such; but it couldn't have been that, for it was Mr Hurst as was driving. More tea, miss?'

'What? Oh, yes, yes please.'

They chatted for a little longer, but even whilst Eleanor was responding to Mary's cheerful remarks and making comments of her own, her mind was elsewhere. Eventually she made her excuses and got up to leave.

'You're very welcome to come again, miss, if you like,' Mary said. 'I'm often on my own as Jem and I haven't been blessed with children. I don't mind my own company but I should be glad to see you.'

Eleanor left, promising to return; but as she walked up the drive, her mind was immediately working on the idea that had come to her in Mary's cottage. Hurst had said that he had not been able to remember the events on the night of the accident. His face had born a mark that was similar to a lash from a whip. What if Mrs Hurst and not her husband had been driving that evening?

CHAPTER FIFTEEN

The more thought that Eleanor gave to the matter, the more she became convinced that she had hit upon the solution to the problem. There were two reasons for this conclusion, one more compelling than the other. The first was the mark on Hurst's face. No doubt those who had dealt with the aftermath of the accident had been preoccupied with Mrs Hurst's death, and her husband's inability to walk. The mark on his face would have been dismissed as a minor injury, probably caused by a branch catching him as he fell.

It was not possible to prove that things had not happened in this way; but Jem Cutler, the first on the scene, had told his wife that the mark had looked like a blow from a whip, and Jem was a countryman, used to seeing injuries inflicted by branches and the like.

This, intriguing though it was, seemed to Eleanor to be less significant than the evidence provided by the condition of Hurst's horses. Clay had told her that they had been distressed, as if ill-treated, when they had been returned to the stables; yet everything that she had ever heard had convinced her that Hurst was a skilful and considerate driver. He himself had said that his greys had never needed more than a very light hand. Suddenly, she recalled how he had driven away from her, hell for leather. He had been furiously angry, but he had driven to an inch round that corner, and she was certain that he had barely used the whip. He could not have been driving on the evening of the accident.

There was only one other possibility, and that was that Mrs Hurst must have been driving. If that were so, then it was she who had beaten the horses, caused the accident, crippled her husband and destroyed her own life and that of her unborn child. It seemed to Eleanor that Mr Hurst should at least be encouraged to consider this question. After all, he was the only person alive who knew the answer. If he could be brought to recall what had happened that night, and if those memories revealed that he had not been culpable in the matter of the accident, then perhaps he might find peace of mind over the whole incident.

The first thing to do, she decided, was to visit Glade Hall. It should be quite easy to persuade her aunt and uncle of the need for her to go. They were well aware of her fear of horses, and would understand that she would want to explain to Hurst why she had seemed to be so ungrateful. Then, once she was over there, she could put before him her theories about what might have happened on the night of the accident. The biggest problem would be that Aunt June would expect to chaperon her, and the last thing that she wanted to do was to make her explanation to Hurst in front of an audience, however sympathetic. It did occur to her that she might ask Captain Richards to take her. He had after all expressed an interest in Mr Hurst's horses. Her next thought was that since Hurst had supposed her to be doubtful of his driving skills, to turn up with a man eager to purchase his matched greys would be less than tactful.

In the event, her problem was solved in a quite unexpected way, for the following morning, as Eleanor and her aunt and some of the company were talking together in Mrs Carlisle's pretty cream drawing-room, the butler came in to announce Mrs Hulce, Miss Reynolds and Mr Playell.

Eleanor was surprised at the pleasure that it gave her to see them again. After all, she did not know any of them very well and she certainly did not care for Miss Reynolds. But for various reasons she had found herself thinking back to the time spent at Glade Hall with nostalgia. Furthermore, the arrival of these three people might easily provide the opportunity of arranging to see Hurst.

She introduced them to her aunt and to the others present, but when she fell into conversation with Isobel, she was surprised to find that lady to be rather reticent. Mr Playell, too, was a little distant in his manner, but Mrs Reynolds seemed to be much the same, and if anything a little more cordial than usual.

Mrs Carlisle sent for refreshments, and they were all sitting round talking generally when Mrs Hulce exclaimed in vexation. 'Oh dear, I seem to have caught some of my lace and I don't want it to tear. Eleanor, would you be so good as to take me to your room and help me to pin it up?'

Eleanor readily agreed, and took her guest upstairs. The two of them chatted generally on the way, but as soon as the door closed Isobel exclaimed, 'Eleanor, what on earth happened yesterday?'

Eleanor went a little pale. 'Yesterday?' she echoed.

'My brother went out driving for the first time since his accident,' Mrs Hulce said, pacing up and down. 'You should have seen his face when he left the house; so happy and full of hope. Then, in what seemed like no time, he returned with a face like thunder, almost

238

screaming to be got down from his curricle. He demanded that the carriage should be burned and the horses sold, and he has been drinking ever since. What did you do to him, Eleanor?' She held out her hands beseechingly.

There were two chairs set next to the fire. Eleanor showed her to one, then sat on the other. She took a deep breath. 'When I was five years old, my father's uncle, who was himself something of a hell-raiser, took me for a ride in his curricle. Mama and Papa were both out, and the servants were not determined enough to be able to stop him. He was drunk at the time, and I remember thinking what a long way up it was.' She found herself shaking and had to pause. 'Excuse me. We set off down the drive at what seemed to me to be a breakneck speed. Uncle was shouting and cursing at the horses, then turning to me and laughing and saying what fun it was. I still remember his great red mouth opened wide, and the noise of his laughter against the sound of the jingle of the harness.

'Then, when we had only been travelling a short time, he took a corner too fast, and I was thrown out. Luckily, there was a haystack close to the corner and I fell into that. Uncle halted the horses, cursing and swearing, and staggered round to their heads, but he must have frightened them, or startled them or . . . or something, because they reared up and felled him and . . . and I saw it all.' She covered her mouth with her hand as her voice quivered.

'Oh Eleanor, what a dreadful tale!' Mrs Hulce exclaimed.

Eleanor summoned up a wan smile. 'I am afraid of horses,' she admitted. 'I do not tell anyone unless I have to because most people seem to think that it is so stupid. I do myself. I cannot tell you how many times I have resolved to conquer this. After all, it makes life so inconvenient. I do not ride, and my relatives know that I can never travel in an open carriage whose design means that I am obliged to face the horses.'

'Then yesterday. . . .'

'Your brother came to ask me to drive with him. I had encouraged him to drive again, after all. I had even told him that I would go with him,' she added ruefully.

'I expect you thought that you would never be called upon to make good your words,' Mrs Hulce surmised.

'No indeed,' Eleanor agreed despondently. 'I just wanted to encourage him, to pull him out of that dark depression, and it seemed to me that it would be better for him to dwell on the things that he could still do, rather than the things that are denied him. When I told him that I would go out with him, I felt sure that I would have left this vicinity before the weather would be good enough for him to invite me for a drive. No doubt it was very foolish of me to make such a promise, but I did not reckon upon this sudden thaw.'

They were both silent for a time, then Isobel said 'I must confess that I came here with no very charitable thoughts towards you. But I did want to see whether there might have been some explanation. Now of course I understand why you reacted as you did. Chris does not. Do you want me to tell him?'

Eleanor shook her head. 'No, I must tell him myself, otherwise he may never understand. But I cannot tell him in front of a room full of people.'

Mrs Hulce thought for a moment. 'I have an idea,' she said. 'Suppose I suggest to Patricia that she and I should go shopping in Warwick tomorrow? Owen can go with us as our escort. We'll stay for luncheon, and come back in the afternoon. But meanwhile, you can tell your aunt that I have invited you to come to see us.'

'All right,' Eleanor agreed. 'I'll wait until we are alone, so that no one else will expect to come. If they do, I'll plead your brother's condition as an excuse.' She paused briefly, then said, all of a rush, 'Do you think that your brother will see me? He was so very angry.'

Isobel leaned forward and grasped hold of Eleanor's clasped hands with one of her own. 'I'm sure he will,' she said. 'I think that you are very special to him.'

Shortly after this, they went back downstairs, and soon the visitors were taking their leave.

In the event, she did not need to resort to any kind of subterfuge in making her arrangements for the morrow. Although Mrs Carlisle had a very keen sense of what was proper behaviour in a young woman, she was well aware that Eleanor's unusual upbringing had given her a greater amount of independence than most gently-bred single ladies enjoyed. 'Go by all means,' said Mrs Carlisle. 'You certainly owe Mr Hurst and his household some attention. Take Gwen with you. She, too, will be pleased to renew her acquaintance with the friends that she made there, no doubt.'

Once the weather had begun to improve, Clay and Briggs together with two other men from Mr Carlisle's stable had gone to investigate the problem with Eleanor's carriage. Once the wheel had been removed and replaced, the carriage had been brought back to Highbridge House, where it had been thoroughly dried out and polished, to bring it back to good condition after its prolonged stay in the wet. It was therefore in her own carriage, driven by Briggs and accompanied by Clay and Gwen, that Eleanor set off for Glade Hall the following morning. This was how the adventure had begun, she reflected.

It was not until the journey had started that she really began to feel nervous. Would Isobel have said anything to her brother about this morning's visit? How would Hurst receive her?

Might he even refuse her entrance? Would he listen to her recital of her fears, and would she be able to tell him about her suspicions concerning the night of his accident? Or would she be sent away with a flea in her ear before she had had a chance to say anything at all?

In order to take her mind off her anxieties about her reception, Eleanor decided to tell Gwen about her theory. Gwen listened carefully. 'Nobody said much about the accident while I was there, miss,' she said. 'But it seems to me that if a gentleman is one as cares about his horses, then he wouldn't never mistreat them, however angry he was.'

'That's what I thought,' Eleanor agreed.

On arriving at Glade Hall, Eleanor found that the coating of snow which had covered everything when she had last been there had completely vanished, and with it the fairy-tale prettiness which the snow had bestowed. It was clear that the house, and perhaps even more so the grounds, were in desperate need of attention. A woman's touch was definitely called for. Refusing even to think about the idea that she might like to be its mistress, Eleanor told herself firmly that it was a good thing that Isobel was to reside with her brother.

This time, instead of stumbling up to the door and fumbling for the door-knocker in the dark, Eleanor had Clay to run up the steps and beat a summons upon the door on her behalf, whilst she and Gwen alighted. It was not many minutes before Plaice came to the door.

'Good morning, Plaice,' said Eleanor pleasantly. 'Is your master within?'

'Oh, ay, he's within,' Plaice answered. His approach to visitors had not improved, Eleanor noticed. She sent her carriage round to the stables, and entered with Gwen following her, and Plaice hovering around them as if he did not know what to do.

'Is Cherry here?' Eleanor asked, taking off her bonnet and cloak and handing them to him. He looked as if he had no idea what to do with them, and Eleanor felt that she would not have been at all surprised to see him drop them in a heap on the floor.

'Yes, he's here.'

'Then will you fetch him, please? Gwen, you may go to the kitchens. I'll send for you when I need you.'

'Very well, miss.'

At that moment the door to the saloon opened and Cherry came out. 'Miss Carruthers,' he said, smiling in his usual restrained style. 'This is an unexpected pleasure.' So Isobel had not said anything about her visit, even to Cherry, Eleanor noted. She did not know whether to be glad or sorry.

'Thank you, Cherry,' she answered. 'How is Mr Hurst today?'

He paused. 'Not so well, miss. That is to say, his spirits are very low.'

'Is he in the salon?' He nodded. 'I'll go to see him. Cherry?'

'Yes, miss?'

'Wish me luck.'

He smiled. 'Of course, miss.'

On entering the salon, she found that Hurst was sitting in his usual chair by the fire. During her stay, she had become used to seeing his hair tied back neatly in deference to visitors. Today, it was hanging loosely about his shoulders, as it had done when they had met for the first time. He was wearing a dark coat with a matching waistcoat but no cravat, and his shirt was undone to halfway down his chest, revealing a shadowing of dark hair. In his hand was a glass of brandy.

'Good morning,' she said, as she moved forward and curtsied. She was rather proud of the way in which her voice did not tremble, despite her nervousness. He turned his head and stared at her, his face set.

'God in heaven, madam, will you never learn?' he said savagely. 'Or do you come with more plans for my rehabilitation, which you will be ready to applaud, as long as they don't involve you?' He turned away. 'But why should I blame you after all? How safe would you have been, driven by a cripple?'

With that, she ran forward and threw herself down beside his chair, grasping hold of his hand. 'It isn't that,' she said.

'Of course it is,' he replied, pulling his hand

245

away with such violence that she fell back on to the floor. 'Do you think I didn't see the fear in your eyes? I understand it; of course I do. But why did you say you would drive with me? Why did you ever allow me to hope?'

'Because I hoped that with you I might be able to overcome my fear,' she replied, not moving from the place where he had thrown her. 'Not fear of your driving; but a fear that I have had for nearly twenty years.'

'Don't lie to me,' he snarled.

'I'm not lying,' she answered, kneeling up again. 'It's horses I'm afraid of; any horses.'

He laughed. 'Horses? Don't be absurd!' At once he saw the change in her face. Now it was *he* who leaned down and grasped *her* wrist. 'Tell me,' he said intensely, his face serious.

As she had told his sister the previous day, Eleanor unfolded to Hurst the whole story of her uncle's foolishness and his death beneath the hoofs of his own horses. This time, as she finished the account, tears were running down her cheeks and to her surprise and embarrassment, she found herself weeping as she had not done for years.

Hurst pulled her close, and allowed her to sob against his chest. He did not normally have a lot of patience with female tears, but somehow Eleanor's were different. On other occasions he had wished heartily that a woman would stop crying because it was tiresome. Now, some part of him wanted her to carry on so that he would have an excuse to keep holding her.

When her sobs began to subside, she murmured, 'I beg your pardon. I don't know why I did that.'

'Perhaps because after it had happened, the right moment never came,' he suggested, taking out a fine lawn handkerchief which he handed to her for her use. 'Everyone's first concern was understandably the death of your uncle. Then after that, they were all so relieved that you were unharmed, that they wanted to forget the whole business as soon as possible, and tried to make you do the same. But what you really needed to do was talk about your fears and then confront them.'

'How do you come to be so wise?' she asked him.

'When I was a boy of about nine or ten, I took a fearful toss from my pony,' he told her. 'Of course, the ideal thing would have been for me to get straight back on him again, but unfortunately I broke my arm and wasn't able to ride for some weeks. To begin with, I didn't even want to go down to the stables but Brewer came to the house every day to find me.'

'Was that the same Brewer who is with you now?' Eleanor asked him curiously.

'The same. He couldn't have been more than a lad himself, but he fetched me, and even though I couldn't ride, he made me talk to my pony and to all the other horses. He made me realize that Bracken hadn't wanted to throw me any more than I'd wanted to fall. If it hadn't been for him, it might have taken me long enough to overcome my fear.' They sat in companionable silence for a few moments. Then gradually, Eleanor became conscious of rough warmth at her fingertips. She looked down and saw that her hand was tucked into the opening of his shirt, and all at once became aware she was sitting on his knee.

'Oh, good heavens,' she exclaimed blushing furiously, and she hurriedly scrambled to her feet.

He did not seek to detain her, nor did he make some flirtatious remark, but said, 'I think a breath of fresh air would do us both good. I'm going to ring for Cherry, but before I do, you might care to look in the mirror.'

She did so, and after giving a small shriek, which prompted a low chuckle from her host, she took a comb out of her reticule and began to tidy her hair. Realizing that Hurst was watching her, she turned to look at him as she was looping up one of the strands that had become loose. 'Beautiful,' he murmured, his eyes on her hair as he fastened up his shirt. She looked away quickly, suddenly feeling hot and flustered.

When she had tidied herself, Hurst rang a small bell which was on the table at his elbow, and Cherry came in response to its summons.

'Bring my outdoor things, would you?' said Hurst. 'Miss Carruthers and I are going out on to the terrace.'

'I'll go to find out where Plaice has put my bonnet and cloak,' Eleanor said. 'If you send for him, we'll probably be waiting until next Christmas.'

Elcanor found Plaice in the kitchen, where Gwen was holding court. It looked suspiciously as if she was taking over the planning of the evening meal. Plaice muttered about some folks not knowing their own minds, but went to fetch Eleanor's outdoor things as she had requested. When she returned to the salon, she found that Cherry was helping his master into his greatcoat.

When both Hurst and Eleanor were ready, Hurst asked Cherry to wheel him out on to the terrace and to the far end. Again, Eleanor noted that the grounds were neglected, unlike the house itself which was structurally in good condition.

'Yes, I know, I need a team of gardeners to do something about this,' Hurst sighed. Once they had reached the far end of the terrace, he nodded his thanks to Cherry, who withdrew. 'When the spring arrives I'll deal with it. To be truthful, up until very recently I didn't give a damn about the place, or indeed about anything else very much.'

The day was fine and bright, and Eleanor breathed in the fresh air, and closed her eyes the better to feel the sun. Moments later, she heard a sound which was enough to make them fly open again. Across the grass, she saw Brewer walking towards them and leading one of the team of horses which Hurst had been driving when he had come to Highbridge.

She turned to Hurst, her face white. 'What is this?' she asked him.

'He's beautiful, isn't he?' Hurst replied. 'I mean Mercury, of course, not Brewer.'

This remark forced a laugh out of her, despite her nerves. Her hand went to her throat. She could not take her eyes from the creature that was coming towards her; a creature which, however irrationally, seemed to symbolize all that she most feared. 'What . . . what do you intend?' she whispered. Her tone was faltering and uncertain.

'Why, just to introduce you, that's all,' Hurst replied. 'You don't have to ride him, or get up in a carriage behind him, or even get close enough to touch him, and he certainly can't get to you from there. All you have to do is look at him and get used to him. He really is very gentle, you know, and just as wary of you as you are of him.'

Cherry had pushed his master right up to the low balustrade, so that when Brewer came up to them with Mercury, Hurst could easily lean across and stroke the horse's nose. 'Well now, lad,' he said softly. 'Are you pleased to see me, eh?' The horse snorted, and nuzzled into

250

Hurst's hand. 'Is it true love, though, or is it this you're after?' He reached into his pocket and took out a piece of sugar. 'Here you are, then,' he said, with a chuckle in his voice as he held out the sugar on the flat of his hand.

Eleanor stood watching. She had taken a step back as Brewer had approached with the horse, but she had not run into the house. Later, looking back on the incident, she found herself admiring the way in which Hurst had chosen this spot, where she could see the horse clearly and yet feel absolutely safe behind the balustrade. Now, she could only stare as Hurst allowed Mercury to take the sugar, not roughly, but almost delicately, and then stroked his head.

'Come closer, Eleanor.' The little cameo which had been played out between man and horse had seemed so much something that she was witnessing and from which she was detached that Hurst's voice speaking to her came as something of a shock.

Rather than coming closer, Eleanor took a step back. 'I . . . no, I. . . .' she stammered.

'Trust me, Eleanor,' Hurst interrupted her. 'That's all I ask. He won't hurt you.'

She gulped. 'You mean, he won't hurt *you*,' she replied.

He chuckled. 'No, that isn't what I mean,' he answered. 'Horses are very much at our mercy, you know. We have far more power over their lives than they have over ours, despite what you witnessed that day. Come over here and show him that he has nothing to fear.'

This was an entirely novel notion. Nobody had ever really talked to her about her fears before. They had been accepted, sympathized with and catered for by her understanding family. But no one had ever tried to help her overcome them, and no one had ever suggested that horses might be nervous too.

She took a step closer. 'Do you mean that the horses ... my uncle ... he might have frightened them?'

'More than likely, I would have said,' Hurst replied in matter of fact tones. He was still stroking the horse, not looking at Eleanor, but praying that she would soon come closer. He desperately wanted her to overcome her fears, but not for anything would he keep one of his prized cattle standing for too long in the cold. He almost held his breath as he heard the rustling of her skirts which told him that she was coming closer. He had been afraid that by mentioning her uncle he had gone too far. 'Would you like to give him some sugar?' he asked.

'No,' she said quickly. 'But can I watch while you give him some more?'

'Of course,' Hurst replied. He took out a piece of sugar and held it out on the flat of his hand as before, and Eleanor watched in wonderment.

'Aren't you afraid he'll bite you?' she asked.

'Why would he do that?' he asked. 'He knows I'd never hurt him.' He patted the horse once again, then said 'Take him back now, Brewer, he's been out for long enough, and so have we, I think.' As the groom led the horse away, Hurst said 'Eleanor, my dear, would you be so good as to ask Cherry to take me inside?'

'But I could—' she began.

'No.' His voice was firm, even stern, in direct contrast to the gentle tones that he had been using when speaking to the horse. 'No, Eleanor,' he went on, his tone a little softer. 'You must leave me some pride, you know.'

She hurried inside to look for Cherry, but he was not in the salon, or in his master's bedroom. Forgetting the little handbell, she stepped out into the hall, but as she did so, the front door opened, and to her surprise and dismay, Miss Reynolds entered, to be followed by Isobel and Owen.

'I do not know when I have been more vexed,' Miss Reynolds was saying. 'All our plans spoiled!' At this point, she noticed Eleanor standing at the other end of the hall, and her face took on an expression that was far from pleased. 'Why, Miss Carruthers! What upon earth can have brought you here?'

'You came to call, but found that we were out, I expect,' Mrs Hulce interposed, hurrying forward to welcome Eleanor. 'Patricia is right that our expedition is spoiled—a tree across the road, if you please, making it necessary for us to turn back—but how fortunate that we did not miss you.'

'Yes indeed,' said Playell as he came forward. 'How are you, Eleanor?'

'I am well, thank you,' Eleanor responded, conscious in the back of her mind of Hurst waiting on the terrace. 'I have just come to find Cherry.'

'Where is Chris?' Miss Reynolds asked, having put her head around the salon door.

'He is on the terrace,' Eleanor replied. 'In fact, I had just come in—'

'On the terrace?' exclaimed Miss Reynolds. 'You left him on the terrace in this weather?' At that very moment, the door to the kitchens opened and Cherry appeared. 'Cherry!' Miss Reynolds exclaimed. 'Miss Carruthers has abandoned Chris on the terrace. We must rescue him at once!'

The two of them hurried away, and Eleanor was left standing with Isobel and Owen. She was very annoyed at having her actions misconstrued, but could not think what to say that would not make her sound as if she were finding excuses for herself.

Plaice came and relieved them of their outdoor things, and Mrs Hulce gave him instructions about bringing a hot toddy to the salon.

'Chris always did have the fair sex buzzing around him like bees round jam,' Playell observed as he escorted Eleanor into the room. 'I might have guessed that his disability would make no difference in that respect. In fact, it might even add to his attractions, as they will all now feel sorry for him.'

'I don't feel sorry for him,' Eleanor replied quickly.

'No, but then you are an exceptional woman,' he answered.

Cherry appeared pushing Hurst, who had taken off his outdoor things, and Miss Reynolds followed in their wake, a hairbrush and ribbon in her hand.

'Now, I am going to make you look more civilized,' she said playfully, advancing with the brush.

'Certainly not,' Hurst replied. 'Cherry will do that.'

'Spoilsport,' Miss Reynolds pouted. 'And I was so looking forward to brushing that beautiful hair of yours.'

'Yes, but if you did that you would be depriving Cherry of one of his favourite occupations,' Hurst replied, smiling.

'Very well, Chris dear,' responded Miss Reynolds, as she handed Cherry the brush. 'I shall just have to watch instead,' and she proceeded to do so in a very proprietorial way.

Eleanor was invited to stay for luncheon and did so, but Miss Reynolds took every opportunity to make it clear that she was now no longer a resident, just a visitor whom they would not expect to see again very soon.

As she travelled home, however, she reflected that despite the expectations of any of the people at Glade Hall, she would have to make another visit. There was a matter on which she had wanted to communicate with Mr Hurst and had not had the opportunity, and that was the business of who had been driving on the evening of his accident.

She thought about the time that she had spent on the terrace and the gentle way in which Hurst had spoken to the horse and fed it with sugar. More than ever, she was convinced that he could not have been the one who had lashed the horses with the whip on the evening of the accident.

She thought, too, about the way in which he had sought to help her overcome her fear. No one had ever tried to do such a thing before, but now that someone had, she could almost imagine that there might come a time when she would no longer be crippled by this awful disability which made her unable to participate in so many of the pleasures that others enjoyed. As they got down from the carriage, after a journey during which Eleanor had addressed not a single word to Gwen, she was suddenly struck by the novel idea that she was as disabled by her fears as was he through his accident. What a strange irony it would be if

256

he were to be the one to enable her to be whole again.

CHAPTER SIXTEEN

It was only a day or two later that Mr and Mrs Carlisle's visitors left, and not a moment too soon, for no sooner had they gone than Mrs Carlisle took to her bed with a high temperature. Mr Carlisle sent for the doctor, who diagnosed an infection, exacerbated by the excitement and extra work that having visitors had entailed.

'A period of rest and quiet will be the best cure,' he told Eleanor and her uncle as he enjoyed a glass of burgundy with them following the visit to his patient.

'All our visitors are gone now, so there is no need for her to do anything but rest,' Mr Carlisle responded.

A servant came in with a message for Mr Carlisle, asking him to attend his steward for a few moments in the book room, so he excused himself, leaving Eleanor with the doctor.

'For how long have you been the physician around here?' she asked him.

He thought for a moment. 'It must be twenty years, now,' he mused. 'Both my son and my daughter were born here, and my daughter is now married with a baby, so yes, I fancy it must be twenty years.'

'Do you attend the family at Glade Hall, or is that area covered by another doctor?' Eleanor asked. She would have liked to have approached the subject rather more indirectly, but she had no way of knowing for how long her uncle would be away, and there were questions that she wanted to ask.

'Yes, I attend that household. Why do you ask?'

She had not anticipated this question, but she had an answer ready. 'I was staying there over Christmas, and nearly had to have a doctor to see my maidservant.'

'I don't believe I have been to Glade Hall since last summer,' mused the doctor.

'That must have been because of Mr Hurst's accident,' Eleanor speculated.

He nodded. 'That was a bad business, last June. A very bad business.'

'Were you called to the scene?' Eleanor asked.

'I was indeed.'

'That must have been a shocking experience.'

'Dreadful, quite dreadful. I had attended Mrs Hurst from her childhood, when she was Miss Glade. She was always difficult, of course, but I would not wish such an end upon anyone.'

'Difficult?' prompted Eleanor.

The doctor thought for a moment. 'She had

258

a very uncertain temper,' he said eventually. 'When she lost it. . . .' He paused again. 'I have sometimes wondered. . . .' He looked at Eleanor shrewdly. 'Young lady, you will make me break my Hippocratic oath.'

Eleanor coloured. 'No indeed, I would not have you do such a thing for all the world,' she said.

'Well, I don't suppose my thoughts on the cause of the accident have anything to do with keeping a patient's confidences. I will tell you plainly, Miss Carruthers, that I have sometimes wondered whether Mrs Hurst so lost her temper whilst they were travelling that she caused her husband to lose control of the horses.'

The sound of footsteps was heard outside the door, and Eleanor said quickly, 'Doctor, may I come and talk to you further about this?'

'Of course. As long as you don't expect me to tell anyone else's secrets. Come tomorrow morning. I shall be in my dispensary, so you may collect some of your aunt's medicine at the same time.'

The village was within walking distance, so the following morning, Eleanor put on her outdoor clothes and stout boots and quietly slipped out unaccompanied, in order to see the doctor.

She had spent a little time pondering over all that she knew about Mr and Mrs Hurst and their accident, and she had then written some of the salient points down on a piece of paper to help her thinking.

The door of the doctor's house was opened by a parlourmaid who welcomed Eleanor, and invited her to come into the drawing-room, whilst she fetched the doctor from his dispensary. Eleanor accepted the girl's invitation to have a cup of tea, and stood looking out of the window into the back garden. It was well tended, showing that whoever looked after it had a liking for flower-beds.

'I hope you have not had to wait too long,' said the doctor from behind her as he came in. 'I was in the middle of preparing a mixture which I did not want to leave half-way through.'

'Not at all,' Eleanor replied. 'I have been looking at the garden.'

'I do a little when I can. My wife used to enjoy the garden and after she died five years ago, I began to take an interest in it myself. I find it helps to take my mind off my problems—and those of my patients.'

After the tea had arrived and Eleanor had poured at the doctor's request, he said: 'Now, young lady, in what way may I be of service?'

'You may recall that I told you I stayed at Glade Hall over Christmas,' Eleanor replied. 'This was rather forced upon me because of the dreadful weather.'

'Yes indeed, it was shocking,' the doctor agreed. 'Fortunately, I only had one lying-in to attend over Christmas, and that was in the village. Go on.'

'I became acquainted with Mr Hurst and his sister and their friends,' she went on. 'Naturally, I heard a certain amount about the accident, and there were a number of things about it that did not seem to me to make sense.'

'And what were those?' the doctor asked.

'Well, first of all, the condition of the horses. Apparently, they had been struck with a whip so that the marks stood out on their coats. But I have seen Mr Hurst with his horses, and I don't think he would ever do that. Those who work for him in the stables do not think so, either.'

'It does seem a little strange,' agreed the doctor. 'But when a man is angry, you know. . . .'

'But I have seen him driving them when he was very angry, and he did not take his temper out on his horses.'

'Indeed? When was this?'

Eleanor coloured. 'He came to take me driving a few days ago. I would not go with him, for reasons that I do not need to explain to you now. But he drove away in a temper.'

The doctor chuckled. 'Well, I am pleased to hear that he is taking up some of his old pursuits. But go on.'

Eleanor looked at her piece of paper. 'When he was found, he had a slash across his face. Did you come to any conclusions as to what had caused it?'

The doctor shook his head. 'To be honest with you, I was far more concerned with discovering if there were any other injuries not visible to the naked eye; and with attending to the correct disposal of Mrs Hurst's body. I suppose I put it down to his scratching his face on a branch as he fell.'

'Do you think it is possible that it might have been caused by a whip?' Eleanor asked carefully.

'A whip?' the doctor echoed in a startled tone.

'You see, I am wondering whether perhaps it was Mrs Hurst driving that night, rather than her husband.'

'It would certainly account for the treatment of the horses and for the mark on Mr Hurst's face,' the doctor agreed. 'But you are forgetting, Miss Carruthers, that the couple were seen leaving the event that they had attended, and those who saw them say that the gentleman was driving.'

'Well perhaps he allowed her to have a turn, in the hope of placating her,' Eleanor suggested.

'Perhaps,' the doctor agreed. He was silent for a time. 'Forgive me, ma'am, for speaking so plainly, for I do not know you very well, but why this acute interest in something that took place six months ago?'

Eleanor coloured. 'It is simply that I have heard more than one person say that Mr Hurst's injuries were a judgment upon him, for driving so irresponsibly. If it could be proved that he was not driving on that occasion, then at least that slur upon his reputation would be removed.'

The doctor nodded, and smiled at her understandingly. 'You have a passion for justice, I can see,' he said. 'But I must beg you, for your own sake, to think very carefully about what you are doing. There is no guarantee that Mr Hurst will ever walk again, and even if he does—'

Eleanor interrupted him, an astonished expression upon her face. 'There is a possibility that his injuries are not permanent, then?'

'Miss Carruthers, the mind can play strange tricks upon us. Probably science will never be able to understand it fully. There is no injury to Mr Hurst's spine or ... er ... limbs that I can discover. But for some reason, his mind will not permit him to walk.'

'This is very strange,' Eleanor murmured.

'It is the first case of its kind that I have experienced, although I have read of such things,' he agreed.

'Does Mr Hurst himself know of this?' she asked him.

'Oh yes, he knows, as does the estimable Cherry, who massages his master's limbs every day, so that the muscles will not waste away. Believe me, my dear, Mr Hurst's condition is no pretence. Some power is operating very strongly upon his mind, preventing him from walking. It is my belief that he will never do so until some other power gives him a more compelling reason for doing so.'

Eleanor sprang to her feet, her eyes shining. 'But do you not see,' she said, 'that the compelling reason might be the disclosure that the accident was not after all his fault? He must be told.' She leaped up as if she might immediately set off for Glade Hall, but the doctor laid a hand on her arm.

'Wait,' he said.

'But—' It was all that Eleanor could do not to shake off his restraining hand.

'I implore you, Miss Carruthers; think carefully. We know already that Mr Hurst's mind has worked powerfully upon his physical condition. Who can say that the shock to his system of making such a discovery in the wrong way would not do more harm than good? We must be very cautious.'

Some of the light died out of her eyes. 'Yes. Yes, you are right. But how to tell him....' Her gaze fell upon the paper that she had brought with her, with her notes written upon it. 'A letter!' she exclaimed. 'I shall write him a letter.'

'An excellent notion,' the doctor answered. 'I do hope that it will yield positive results. Who knows, perhaps he may come walking in here one day to tell me all about it.'

'Perhaps,' Eleanor answered. She got up to leave; then, thinking of something that he had just said, she turned to the doctor once more. 'Did you know him before he had the accident, sir? I know that he did not come from here originally.'

'I met him a few times,' the doctor replied, ringing the bell so that Eleanor's outdoor things could be brought.

'How tall is he?' she asked him, colouring. 'Is he taller than me?'

'Does it matter?' the doctor asked her quizzically.

She smiled and shook her head. 'It doesn't matter at all,' she responded. 'All that matters is that he should be well.'

Once back at Highbridge House, Eleanor lost no time in sitting at her writing-desk and setting down her thoughts and the results of her investigations for Hurst's perusal. The business took longer than she had expected. She knew exactly what she wanted to say; but as she began to write, she was suddenly assailed by a fear that Hurst would think that she was interfering in his private concerns. She now perceived the wisdom that the doctor had shown in advising her not to hurry over to Glade Hall and blurt everything out. It was therefore not before she had made and discarded six attempts that she managed to achieve a result that she felt conveyed the facts of the case, and her concern, but did not look as if she were prying.

Having finished the letter, she got up from her seat and went to find the driving-gloves that she had given him. She had taken them with her to Glade Hall when she had visited him there, but with all the challenge and excitement of seeing Mercury at close quarters, she had returned home with them still in her cloak-pocket. Carefully she parcelled up the gloves with the letter and went downstairs with them, giving instructions to the butler that they were to be sent to Mr Hurst at Glade Hall without delay.

*   *   *

Patricia Reynolds was beginning to feel a little anxious. She had felt absolutely certain of her power to ensnare Chris Hurst when she had arrived at Glade Hall. He was trapped there by his disability. She was sure that he had been without female company for some considerable time. It surely followed that he must be desperate for the solace that only a woman could bring. It was therefore very frustrating to find that he seemed to be eluding her.

Orphaned at an early age, Patricia Reynolds

had always been able to get exactly what she wanted. She had been brought up by an elderly uncle, who was also one of her trustees, and from her youth she had discovered that a judicious tantrum at selected moments would rapidly secure the result that she hoped for. As she grew older, she came to understand that guile could be just as useful, but she had never lost that determination to get her own way, no matter what the cost to others.

Hurst had attracted her from the moment that she had first seen him. He was handsome, a little older than the beaux who congregated around her peer group, and with that world-weary air that hinted of experiences that were far out of reach of a young woman in society such as herself. There was also that sobriquet, the Hell-raiser, that gave him added desirability, for she had always had a weakness for rakes. The fact that he was a married man and therefore unavailable only added to his attraction. He had certainly indulged her with a flirtation or two when they were both in London, but their relationship had not progressed any further than that, other than in her imagination.

His accident had put paid to her interest for a time. It had never even occurred to her that someone who had suffered such a misfortune would have been glad of a visit or a letter. Once he was out of the way, she had turned her thoughts seriously to making a good marriage and her aim had been to ensnare as high-ranking a man as she could find. Her fortune was respectable rather than large, but she was very attractive and by dint of putting forth her best efforts, she had managed to secure an offer from Viscount Drysdale, heir to the earldom of Harne.

Her trustees had been delighted at her success, and she herself had been very pleased with her achievement. Unfortunately, however, once she had ensnared Drysdale, she ceased to be interested in him. He was handsome, smiling, attentive, deferential, and terribly dull. On the other hand, his father, Hugo Strickland, fifth Earl of Harne, while striking rather than handsome, was also attentive, at times enigmatic, teasing rather than deferential, and definitely not dull. Harne and his lady cordially disliked one another and lived in the same house only when they had to, and whilst Lord Harne had never been faithful to his lady, Lady Harne had never expected it. After receiving one slanting look from his future daughter-in-law, the earl had decided that she was fair game. Harne the hunter, as he was known in town, was very hard to resist, especially when the lady in question already had a decided weakness for rakes.

Their encounter on that fateful afternoon had been quite unplanned. Patricia's arrival at Harne House had been expected but Lady Harne's memory was notoriously bad, and she had gone out with her son to look for a gift for her future daughter-in-law.

On arriving at the house, Patricia had been shown into the drawing-room where Lord Harne was enjoying a glass of burgundy. From that point forward everything had gone wrong. Harne should have sent for his elderly aunt to join them, but he had left the old woman sleeping upstairs. He should have offered Patricia ratafia, not poured her a glass of the rich red wine that he was drinking, and Patricia should not have accepted the first glass, or the second.

She had not been drunk—far from it. But she had felt deliciously free from responsibility, and Harne, with his swarthy, virile looks and flashing eyes seemed everything that was desirable. So when she had stood up to walk over to the window, she had carefully stumbled when she was close to him and predictably, he had caught her in his arms. Then the kissing had begun, and once she had started to respond to his caresses, she did not seem able to stop. It had been dreadfully bad luck that when Lady Harne had entered the room with Drysdale and Ruth Presse in tow, Patricia should have been sitting on Harne's knee, his lips fastened to hers, her skirts thoroughly disarranged and his right hand exploring her bodice.

After that, flight from London had been inevitable. Her engagement had been broken,

Ruth Presse, her eyes sparkling, had gone away with a juicy tale for the whole of London to enjoy, and Harne, looking regretful, had found time to whisper 'Marriage ain't much fun, sweetheart, take my word for it. If you want to go to Paris, I'm your man.'

Flight was the only solution. Before the rumours had even begun, she had declared to her current chaperon her intention to leave town and recover from all the excitement of the season. She would go to her estate in Somerset. Then she could decide what to do. It was only after she had set out that she had considered carefully how close to Bath her estate was. Bath was a hotbed of gossip, relatives of Lady Harne lived there, and it was only too likely that there would be people there who would already have heard the scandal. Somerset would not do.

It was then that she thought about Hurst. Crippled, alone, and with every prospect of remaining so, would he not be delighted to see her? No one else would want to marry him now, she reasoned. Why should she not do so? He would still be handsome, no doubt. Marriage to him would cover the scandal in London with respectability. Furthermore, his state of health meant that there would still be the delicious possibility of carrying on an affair with Harne—an affair that Hurst would be unable to do anything about! The more she considered the matter, the more she liked it.

As she had thought about how to proceed, she had recalled that Hurst's sister, Isobel Hulce, was widowed and also living in Somerset. Making a sudden decision, she had gone to see Isobel, thinking that this renewal of aquaintance would enable her to pick up the threads with Hurst again. The news that Mrs Hulce was planning to spend Christmas with her brother had been beyond anything she could have hoped for. Then when Owen Playell had appeared, her decision was confirmed. With this fortuitous combination of circumstances, it seemed as if the Fates were at last on her side. So enamoured was she of her plan, that when she arrived at Glade Hall, she already considered Hurst to be as good as hers.

The discovery of Eleanor Carruthers in residence had come as a very rude shock, for she had certainly not expected any competition. Nor had she expected Hurst to be as elusive as ever. According to her own reasoning, he ought to be grateful for her interest and only too ready to fall in with her schemes.

It did not take long for her supreme self-confidence to reassert itself. Eleanor Carruthers was used to travelling all over the world. She would hardly be prepared to tie herself to one location for the sake of one man. Furthermore, she was not in the least like the kind of female that normally appealed to

Hurst. He liked small, dainty fragile women, not buxom Amazons with minds of their own. When the weather cleared she would be gone to stay with her relations, then the field would be clear once more.

It came as a disappointment to Patricia to find that even with Eleanor out of the way, she seemed to be no nearer her objective. Meanwhile, the time would soon come when they would all have to be gone. It was fast becoming a matter of urgency that she must make Hurst see that he really needed her.

With this in mind, she decided to offer to read to him at bedtime. She spent a little while earlier in the day searching in the library for a novel that would be sufficiently horrid for her to become shocked and therefore need to cast herself upon his chest. Having done that, she waited until she was sure that the rest of the household had retired for the night, then she tiptoed downstairs, book in hand, wearing her most becoming nightwear. Given the angle at which Hurst's bed was set, she decided that entering his chamber from the salon would give the best chance for her to be seen in the most flattering light.

She tiptoed into the salon, but paused at the bedroom door because she could hear the rumble of male voices. Thinking at first that it might just be Cherry bidding his master goodnight, she listened more closely, only to discover that Hurst was talking to Owen

Playell. Having absolutely no compunction about overhearing other people's conversations, she stepped a little closer.

The men were discussing for how long the visitors might be staying. 'I have commitments in town which I must not break, so I think I will have to go in a few days,' Playell was saying.

'Now that you have visited me once, I hope that you will make a habit of it,' Hurst replied.

'I'll be glad to. Perhaps we'll see you in town, too.'

'I think not,' Hurst answered with a sneer.

'But my dear fellow—'

'Owen, I can cope here amongst my own people, upon my own territory, and only being sought by people who care enough to have more than a casual interest in me. Do you want me to become some sort of peep-show? The rake tamed? The hearth- sitter instead of the Hell-raiser? No, I thank you. I shall remain here.'

'But not alone, at least,' said Playell with a smile.

'No, and I have you to thank for that,' Hurst replied. 'I little thought that when you arrived, you would bring me the very solace that I needed.'

'I have to confess I never thought that everything would turn out so well,' Playell admitted. 'You must be sure to invite me to visit you in the future so that I can see how things are going.'

'Of course. You have a standing invitation to join us at any time.'

Hardly able to contain herself for glee, Patricia tiptoed away from the door and hurried upstairs. The conversation that she had overheard could only mean that Hurst intended to propose, and then celebrate a quick marriage by special licence. Well, that would suit her very nicely, for all kinds of reasons. She must get a good night's sleep to look her very best on the morrow.

Downstairs, Owen poured himself another glass of wine. 'More for you, Chris?' he asked.

Hurst shook his head. 'For the most part I take care not to drink very much after leaving the dining-table,' he said. 'Once Cherry is abed, I try not to disturb him too much.'

The two men shared a companionable silence. Hurst was sitting up in bed, whilst Playell lounged in an armchair close by. Eventually, Playell said, 'You know, you could have more company than your sister.'

'Spare me,' exclaimed Hurst, lifting up his right hand in a defensive gesture. 'I very much fear that if Patricia attempts to smother me with any more kindness I will expire from the pungency of her perfume!'

Playell smiled, looked down into his glass and swirled the liquid around a little before saying, 'I wasn't referring to Patricia.'

Hurst turned his head to look at his friend.

274

'Weren't you?' he said. With some surprise he realized that at some point over the last few days, he had begun to think that this might even be possible.

CHAPTER SEVENTEEN

The following day, Patricia dressed with particular care. So anxious was she to give Hurst every opportunity of declaring himself that she was downstairs before noon, a circumstance which drew congratulations from all present.

'I do believe I am getting used to being in the country,' she remarked. 'This is a charming place in which to live.'

'I am delighted to hear you say so, Patricia,' Hurst answered, causing her heart to leap as she read more into his polite words than he had ever intended.

'Of course, these rooms could do with some refurbishment,' she went on looking round. 'I know of some excellent establishments in town that could give you every assistance.'

'You are very good, but I think that using local tradesmen would be more tactful.'

Miss Reynolds shrugged. 'As you please,' she replied carelessly.

It was after luncheon, when they were all present in the salon, that Playell brought up the subject of their departure. 'I have engagements in town before very long, so I wondered whether we might leave on Monday, if that is agreeable to you?'

He was looking at Patricia as he spoke, but as Patricia knew perfectly well that she would be staying, although Hurst had not said as much, she in her turn looked at Isobel. There was a short pause, at the end of which Playell said, 'Patricia?'

'Oh, yes. Of course, I had forgotten that we came in my chaise. You are welcome to use it by all means, as long as you send it back.'

There was an awkward silence, broken again by Playell, who said, 'Naturally, I shall expect to be taken to wherever you are going. You can set me down in London, or at an inn on the mail route, if need be.'

'But Isobel....' faltered Patricia, beginning to guess the truth.

'Isobel has consented to reside with me,' said Hurst, smiling. 'Am I not a fortunate man?' He had suddenly recalled how Patricia had crept down to his room one night. Could she have convinced herself that he would invite her to stay with him permanently?

'Reside with you? Isobel?' breathed Patricia, astounded.

'Yes, Isobel,' Hurst replied. 'Why, my dear, whom else did you think I might mean?'

'Why, no one,' Miss Reynolds replied, tossing her head and hoping that no one had seen the flush of mortification on her cheek. 'For how long, I pray, has this scheme been a-hatching?' She whirled upon Isobel. 'I suppose that I was just a convenience for you to batten on to for your journey here!'

'Now, steady on, Patricia,' said Playell.

'It's all very well for you,' Miss Reynolds replied angrily. 'I expect you were in upon the scheme from the very beginning.'

'Patricia, this is not fair,' said Mrs Hulce, speaking for the first time. 'You know very well that I had already arranged to visit Chris when you arrived. If anything. . . .' She stopped abruptly, reluctant to continue.

Miss Reynolds, however, had no such compunction. 'You mean, *I* was the one who battened upon *you*,' she said rudely. 'I should like to know how that can have been when I was the one with the carriage and you were the one about to take the common stage because you hadn't a penny to bless yourself with!'

'Enough,' said Hurst sharply, his brows drawing together. He turned to his sister and Playell. 'Would you leave us for a short while? I think that I need to clear up this little misunderstanding with Patricia.'

'We'll go into the library,' said Playell, opening the door for Isobel who hesitated, then left the room with him.

'You forget yourself, Patricia,' said Hurst as soon as they had gone. His tone was sharper than he had been wont to use with her. 'I

277

acknowledge that in the matter of not telling you of Isobel's new arrangements we have been a little remiss—'

'Well, I'm glad you have the grace to say so,' responded Miss Reynolds tartly, still very angry because of the dashing of her hopes.

'But only in that,' Hurst went on firmly. 'Isobel had no idea that I would invite her to come and live with me here; nor had I even thought about it beforehand. The question was only decided a matter of days ago.'

'Days ago. I see. And I suppose I am the last to hear about it.'

'Possibly,' he answered. 'However, there is another little matter that needs to be cleared up between us. Patricia, you never could manipulate me, and just because I'm in this chair you aren't going to begin now.'

'I don't know what you mean,' she answered defensively.

'I think you do. You've been kicking up a scandal in London, in front of Ruth Presse, of all people. Yes, I do know about it, so you needn't deny it.'

'I suppose Owen told you a pack of lies,' she said angrily.

'Owen did tell me, yes. But you forget that the post has been getting through over the past few days. I've had a letter from Horry Walpole who has told me exactly the same thing. The only reason for your coming up here was to see if you could persuade me to cover up your misdemeanours, but I'm afraid you're out of luck, my dear. You'll have to look somewhere else for an idiot.'

At this unfortunate moment, the door opened and Plaice came in with a parcel. 'Groom came with it from Highbridge House,' he muttered. 'What shall I do with it?'

'You may give it to me,' said Patricia, her eyes sparkling with malice. 'I'll give it to your master. Or maybe not,' she added, after Plaice had left.

'Patricia,' Hurst said, holding out his hand.

'I expect you're going to be polite to me now, aren't you?' she asked.

'Just give it to me,' he said, his tone still calm.

'You'll have to be a good deal nicer than that to get your precious parcel,' she answered, turning it over in her hands. 'I wonder what's inside?'

'Patricia, I'm warning you,' he said. Inside he could feel his temper begin to rise.

'It's from her, isn't it? I knew she would cause trouble, as soon as I came in and saw her standing by your chair as if she owned the place,' Patricia spat out. 'I expect she knows all about your plans to move Isobel in here, doesn't she?'

Hurst did not need to enquire to whom Patricia was referring. 'She knows, yes, but—'

'I thought so. Our arrival really put her nose out of joint, I expect. No more sneaking down the stairs in order to spend the night in your bed.'

'That's your kind of trick, not hers,' he retorted.

'Oh yes? She has all the virtues, no doubt. And another thing—I heard the other day that she's afraid of horses! Imagine that! Being afraid of horses when you look so much like one!'

'Patricia, I'm warning you,' he said again. 'Give me that parcel, or—'

'Or what? Do you know, I think you're going to have to beg me for it—if you're so anxious to get a parcel from that drab of yours!'

Suddenly, the anger inside him rose to such a pitch that he found himself bellowing, 'In God's name, give it to me!'

It was only when Patricia dropped the parcel as she stared at him open-mouthed that he realized he was standing.

With a gasp, Patricia fled from the room, and Hurst shouted, 'Playell! Cherry! Anyone!' Playell was the first to arrive, with Isobel on his heels. He stopped so abruptly in the doorway that she cannoned into him from behind.

'My God!' Playell exclaimed. He ran to his friend's side. 'Do you want to sit down?'

'Owen, I've been sitting down for the past six months,' Hurst replied. 'I want to walk to that table.'

'Can you?'

'I don't know,' Hurst replied frankly. 'But I'm going to have a deuced good try.'

With Playell supporting him, he did manage to walk across the room to the table and back again, but that was as much as he could achieve. Cherry came in as he was completing his walk. He paused just inside the doorway, and when Hurst looked at him he could see that there were tears running down the manservant's cheeks. Loath though he was to admit it, he was not very far from shedding a few himself.

'I'll sit down again,' he said. 'Lord, I feel as if I've walked half-way across London. Fetch us some wine, will you Cherry? And bring a glass for yourself.'

The manservant did so, and when they were all settled with a glass each, Playell asked, 'How did this come about? Did you just decide to get up?'

'It was Patricia,' Hurst replied. 'She made me so angry.' He looked around on the floor then said, 'That parcel; bring it here, would you old chap?' Playell picked it up and handed it to him. Hurst looked down at it, smiling. 'I think I know what this must be,' he said. He opened the parcel, and sure enough, the gloves were inside: with them was the letter over which Eleanor had spent so much time and trouble. 'By your leave?' he said, picking it up to read it. Cherry left the room.

'Back to the library,' said Playell cheerfully

to Isobel.

'This is wonderful news,' Isobel said sincerely, when they were back in the library. After the Christmas-morning service, the fire had been lit in there every day, and the room was warm and comfortable.

'It is indeed,' he agreed, with a sideways glance at her. 'I was not sure how you might feel about it, however.'

'Why should you not be sure?' she asked him in honest puzzlement. 'It is what I have been praying for.'

He thought for a moment. 'Yes of course,' he agreed, 'but this does change everything.'

Isobel straightened her spine. 'You are surely not going to suggest, sir, that I could possibly be so wicked as to hope for my brother to remain disabled so that I might be sure of a home?'

'No, of course not,' he replied hastily. 'Only that you might want to think about making other plans.' He came closer and took her hand. 'It is my earnest wish that you might feel you could consult me concerning those plans. I hope I am not speaking out of turn, or too soon.'

She smiled at him, and gently drew her hand away. 'A little too soon, perhaps,' she replied, indicating her mourning attire. 'But not out of turn.'

A few minutes later, they returned to the salon, to find Hurst gazing into the fire. It seemed to both of them that his position was subtly different from that which he had taken up on previous occasions. Then he had looked fixed in his place. Now, he looked as if he might get up at any moment.

Isobel ran over to him, put her arms around his neck and kissed him. 'Oh Chris, I'm so happy for you,' she said. He smiled, but his expression seemed to indicate that he was miles away. He picked up the letter that Eleanor had sent him, and held it out.

'Read it, both of you.' They did so, Isobel holding the paper, Playell looking over her shoulder in an attitude which seemed to be a foretaste of the intimacy that would one day be part of their relationship.

After Hurst had given them a chance to master its contents, he said, 'It's most extraordinary, but as I read this letter, it was as if a closed door in my mind was suddenly opened, and I remembered what had happened that day.

'We were both angry when we left that ball. Priscilla had just told me that she planned to leave me and set up house with her lover, keeping our child to be brought up between them. No doubt I could have prevented that, but her blatant statement of that intention made me furiously angry.

'We were shouting at each other; I don't remember what was said. Anyway, she began to struggle with me. Her anger lent her strength, and because I was having to concentrate on controlling my team, I allowed her to get hold of the whip. She struck me across the face with it, and wrenched the reins from my hands. I suppose I must have been half unconscious from the blow at that point. I don't know for how long she drove; not very long, I suppose, given where Jem Cutler found us; but this I do know: it was she who was driving and she who overturned us. Eleanor was right. I was not blameless over the unhappiness in my marriage, but I was not responsible for that accident.'

*   *   *

Patricia joined them all for dinner that evening. Clearly by her manner she was disposed to be courteous, if not cordial, but she did state her intention of leaving the following day. 'I can take anyone in my carriage, but I do intend to go to my own home in Somerset,' she said.

'Naturally, I shall be at your service, should you wish for my escort,' Playell said politely.

'I am obliged to you, but I have a notion to travel by a roundabout route,' Miss Reynolds responded in an airy tone. 'In any case, I am sure you will be needed here for a time.'

'That is very thoughtful of you,' Hurst replied. 'I shall be glad of Owen's help, for I intend to set off for London as soon as possible.' To everyone's delight, Hurst had managed to walk to the table, but he was still rather shaky on his legs, and needed the help of his friend.

'London?' exclaimed Playell. 'But I thought that you would want to see ... that is, I thought you might want to ... to recuperate, you know.' Patricia narrowed her eyes at his little slip-up, but said nothing.

Hurst laughed. 'I do indeed have reasons why I intend to return here as soon as possible,' he said. 'But I need to go to London, for sundry reasons with which I will not burden you. But you will accompany me, won't you, old fellow?'

'With all my heart,' Playell replied smiling broadly.

Later on, after the ladies had gone upstairs, the two men sat talking.

'I can still hardly grasp that this has happened,' Hurst said, as he savoured the pleasure of at last being able to enjoy another glass of wine. 'To be able to walk again; the doctor said that it was possible, but I don't think I ever really believed it.' He paused. 'I just wish it hadn't happened in the way that it did.'

'What do you mean?' Playell asked him, surprised.

'I wish that it had been the letter that Eleanor sent that had got me out of my seat, rather than that witch, Patricia,' Hurst responded ruefully.

'Perhaps it was inevitable,' Playell suggested. 'Perhaps you just had to be so angry that you did not even think about it. But this changes everything now, doesn't it? I mean to say, you will be back, won't you? To see her?'

'Can you doubt it? But I meant what I said at dinner. I won't approach her until I'm steady on my feet, wearing clothes that fit me. But I will write to her before I go to London.'

'Will you inform her about what's happened?'

Hurst shook his head. 'I think I'll surprise her,' he answered. 'I'll tell her that I've gone to consult with a London physician about my condition.'

*   *   *

When Miss Reynolds appeared for breakfast the following morning in her carriage dress, it became clear that she really did intend to leave that day.

'At least it should be an easier journey than when we came,' said Isobel, then she blushed because she was not going back with her friend.

'Yes, it should,' Patricia agreed. 'At least there is no snow this time. I just hope that the thaw has not caused any of the roads to become too waterlogged.'

'You are welcome to return, if you have

286

problems,' said Hurst. 'This Christmas must certainly rank as being one of the most unusual that I have ever spent.' The whole company agreed.

When Miss Reynolds came downstairs later, the hall was empty, apart from Plaice, who was crossing the hall with a letter in his hand. 'What have you there?' she asked him.

'Letter to go to Highbridge House,' he said. 'I was just taking it to the stables for Brewer to deliver.'

'Give it to me,' said Patricia. She saw that it was addressed to Miss Carruthers. The writing was in Hurst's distinct, bold, sloping hand. 'I'll take it,' she said. 'I'm going to call on Miss Carruthers as I leave. There's no need to tell anyone that I've done so.' She put the letter into her reticule, then pinning a smile on to her face, went into the salon to make her farewells.

*　　　*　　　*

If Eleanor was surprised to receive a visit from Miss Reynolds, she certainly did not show it. Mr Carlisle had succumbed to the fever that had laid his wife low, and Mrs Carlisle was sitting with him, so Eleanor entertained the visitor alone in the green drawing-room which looked out on to the garden. She rang for refreshments and after they had been brought and both ladies had a cup of tea, Miss

Reynolds said, 'I thought that I would drop in and see you, as we are all leaving Glade Hall. It has been such a lovely visit.'

'You are *all* leaving?' asked Eleanor. 'But I thought that Isobel was remaining, to reside with her brother.'

Patricia could feel anger rising up inside her at this confirmation that even Eleanor Carruthers had been told about this before she had been informed. She gave no outward sign of this, however, but simply said airily, 'Oh yes, but everything has changed now. The most wonderful thing has happened! Chris is able to walk again!'

Eleanor could not help the look of happiness that suffused her face at this news. 'That is indeed wonderful,' she agreed. 'How did it happen?' She was thinking of the letter that she had sent him.

'Oh, it was the most romantic thing,' exclaimed Patricia artlessly. 'He and I were alone together; just talking, you understand,' she added coyly, 'when all of a sudden he stood up and took a step towards me. I could have wept for joy!'

'I am sure,' Eleanor responded feeling suddenly deflated.

'So now, he is to go to London to consult his physician who, I am sure, will recommend some time spent in sunnier climes. Just think of it, Miss Carruthers, Italy in the spring! I have always wanted to honeymoon in Italy.'

She smiled as if already anticipating joys to come in Hurst's company.

'Italy is very lovely in the spring,' Eleanor answered colourlessly. 'So you are to be married, then? I wish you joy, Miss Reynolds.'

Patricia cast her eyes down modestly. 'It is not precisely fixed, as yet,' she said, 'but there can be no doubt of it. He was only holding back before because he did not want to burden me with his disability. But thankfully, all that is behind us.'

'Yes indeed,' Eleanor agreed. 'Are Mrs Hulce and Mr Playell to go to London as well?'

'Yes, they are,' Patricia replied truthfully.

'Then I trust that you will send them my compliments, and accept my best wishes to yourself and Mr Hurst on your future marriage. I am so pleased he is better.'

'Yes, I know you are,' replied Patricia. 'Do you know, Miss Carruthers, when I first met you I was silly enough to imagine that you might be a rival? Wasn't that ridiculous?'

'Ridiculous,' Eleanor agreed, laughing politely.

'But now, we can put all that silliness behind us, can't we?'

Yes, Eleanor thought to herself, now I can put it all behind me; all the silliness of imagining that I could ever compete with a dainty little thing like her—the kind of woman that he clearly prefers. I can put behind me that stupid, arrogant idea that by my detective work I could make him fall in love with me, when all he needed to do was fall into her arms. I can put it all behind me, but can I ever forget it? Can I forget how it felt to be held in his arms and kissed by him? Can I forget looking into his eyes, and believing that he wanted to walk by the Neva with me as much as I wanted to be able to take his arm?

Well, now he would be able to walk by the Neva again, but with the woman of his own choice. This was such a depressing thought that after her visitor had gone, Eleanor hurried upstairs to her room in order to fetch her outdoor things. That done, she went outside and walked until she was tired; but it was no good. The first thing that she saw when she came back to the house was a fine holly bush full of berries; and the very sight of it succeeded in doing what none of Miss Reynolds' barbed remarks had done; it broke down her composure and brought tears to her eyes.

* * *

Patricia Reynolds hurried away from Highbridge House with the satisfied feeling of a job well done. She suspected that probably Hurst and the Carruthers woman would eventually resolve their differences; but she had not been able to resist the temptation to take Eleanor down a peg or two. Not that she had shown it!

As she drove away, however, the brief sense of satisfaction gained through crowing over her rival began to evaporate. What could she do now? Thanks to her foolishness with Harne—deliciously wicked though he was— she had thoroughly burned her boats in London. Her penchant for rakes and vagabonds had caused her to sail rather close to the wind before, but the scandal in which she had now become embroiled meant that absence from English shores was the only solution. She had told the others, for pride's sake, that she would go to her estates in Somerset, but even they were not safe, close as they were to Bath, that hotbed of gossip.

She continued to be very preoccupied that day, and Pettit, often the recipient of her mistress's confidences, found herself addressed in little more than monosyllables. The truth was that Patricia's spirits were gradually sinking lower and lower. Where could she go? To whom could she turn? It all seemed so hopeless.

As evening was drawing in, they were approaching Bedford, so after consulting with her coachman, Patricia decided to stay for the night at the Swan. She was not known there, but it had a good name, and after all, she had to stay somewhere. With any luck, she would not be recognized.

She was just waiting to be attended to, and longing to get to her own room, when a voice that she knew very well said, 'Patty, my dear! This is most fortuitous.'

There was only one person who had ever called her Patty. She turned round, and there behind her was the Earl of Harne, looking at least twice as wicked as usual and just as manly.

She eyed him suspiciously. 'Is Lady Harne here?' she asked him.

'No, she's suing for a divorce,' he replied, grinning. 'She's tired to death of me stirring up scandal, so she's decided to create some of her own.' He looked at her keenly. 'But what of you, Patty? You look blue-devilled.'

Suddenly, it all swept over her, the humiliation, the scandal, the loneliness, and after exclaiming, 'Oh, Harne!' she burst into tears.

The Earl of Harne was not a man to miss such a glorious opportunity. Without a moment's hesitation he swept her up into his arms, and headed for the stairs. 'Landlord!' he said peremptorily. 'My wife is unwell and I am taking her to my room!' As he climbed the stairs, he whispered in her ear. 'My room— then Paris; yes?'

She grasped hold of his lapel, her eyes shining through her tears. 'Oh Harne, yes *please*!'

CHAPTER EIGHTEEN

'Eleanor, my dear, we had counted upon a much longer stay than this,' said Mrs Carlisle reproachfully. 'You have only been with us for a mere three weeks, and I have been ill for part of that.'

'Yes I know, but you see from this letter that my friend is very pressing,' Eleanor replied with a smile, as she handed her aunt the piece of correspondence that she had just received. 'Her baby is to be baptized and she wants me to be a godmother. Just think! I never thought that I would ever be anything half as grand.'

'Well, I suppose I shall have to let you go,' sighed Mrs Carlisle. 'But you must promise to come back to see us again very soon.'

'I shall visit you again before I go to join Papa and Monica, I promise you.'

'Monica!' exclaimed Mrs Carlisle who had very old-fashioned ideas in some matters. 'Is that any way to address or speak of your stepmother?'

'Monica herself asked me to do so,' Eleanor replied. 'And as she is three years younger than I am, to be calling her Mama would sound a little absurd.'

'Three years younger!' exclaimed her aunt, giving voice to sentiments that she never usually expressed except to her husband. 'Why, you yourself—'

Eleanor's smile vanished. 'Yes, perhaps, but it was not to be, was it? Now, if you will excuse me, Aunt, I shall go and supervise Gwen while she packs.'

In truth, the invitation from Molly Bradshaw had come as a welcome relief. Highbridge House was just too close to Glade Hall for comfort, and its solitude gave too much time for thought. A stay in a busy bustling household in which her goddaughter-to-be was the third child would make a welcome change, and might even help her to forget the man who had so easily forgotten her.

By the time Eleanor was ready to leave the next day, Mrs Carlisle had almost become reconciled to her departure. 'Now do write to us and tell us all about the baby and the ceremony,' she said, as she and her husband escorted their niece to the waiting carriage. In accordance with Eleanor's known wishes, her coachman had driven past the steps so that she would not have to pass the horses on her way to the carriage.

She paused on the top of the steps, walked down them, then slowly and very hesitantly, she walked to the leading horse nearest to the house, stretched out her arm to its fullest extent, and touched its coat with her hand. Mr and Mrs Carlisle looked at one another astounded, but Eleanor was unaware of their astonishment as she said quietly to herself, at least he has given me that.

As she was going back to embrace her aunt for the last time they all heard the sound of a carriage approaching, and soon a curricle was seen coming up to the house pulled by splendid matched grey horses at a smart trot. Eleanor stood still as the equipage halted and the driver sprang down and walked towards them with athletic grace. He was taller than she had expected; at least six feet at a guess.

She had told herself that she would never meet him again. Now, confronted with that very eventuality, she found herself quite unable to think of anything to say. It was her uncle who spoke first. 'We had heard of your good news, Mr Hurst, but it is even more pleasing to see you standing on your feet.'

'I can assure you, sir, that it's just as pleasing to me,' Hurst responded. He looked down at Eleanor, noted that she was in her travelling costume, turned to examine the back of the coach, then looked back at Eleanor again. 'You are leaving,' he said, with a slight frown.

'Yes, but I am sure that she can come inside for a short time and hear more about your recovery,' said Mrs Carlisle warmly. 'Come, sir.'

'No, Aunt, you are mistaken, I cannot come in,' said Eleanor in tones that were not entirely steady. 'I must not keep the horses standing.' She turned to Hurst, a forced smile upon her face. 'I am glad to have seen you, but must bid you farewell.'

'The devil you will!' he replied, his frown more pronounced.

'I am glad that you have recovered, and I hope that you and Miss Reynolds will be very happy upon the Continent,' she told him, proud of the steadiness of her tone.

'The Continent? Miss Reynolds and I? What is this all about?' he demanded, on his face an expression of complete bewilderment.

Mr Carlisle took a decision. 'Briggs, walk the horses. Eleanor, come inside at once, and Mr Hurst, please join us. There is more here to be discussed than can be aired in a seemly fashion on the steps outside.'

Eleanor made one fleeting gesture towards the carriage, which had seemed to represent both relief and escape, then allowed herself to be led inside, and relieved of her bonnet and cloak, whilst Hurst surrendered his own outdoor garments to the waiting butler. Then Mrs Carlisle linked her arm with that of her niece, walked with her into the salon, welcomed Mr Hurst in as well, then just as deftly removed her husband from the scene.

Eleanor sat down, suddenly feeling that her legs might give way underneath her. Hurst walked across to the fireplace and stood with one foot on the fender. He was wearing a dark-blue coat and buckskin breeches with top-boots polished to an amazing shine. She had never seen him standing up before. He was well built and beautifully in proportion, she noted. Suddenly realizing that she was staring at his well-muscled legs in a way that was quite improper for a young lady, she looked up at his face and then seeing his grin, she turned away, blushing. He looked as if he could read exactly what she was thinking!

'Why were you leaving, Eleanor?' he asked her quietly.

'I have been invited to be a godmother. Is that not exciting? My friend, Molly Bradshaw. . . .' She fell silent, conscious that she was beginning to babble.

'That might explain a short visit, but you have your entire luggage there on the back of the coach. Did you not want to see me again?'

Not want to see him? When she dreamed about him every night, and when every other waking thought was about him? 'I did not expect you to return,' she answered.

'But I told you in my letter that I would do so,' he replied.

'Your letter?' Her face was honestly puzzled.

'Yes, I sent you a letter, on the very day that. . . .' A look of comprehension came over his face. 'Patricia,' he said. 'Now I see. I gave the letter to Plaice to be delivered to you. I'll wager that it went into Patricia's reticule instead.'

'But when she was here, she gave me no letter,' Eleanor said, still not understanding.

'She came here? Tell me, my love, what

pretty lies did she spin?'

Eleanor coloured at the endearment. 'She said that you could walk again, and that you were going to London with her,' she murmured, looking down at her hands. 'Then you would be going to Italy together, on your honeymoon.'

'That is not very likely, considering that I would not even walk twenty paces in her company if I could avoid it. I indulged her with a flirtation or two in London last year, but anything more romantic between us only existed in her imagination.' He left the mantelpiece and walked over to her. 'There is only one woman I want to honeymoon with, and I have come all the way back here to tell her so.'

'But why did you go away?' she asked him, standing up. It seemed strange to be looking up at him. 'Why did you leave and let me hear your wonderful news from that detestable woman?'

'I'm sorry, Eleanor. I never intended that to happen. I wrote a letter to you, as I've already said, telling you that I was going to London to consult a physician, but not mentioning my recovery.'

'But why?' she asked him again.

He took hold of her hand. 'It was partly vanity, I fear,' he replied. 'For one thing, I wanted to exercise these rusty limbs of mine at Jackson's boxing saloon and Angelo's fencing academy. After such a long period without exercise, I could not move about with my usual ... ah ... grace. For another, I needed to purchase some new clothes. Cherry altered all my other garments so that they would be comfortable for someone who was obliged to sit all the time. I wanted to cut a fine figure in front of you, wearing clothes that fitted me properly.'

She thrust his hand away. 'But why should you think that I would care for that?' she demanded angrily, tears coming into her eyes. 'I always loved you, always, just as you were! What did it matter. . . ?'

'Eleanor!' he groaned and caught her to him. Then his mouth was on hers, and suddenly all the misunderstandings melted away in the wonder of the kiss that they shared.

When at last their lips parted, Hurst said, 'I did have another reason for going to London, and one which I hope you will approve.' He reached inside his coat, then, after pressing one light kiss on to her willing lips, went down on one knee before her, and held out a ring. 'Only sapphires for you, my heart. Will you marry me?'

Her smiling response brought him to his feet to take her in his arms once more.

'I shall have to get used to looking up at you,' she said as soon as she was able. 'I rather like the way you look from this angle.'

Hurst stepped back, keeping hold of her

hands. 'I think you look enchanting from any angle,' he replied, 'and especially from this one.' He glanced down at her modest décolletage, and grinned wickedly.

Eleanor coloured, but said spiritedly, 'By the way, whose gown was I wearing on the night I arrived at your house? It was a good deal too . . . too. . . .'

'Snug?' Hurst suggested. 'You need have no qualms, my dear. It was delivered to the house in error, and you were the first to wear it. I thought it very becoming.'

'Your eyes were a good deal too busy, sir,' she told him severely.

He lifted her hands to his lips and kissed first one then the other. 'Yes, I know,' he agreed in a regretful tone. 'Would you be able to tolerate it, do you think, if I promised that from now on they would only be busy looking at you?'

'I think that that would be quite satisfactory,' she murmured, just before he kissed her again.

*   *   *

Needless to say, after that, all Eleanor's luggage was taken off the carriage again, and carried upstairs. 'Plaice would be grumbling fit to burst by now,' Hurst observed, to Eleanor's amusement. Mr and Mrs Carlisle, who had noted more about Eleanor's recent demeanour than she would ever have guessed, were delighted to see her happy again, and

300

invited Hurst to dine with them, which invitation he was only too happy to accept.

'When Eleanor was younger and her father went abroad leaving her in England, I was sometimes appointed as her guardian,' Mr Carlisle told Hurst when the two gentlemen spoke privately in Eleanor's uncle's study. 'Now, of course, she's of age, and she can please herself.'

'That may be so,' Hurst agreed, 'but although Eleanor may not need her father's consent, I am sure she would like his blessing. I intend to write to him informing him of our plans, then if Eleanor agrees, I think we should marry quite soon and travel to see her father and stepmother for our wedding-tour. Do you think that she would like that?'

Mr Carlisle was of the opinion that Eleanor would like it very much. So, too, was Eleanor when Hurst told her about his idea. The newly engaged couple met before dinner, and as they were both down before their hosts, they managed a little more private conversation.

'Chris, I think it's a wonderful idea,' Eleanor exclaimed. 'Then Monica can give a ball for us when we arrive, which she will love.' She glanced up at him demurely. 'Monica is small and dainty,' she told him. 'Just the kind of female who appeals to you.'

'Just the kind of female who *used* to appeal to me,' he corrected her. 'My tastes have changed recently.' After a few moments, he said: 'By the way, I have not yet thanked you for the efforts that you made to discover what really happened on the night of the accident. It had never occurred to me, nor to anyone else, I believe, that I might not have been driving at the time. I know it doesn't change the tragic consequences, but it does ease my mind. You see, I really couldn't remember what had taken place. My belief was that I must have been so thoroughly drunk that I did indeed drive recklessly and destroy two lives. At least now I can be certain that I did not cause the accident.'

They were both silent for a time. Then eventually Eleanor said, 'I was so hoping that my letter would give you the encouragement that you needed to be able to walk again, but Patricia told me that you stood up for her and fell into her arms.' She turned away, fidgeting with the ring on her finger. He caught hold of her hands and stilled them.

'It's true that I stood in her presence; but the reason for that was because she made me so angry that I couldn't think straight.'

'What did she do to make you so angry?' she asked.

'She insulted you, my darling, and refused to give me the parcel that you had sent. So you see, although I had not read your letter at the time, it was my need to defend you that got me to my feet. Strangely enough, I think that in the end she was really quite disappointed at my recovery.'

'Disappointed!' Eleanor exclaimed, sitting up straight. 'How could she be?'

'Surely you must have noticed how she enjoyed petting and fussing over me,' he reminded her. 'Besides, I fear she had a very ignoble plan in mind.'

'And what was that?'

'I think that she was hoping to use marriage to me as a cloak of respectability to cover affairs with such men as the notorious Earl of Harne.'

'Not Harne the hunter!' Eleanor protested.

'Oh, so you've heard of him too, have you?' Hurst asked suspiciously, putting one finger under her chin to tilt her face towards him.

'I think that everyone must have done, but I was never allowed anywhere near him,' Eleanor replied virtuously. 'Papa was by far too protective of me.'

'And quite rightly,' Hurst agreed. 'Anyway, Lady Harne has now threatened her husband with divorce, Harne has disappeared from London and Patricia's whereabouts are unknown. But a lady who looked rather like her was seen boarding the packet at Dover in Harne's company, so I suspect that we shan't be seeing much of her in the future.'

'I cannot say that I am really sorry,' Eleanor admitted. 'She was my least favourite of all your guests.'

'I hope you liked the other two,' Hurst put

in.

'Certainly,' she replied. 'I liked both Isobel and Owen very much.'

'I am glad you like Isobel, for she will be making her home with us but not, I suspect, for long.'

She clapped her hands. 'Are they to make a match of it?' she said excitedly. 'Oh, I am so pleased.'

'Nothing can be settled until Isobel is out of mourning, but I believe they will do so; which leads me to say, Miss Carruthers, that you led me a fair dance, first making me think that you were attracted to Owen, and then telling Isobel that you had another attachment. It was then that I realized, my darling, that whatever my disability, I still had a man's feelings. To imagine you belonging to someone else was torture indeed.'

'No one else ever had a chance,' she told him, lifting his hand to her lips.

He snatched it away. 'No. You are not to do that,' he said sternly.

'Why not?' she asked him in surprise.

'Because I am not worthy of you, sweetheart. You've heard that I was called the Hell-raiser, I dare say. Well, it was a name that I certainly earned, for I've been raising hell ever since I was old enough to go on the town. Then that accident brought me low and for a time all I did was rail against fate and get drunk and swear at Cherry and Plaice and anyone else

304

who would come near me. By the time you met me, I had got past that stage but I still could not see that life could possibly have anything good in store for me.'

'Did you miss your life in London?' Eleanor asked him curiously.

'Strangely enough, I didn't,' he replied. 'When I thought about the things that I wanted to do, they were always fencing or boxing, or country pursuits, or simple things like walking from one room to another or even climbing library steps.'

'Or holding them,' Eleanor suggested.

'Or holding them,' he agreed, putting his arm around her and giving her a little squeeze. 'Of course, I began to want the company of a woman. And I am sorry to have to tell you this, my darling, but as far as I was concerned, I felt as if any woman would have done. Then dear Owen Playell sent me a wench for Christmas.'

'No he didn't,' Eleanor declared, indignantly.

'Well, I thought he had at first. But you turned out to be unlike any other woman I'd had close contact with. You were beautiful, intelligent, interesting, and yes, you were sympathetic, but you were not prepared to let me wallow in self-pity. Thanks to you I began to see the world in a different way; to understand that things that I had thought were not possible could actually be done. And, of course,' he went on studying his nails, 'I never found it easy to take my eyes off that glorious figure of yours.'

'Chris!' Eleanor exclaimed, blushing.

He cradled her face gently with his hands. 'I love the way you do that,' he said before kissing her. 'Then Patricia arrived and offered herself to me on a plate. That was when I really knew that I had changed. She was very pretty and very available, and twelve months ago, I don't suppose I would have hesitated, but the strangest thing happened. I found that I didn't want her, because by that time the only woman I wanted was you.'

'So when she came down to you on Christmas Eve, you sent her away with a flea in her ear?' Eleanor asked.

'I certainly did,' Hurst answered. He paused, a curious expression on his face. 'How did you know that?' he asked her.

Her colour deepened. 'I was on the point of coming downstairs myself,' she admitted.

He chuckled, then pulled her into his arms. 'Stap me,' he murmured, his lips very close to hers. 'I nearly did get a wench for Christmas after all.'